PRAISE FOR PAMELA FAGAN HUTCHINS

2018 USA Today Best Seller
2017 Silver Falchion Award, Best Mystery
2016 USA Best Book Award, Cross-Genre Fiction
2015 USA Best Book Award, Cross-Genre Fiction
2014 Amazon Breakthrough Novel Award Quarter-finalist, Romance

What Doesn't Kill You: Katie Romantic Mysteries

"An exciting tale . . . twisting investigative and legal subplots . . . a character seeking redemption . . . an exhilarating mystery with a touch of voodoo." — *Midwest Book Review Bookwatch*
"A lively romantic mystery." — *Kirkus Reviews*
"A riveting drama . . . exciting read, highly recommended." — *Small Press Bookwatch*
"Katie is the first character I have absolutely fallen in love with since Stephanie Plum!" — *Stephanie Swindell, Bookstore Owner*
"Engaging storyline . . . taut suspense." — *MBR Bookwatch*

What Doesn't Kill You: Emily Romantic Mysteries

"Fair warning: clear your calendar before you pick it up because you won't be able to put it down." — *Ken Oder, author of* Old Wounds to the Heart
"Full of heart, humor, vivid characters, and suspense. Hutchins has done it again!" — *Gay Yellen, author of* The Body Business
"Hutchins is a master of tension." — *R.L. Nolen, author of* Deadly Thyme
"Intriguing mystery . . . captivating romance." — *Patricia Flaherty Pagan, author of* Trail Ways Pilgrims
"Everything about it shines: the plot, the characters and the writing. Readers are in for a real treat with this story." — *Marcy McKay, author of* Pennies from Burger Heaven

What Doesn't Kill You: Michele Romantic Mysteries

"Immediately hooked." — *Terry Sykes-Bradshaw, author of* Sibling Revelry
"Spellbinding." — *Jo Bryan, Dry Creek Book Club*

"Fast-paced mystery." — *Deb Krenzer, Book Reviewer*
"Can't put it down." — *Cathy Bader, Reader*

What Doesn't Kill You: Ava Romantic Mysteries

"Just when I think I couldn't love another Pamela Fagan Hutchins novel more, along comes Ava." — *Marcy McKay, author of* Stars Among the Dead
"Ava personifies bombshell in every sense of word. — *Tara Scheyer, Grammy-nominated musician, Long-Distance Sisters Book Club*
"Entertaining, complex, and thought-provoking." — *Ginger Copeland, power reader*

What Doesn't Kill You: Maggie Romantic Mysteries

"Murder has never been so much fun!" — *Christie Craig,* New York Times Best Seller
"Maggie's gonna break your heart—one way or another." — *Tara Scheyer, Grammy-nominated musician, Long-Distance Sisters Book Club*
"Pamela Fagan Hutchins nails that Wyoming scenery and captures the atmosphere of the people there." — *Ken Oder, author of* Old Wounds to the Heart
"You're guaranteed to love the ride!" — *Kay Kendall, Silver Falchion Best Mystery Winner*

DEAD PILE (MAGGIE #3)

A WHAT DOESN'T KILL YOU ROMANTIC MYSTERY

PAMELA FAGAN HUTCHINS

SkipJack Publishing

We skip the old school jack.

To Eric. Thanks for helping me find my inner romantic and deal with my old junk.

ONE

Maggie tilts her chin, pushing up the back of the slate-colored pony-tail beanie framing her black bun. All the better to lock eyes with the cowboy looking down at her. He's leaning against the door of a red barn, looking like an ad for Marlboro cigarettes. Or sex. A hand-lettered sign on a weathered board hangs overhead. PINEY BOTTOMS RANCH, SHERI-DAN, WY. She likes the one even better that's just visible inside the barn above the window into the office. WYOMING: WYNOT?

"Nice belt buckle," he says, using it to pull her to him with a jerk.

She catches herself with her hands around his waist. Her chest bumps a little below his, through the bulky Carhartt jackets they're both wearing. Her legs are longer, but he's still got a few inches on her. "Got it off a dead-beat bull rider." In truth, the buckle was part of Hank's haul when he won the bull riding championship at the 2002 Cheyenne Frontier Days Rodeo.

He displays two killer dimples. "I hope you didn't catch anything."

"Just him." Her stomach flip-flops, its usual response to the damn hollows in his cheeks. "But you wouldn't believe how long it took to reel him in."

A single snowflake falls on the cowboy's nose, then another on her own. The snow tickles hers. Melts on his. She sneezes.

He lifts a faded navy-blue bandana to wipe his cheek. "Nice. I think you missed some of my face with that. But not much."

"So you don't want to kiss me?"

The cowboy—Hank Sibley—growls deep in his throat. "Like hell I don't."

His lips are cushiony and warm despite the cold air, like the bed they'd heated up that morning. Maggie melts into the kiss, merging their respective ChapStick flavors—cherry for her, spearmint for him—and drops a hand to his muscular buns.

"Get a room." A much shorter man with twinkling dark eyes and the dark skin and hair of his Mexican heritage doesn't break stride as he heads past them into the barn. Gene Soboleski, Polish last name courtesy of his adoptive parents.

Hank and Gene have been partners in their Double S Bucking Stock business for nearly two decades. Friends longer, from their early days riding bulls for beer and gas money through their later success that seeded the purchase of Sassafrass, the original broodmare for their bucking broncos. But Gene's only recently become Maggie's stepbrother, thanks to the union of her mother and his birth father, after her lifetime as an only child. Not only that, the marriage came with a stepsister, too: her best friend, Michele, back in Giddings, Texas, where Maggie's industrial and homestead salvage business, Flown the Coop, lies in tatters.

Hank talks against Maggie's lips. "Get a life. Or a woman of your own."

Maggie releases Hank after one more long, slow kiss. She isn't stopping on Gene's account. But she doesn't want to scandalize Andy, the Double S's Amish hand, at least not this early in the morning. The top hand, Paco, she's not so worried about. Number one, because he's on vacation. Number two, because he'd probably yell "Let 'er buck" and slap Hank on the ass.

She murmurs into Hank's neck. "Take me for a quick ride before it snows."

"I thought I already did, music girl."

Maggie has mixed emotions about the nickname. Hank had called her that when he first met her, fifteen years before, in her old life. But it's outdated now. *Junker girl, more like.*

Gene walks back by carrying a bale of hay. "La la la. Don't hear you."

She sticks her tongue out at Hank. "Not that kind of ride. I want to ride my horse."

"That pregnant Percheron, big as an elephant, stubborn as a mule?"

Gene rounds the corner out of the barn. His voice is tinny in the cold. "First you'll have to catch her. Miss Houdini has done it again."

Maggie runs to join him. There are horses everywhere in the paddocks, the ones leaving later in the week for the Prairie Rim Circuit Finals Rodeo in Duncan, Oklahoma. But the big black mare is nowhere to be seen, her solo paddock empty. "Lily's out?"

"Yep. That damn mare's a pain in the ass."

Behind them, Hank says, "She's your horse, all right, Maggie. Every time I turn around, she's run off again."

Maggie shoots him a slit-eye look. "Funny."

To Gene, Hank says, "We'll find her."

"Better do it fast. This is supposed to be our first good storm of the season."

As if in response, a gust of wind from the north blows in. Maggie raises the collar on her jacket. Poor Lily. She's due in a month. Most horses gravitate toward a herd. But not her. The mare is a loner, which makes her harder to find and harder to catch. Maggie shivers. These are no conditions for Lily to be out alone in.

"It's only October. Is this weather unusual?" She heads back for the barn, following Hank, Gene following her.

Both men guffaw.

Hank swats her on the tush as she passes him to enter the dark, cavernous interior. "What would Pretty-shield say?"

Maggie had been reading and rereading the book about the Crow medicine woman, which Hank had bought her on a trip through the Montana reservation. She's gone her whole life not knowing she is one-eighth Crow on her father's side, until the previous month. As a Crow-come-lately, she's making up for lost time.

"It's not like a Ouija board. Or an almanac. It's a biography."

Gene says, "The October moon has a lot of different names with the Native Americans in the region, Maggie May. The Cheyenne call it the moon of the freeze on the stream's edge. The Shoshone link it to rutting season. The Lakota named it for the wind that shakes off leaves, the Arapaho for falling leaves, and the Sioux for changing seasons. Seems like those last three all had the same idea."

"I'm not hearing anything about snow, though." Maggie tosses her head and feels her bun flop.

"Ah, but we are nearly on the face of the Bighorn Mountains."

"So will it be safe for us to ride out in this?"

Hank dimples up. "This is nothing."

"It's still in the nineties in Giddings."

"That's hellfire hot to me. Oh, sorry. I didn't mean it that way."

For a moment, Maggie lets herself remember her darling house and cute shop, then shuts it down. It hurts to think about her murderous former bandmate going on a torching spree the month before. Besides her store and house—including all the priceless original artwork painted by Maggie's deceased birth mother—the fires killed Maggie's tenant and an old boyfriend, country star Gary Fuller, and nearly burned up Hank to boot. The fires lit off a conflagration of publicity that has been the last thing Maggie wants. She's glad to have Hank's family ranch, Piney Bottoms, as a refuge while she's waiting on the insurance payout she needs to rebuild her business. She's even more glad that she and Hank are *finally* together, after their years of crossed wires and missed opportunities. His recent almost-fiancée, Sheila, doesn't share Maggie's gratitude. "It's okay. I know what you meant."

"But now you look sad."

"I was just thinking of all Gidget's paintings I lost in the fire." Maggie hadn't known her birth mother while she was alive. An image flashes in her mind of her favorite, *Front Porch Pickin'*, which had depicted a guitarist both melancholy and joyful. "It was all I had of her. Sometimes it gets to me."

"I know. I hate that for you."

Maggie is lost in memories until a floppy-eared head bumps her knee. She bends to pet Louise, the short-legged union of a determined corgi and surely embarrassed border collie. But the dog's nudge is a hit and run. Louise trots past her and up the stairs to the hayloft to hunt rats.

Suddenly Maggie realizes Hank is leading two geldings to the hitching post inside the mouth of the barn, when she hadn't even realized he'd gone. She was more than lost in memories—she'd fallen into a mental black hole. She snaps herself out of her thoughts and moves to help him with them. The horses are lookers. A buckskin and a blue-roan with a graying muzzle. In the distance, she sees Andy in an animated conversation with another man, who she assumes is Amish because of his long beard and distinctive hat and dress.

Hank eyes her over the withers of the buckskin. "Thought I'd lost you there for a few minutes."

He's been worrying about her too much lately. Yes, she's had a tough time. Is having a tough time. But inside, she chafes at herself that she's showing weakness. Outside, she puts up a smoke screen. "Sorry. I should have had that second cup of coffee. Who's that talking to Andy over there?"

Hank's eyes flick to the bunkhouse then back to the buckskin. "That's his father. Reggie Yoder."

"They don't look like they're happy with each other."

"Reggie is hard on Andy."

Gene walks in with a brown-skinned young man whose long black hair is braided, jeans creased, and worn boots oiled. "Hank, this is Michael Short. He's looking for a job."

Hank strides toward Michael, arm out, and the two men shake.

"Nice to meet you, sir. I'd love to work on your fine ranch."

"I'm sure Gene told you we're not hiring full-timers right now, but that could change in the blink of an eye."

"Yes, sir, he did."

Gene nods. "You and Maggie better get going. I'm going to chat a little more with Michael while I give him a tour."

Hank puts a hand on the blue-roan's neck. "Nice to meet you, Michael."

Gene escorts Michael back out of the barn.

To Maggie, Hank says, "You'll take Don Juan. He was my mom's last horse." A shadow crosses his face. His mother's riding days are over. She's wheelchair-bound and has Alzheimer's. She still lives at the ranch, with Hank and a live-in helper, although Hank still provides a great deal of her care. It's a round-the-clock job bigger than any one person.

"So you're not using me as a crash-test dummy on some up-and-comer— that's good."

The up-and-comers will get a road test at the rodeo that weekend. It will be Maggie's first time seeing the Double S buckers in competition, and she's looking forward to it. Like really, really looking forward to it, even though she was never much into rodeo before Hank.

"Last thing I'd ever want is to harm a single hair on your pretty head." Hank hands her a brush and takes another to the buckskin's coat. "Lily likes Don Juan best of all the riding horses. She likes sweet feed even better, so you'll be carrying a feed bag full with you. I'll take Tatonka here." He bends to reach under the roan's stomach, then catches himself with his hands on his knees, grimacing.

Maggie pauses, brush poised over Don Juan's back. "What is it?"

"Another one of my damn headaches. They're coming on fast with no warning." He drops his brush and crouches on his boot heels, elbows on knees, head in hands.

Maggie tosses her brush into a bucket and hurries to him. Her fingers graze his shoulder. She knows he doesn't want anyone in his space when a headache hits. "Where's your prescription?"

Hank's eyes are squeezed shut. "Back pocket."

She pries the pill out of his tight jeans, retrieves a bottled water from a refrigerator that doubles as a holder of human drinks and of animal medications, and brings both back to him, first removing the pill from the wrapping he has trouble mastering when his head crashes. "Here."

He opens his mouth for the pill, accepting it on his tongue. She puts the bottle to his lips. He drinks, swallows, grunts.

"You want a cold rag?"

"No."

"Maybe I could help you into the office?"

He snaps at her. "Quit hovering."

"What did I do?"

"Just leave me the hell alone."

Normally Maggie has a smart comeback for any situation, but his volatile response short-circuits her system. She stands frozen for long seconds. Her eyes burn. Her breath comes out in little puffs of vapor cloud. His abrupt personality change stings. Feeling bad isn't an excuse to act like a jerk, but now's not the time to discuss it.

She picks up the brush he dropped and begins grooming Tatonka. When she's finished, she continues with Don Juan. She's unsure whether Hank will be able to ride, but she needs to do something. Slowly she curries their manes and tails, then picks their hooves. She scrapes botfly eggs off their legs. When the horses are both groomed to the nines and saddled, she gives them sweet-feed mash and hangs a bag of feed for Lily on Don Juan's saddle horn. Half an hour has passed. She puts bridles on the horses. Snow begins to accumulate on the ground in the stable yard. Hank hasn't moved. She's run out of ways to stall with the horses.

"Hank?" she whispers.

He startles. "Yeah?"

"Are you okay?"

"I musta dozed off." He rolls his head, stretching his neck. "I'm feeling a little better. I think we caught it in time."

"Amazing you can sleep in that position."

He holds a hand up to her, and she takes it. "Thanks for helping me."

"You didn't seem to appreciate it much earlier."

He puts a little weight into her hand as he lumbers to his feet. "What?"

"You weren't all that nice."

He looks confused, then he closes the blinds to his emotions with a snap, leaving only blankness. "I'm sorry. I was out of my head."

She doesn't know what worries her more, the fact that he's being evasive and doesn't seem to remember his behavior, or the pain and personality change. "Have you been to a doctor?"

"That's how I get the magic pills."

"I mean recently."

He checks the cinch on his horse. "Yep. Every three months."

"Wait, what? How long has this been going on?"

With his back to her and voice matter-of-fact, he says, "Nearly fifteen years."

Maggie feels as confused as Hank had looked moments before. "Why am I just now learning about it?"

"You've seen me have headaches before."

"You know what I mean."

"Whining like a child isn't the bull rider way."

"Would you stop fiddling with that horse and talk to me?"

He turns and meets her eyes. "Let's ride out. I'll tell you on the way."

TWO

THEY MOUNT UP. Maggie's not an expert rider, but Don Juan feels solid underneath her as she adjusts her reins. Louise runs down from the hayloft and follows them into the stable yard. Maggie's Texas goats, Omaha and Nebraska, are visiting Wyoming, too, and they bleat at her.

"Lawn mowers, do your thing," Hank had said after breakfast, and staked them in the yard on the barn-facing side of the main house, a white two-story wooden structure, where Maggie is staying with him.

Apparently they don't want to do their thing without Maggie anymore. Or maybe they're nervous with the change in weather. Fuss buckets. She makes a mental note to put them up when she and Hank get back with Lily.

Hank clucks and Tatonka takes off at a trot. Man and horse lead the way through several gates, heading south, until they—and Louise—are riding across a pasture so large there's no opposite fence in sight. Theirs is not a long-term partnership. Hank's go-to gelding, Wolf, had died a month before. But Tatonka moves like he's reading Hank's mind, which Maggie knows is partly training and partly Hank's clear body cues and leg pressure.

Hank gestures at the monochrome before them in shades of white varying from marshmallow on the ground to ash in the sky. "Lily has a few favorite spots. We'll check those first."

Don Juan is a slow-goer. Maggie fans her legs at his sides as he falls behind Tatonka. Big flakes swirl around Hank's body, and snow puffs explode from Tatonka's hooves. With ten yards separating them from Maggie, they look like a scene in a snow globe.

Hank swivels his head back toward her. "Smack your thighs with the reins. That usually does the trick."

She smacks, but Don Juan doesn't so much as flinch. She tries again. Once, twice, three times, with increasing velocity. Her thighs sting from the smacks, and the last time she does it, she catches the saddle's pommel. It makes a sharp sound. Don Juan snorts and speeds up to a reluctant trot.

In the distance, she sees the black silhouettes of cattle, all facing the same direction, huddled together. Their backs are dusted white. Louise cavorts like a puppy, snapping at falling snow. The wind is gusty, but not ferocious, and it's strangely less cold than she'd expected. If she wasn't worried about Hank and Lily, in fact, the ride would be lovely. She can even make out the Sibleys' tall, rustic cabin on the mountain and the road winding up to it. Austere. Beautiful. Mysterious. Hank has promised to take her up to see it soon.

"Okay, cowboy, we're riding. Time to talk," she says as Don Juan catches up to Tatonka.

Hank shifts his weight back in his saddle. Tatonka slows to match pace with Don Juan. "You remember me telling you I retired from bull riding because I got hurt?"

"Yes." She glances at him.

"I came here to recover."

"Right."

He nods.

She does a mini eye-roll. "Thanks. That clears it all up for me."

He twists in the saddle, stretching his lower back one direction and then the other. "Bull riders get hurt. Often. I was always too tall for it, really, and prone to whiplash."

"Okay. And?"

"I went down at NFR."

It takes her a second to remember that NFR is the abbreviation for the National Finals Rodeo. "After winning in Cheyenne?"

"Yes. A few months after that. I hurt my head pretty bad, along with some other parts. Another in a long line of head injuries, to tell the truth. It took a long time to heal. Never did completely. I've been on meds and seeing doctors pretty much ever since."

She reaches toward him, trying to touch him. "I'm sorry. I didn't know."

He lifts his hand and brushes hers, then their horses skitter too far apart for them to maintain contact. "It's called traumatic brain injury. Although we didn't have a name for it back when I was riding. Like football players, boxers, and soldiers get."

"And bull riders."

"Yep." His face is stony.

Maggie sees a long-legged mating pair of sandhill cranes alight from the snow. The big birds don't appear flight-worthy, but they lumber skyward where their awkward size turns into effortless grace. They're headed south, it appears, but behind schedule. It makes her feel restless. For a brief moment, a flicker of worry about the wreck of her professional life distracts her. Then another flicker pushes it away. An image of Hank, riding at Frontier Days. Wearing a cowboy hat. "Wait, didn't you wear a helmet?"

"No. And don't ever mention that in front of my mother."

"Why?"

"It was always a point of contention. And arguing about it again doesn't fix anything now."

The horses lean into a climb. By the time they crest the rise, they're both breathing hard.

"But it's under control, right?"

"As much as it can be." He cuts into a stand of aspen trees.

"What's that mean?"

"It gets worse over time. Makes me more susceptible to things."

"What things?"

He looks straight ahead, his jaw tight. "Darkness. Mood swings. Confusion. Forgetfulness."

The gnawing in Maggie's stomach from earlier restarts with intensity. This sounds serious. And Hank has a history of neurological issues in his family anyway. Father dying of Lou Gehrig's disease. Mother with Alzheimer's. She wants to crawl into his saddle and hold him to her. If she's scared, how must he feel? But she knows the last thing he wants is to be coddled.

"Okay, then. Good thing you told me so I can help."

He shrugs. "I appreciate you wanting to, but I don't see how you can."

"Don't underestimate me."

Truth be told, she doesn't see how she can yet either, but she's always believed her refusal to give up when the odds are against her is one of her best traits. They break from the aspen grove. Before she can think of a response, Hank points.

"There she is."

Maggie doesn't see anything but white on white. "Where?"

"Take your sunglasses off. You'll see better."

"It's glary."

But Maggie tucks them down the front of her jacket. She blinks away the glare and the falling flakes. When her eyes adjust, she sees steam rising from an irregular shape in the snow. A black tail swishes and snow scatters. Lily.

"Why isn't she moving?"

"My guess is she's got a halter and lead tangled in something."

"Why would she have them on?" Maggie's voice holds a note of rising panic. She knows the Double S horses are left bare to prevent exactly this.

"Someone probably left her tied up after feeding her. It's good for her. Teaches her patience."

"Teaches her she can break lead lines, too, looks like."

"I imagine she pulled it loose, and we're running shorthanded with Paco on vacation, so no one had been by to put her up yet. We don't tie her off with hard knots. She's broken a hitching post or two before. Damn mare is strong as a freight train."

"And obviously clever."

Don Juan nickers at Lily. Lily is watching them, but she doesn't answer the gelding. Maggie jumps off her horse when they're twenty feet away.

"Wait, Maggie. I'll get her untangled."

"No. Let me, please."

Hank unsnaps a belt scabbard. "Take this. You'll probably need to cut the end of the line to get her loose."

"Thanks." Maggie hands Don Juan's reins to Hank. She attaches the scabbard to her own belt, then unties the feed bag and slings it over her shoulder.

"You always need to carry a knife out here. To deal with whatever comes your way, in case help doesn't."

"I don't have one."

"Keep that one for now." Hank tosses her an extra halter and lead rope he'd coiled on his saddle horn. "And if all else fails, just take off her halter and put this one on."

Maggie trudges toward Lily. The snow isn't deep, but it's wet. Don Juan tries to follow the feed bag, but Hank holds him back.

Lily's line is tangled in tall, thick brush. She strains toward the feed bag, tossing her head and ignoring Maggie altogether. "*Buh-buh-buh, buh-buh-buh, buh-buh.*"

Maggie laughs at her eager sounds. "Lily, you're a mess." She slips the feed bag over Lily's ears and pats her muscular neck.

A buck jumps out of the brush not fifteen feet from Maggie and Lily. Maggie jumps. Lily doesn't. Maggie checks the mare carefully for injuries, but doesn't find so much as a scratch. Lily's round belly looks warm and inviting, so Maggie presses her cheek against it. Inside, a hoof strikes out and thumps her.

Maggie laughs delightedly. "I felt the foal kick."

Hank grunts, but he smiles. "Cut her loose and let's shake a leg. We have to pony her back, and she's going to want to slow us down."

"Pony?"

"Lead her along while we're riding."

Maggie examines the line. "She's wrapped it up tight."

"Can you salvage some of it?"

Maggie loosens the upper coils of the rope, making her way to the bottom. "All but about two or three feet."

"That's worth saving, but we'll have to use the longer line to pony her."

Maggie pulls the knife from the scabbard. It's black, with the Double S brand. "Cool knife."

"We used to have a bunch like that. I think it's the only one left now."

She saws through the lead. It's harder than it looks, what with bad footing and prickly bushes. When the line and horse are freed, she exchanges the old line for the new line and leads Lily to Hank, then removes the feed bag, but not without a tussle.

Hank takes the rope and hands Don Juan's reins back to her. "Let's get out of here."

Maggie clips the old lead line to a ring on her saddle and puts the feed bag over the horn. As she mounts, she catches a glimpse of sun through breaking clouds. In the near distance, she sees big, dark birds circling. "Are those golden eagles?"

Hank glances up, then turns his attention back to Lily, who's trying to bite Tatonka. He twirls the end of her line between the two horses. She quits her attack, but she doesn't back away. "Nope. Buzzards."

Maggie points at a large snowy hump with a few trees to one side. "Is that another animal out there?"

"Probably."

"Should we go help it?"

"Take a closer look."

Maggie squints. "Oh. Is it dead?"

"It, and about ten others."

"What the hell?"

"It's our dead pile."

"Your what?"

"Where we put the livestock that die."

Maggie is drawn to the pile of carcasses like a fly to manure in August. She leads Don Juan toward it.

"Where are you going?"

"I just want a closer look."

"Be careful. There's a buffalo jump on the other side of it. Rock at the bottom."

Maggie knows what a buffalo jump is from reading about Pretty-shield and other Crow, who chased buffalo to low cliffs, where some of the fleeing beasts would fall over. Women would wait at the bottom, knives ready, to finish them off. "Okay."

"When our pile gets too big, we burn it. Then we push what's left over the jump with the tractor."

As Maggie draws nearer to the pile, Louise joins her and bounds up to it. "Oh no, bad idea."

The dog ignores her. She dives in, and soon her head completely disappears. Maggie looks away. Louise barks. Her wagging tail is about the only thing visible when Maggie turns back to her, reluctantly. "Come on out now."

Louise growls and tugs, growls and tugs. The top of the pile shifts on one side. The dog falls backward, a cowboy boot in her mouth. A bright red one with hand-tooling and high heels.

"Hank, Louise has found something, and it's not a cow."

"Could be a horse," Hank hollers. "Everything dies eventually."

"Horses don't wear cowboy boots."

"What?" Hank gives Tatonka a firm "Yah," and they canter to the pile, reaching it just as Maggie does.

The horses stop as one, unwilling to go any closer. Louise wags her tail beside them, the boot still in her mouth.

"Hank, what the hell is going on?"

But she doesn't have to ask. Thanks to their closer perspective and to Louise and her tunneling and tugging, they can both see another distinctive red high-heeled boot in the pile, as well as the back of a dead man's belt that's easily readable even upside down: PACO.

Hank pulls out a satellite phone.

"What are you doing? Shouldn't we help him?" she asks, even though the rational part of her knows Paco's past saving.

Hank is already speaking into the phone. "We've got a suspicious death out at Piney Bottoms Ranch. I think it's our top hand. Paco Lopez. And he's frozen in our dead pile."

THREE

Maggie shakes like thunder from the wet, the cold, and the shock of finding Paco's body. Back at the barn at Piney Bottoms, she and Hank update Gene and Andy. Hank had called Gene earlier with the bare bones of the news. There's not much to add. Just that they expect someone from the sheriff's department any minute. Then she and Hank turn out the horses in silence. They retreat to the main house, where Hank shuts Louise in the mudroom out back.

Maggie dashes upstairs. All she wants is hot coffee and dry clothes before law enforcement arrives. Luckily, Trudy, the ranch cook, has a large pot of coffee percolated by the time Maggie returns in fresh jeans and one of Hank's University of Wyoming sweatshirts. Maggie groans with pleasure when she recognizes the smell of the Panama dark roast from Pine Coffee Supply, the new house coffee.

In the dining room, Maggie heads for the sideboard, which holds the coffee and beverage service. Calling the space a dining room is really a misnomer, though. It's more a mess hall with a long plank table for ten at its center. The entire room is paneled in whitewashed shiplap. Rusted relics hang from the walls, a testament to the ranch's history. A PB branding iron. A wooden-handled scythe. Barbed wire. The dining area opens into an industrial-size kitchen with all modern appliances except for a big wood stove. White shiplap in the kitchen contrasts with dark green painted cabinets and thick plank countertops.

The cook is nowhere to be seen. As Maggie's stirring sugar and cream into her mug, a horn honks outside.

"Who is that rude person out front?" a querulous voice asks.

A wheelchair appears, in it the wizened body of white-haired Mrs. Sibley, and, pushing the wheelchair, Laura, Hank's dark pixie sister. Maggie imagines Mrs. Sibley as a younger woman. She must have looked a lot like her flinty, pretty daughter. Laura's wearing a T-shirt that shows off lithely muscled arms that Maggie envies. Laura's come by them honestly. A ranch kid turned jockey, she's retired now and running an equine camp for troubled youth in New Mexico, on the family ranch managed by her husband.

Hank is right behind them. "It's okay, Mom. I've got it." He kisses his mom's cheek. His face has drawn in and his eyes have sunken, just in the last ten minutes.

Maggie's afraid his headache is back. She pours Hank a cup, black, then backs out of his mother's sightline. It's usually better if Maggie doesn't attract her ire. Evangeline "Vangie" Sibley isn't Maggie's biggest fan.

Laura is up to speed on Paco. She nods at Hank. "Let's go get some tea, Mom."

"I want coffee."

"The doctor says you need to stay away from it."

The older woman pouts. "I want to greet our company."

Laura laughs. "I'm your company, Mom. I just got here last night. Let's go have a visit."

Louise chooses that moment to set up coyote-worthy howling from the mudroom.

Mrs. Sibley's nose wrinkles and her mouth puckers. "Do something about that dog. You know I don't allow ranch animals in the house."

Laura's reply is inaudible as she pushes her mother toward the kitchen. Hank slams his entire cup of hot coffee and winces. He thunks it down on the sideboard, then heads toward the front door. Maggie follows him, still sipping from her mug.

"She didn't even look at me. Laura, I mean. She hates me, too."

"No one hates you." Hank pulls the door open and squints as sunlight blasts him in both eyes.

"Yeah, right." Maggie dons sunglasses from the pocket of the jacket she left hanging on a peg by the door, then puts the jacket on, too. Her head, still protected by her knit beanie, is starting to itch. She rubs the beanie against her scalp.

The cold is sharp now, and it freezes the hairs inside Maggie's nose. The sky is a brilliant baby blue, with the snow a blanket of rainbow crystals sparkling in the sun. She thinks she can make out the circling buzzards over the dead pile in the distance. In the opposite direction, a single set of tire tracks snake from a white sheriff's department Ram 1500 truck back toward the ranch gate. The rumbling engine silences. A grizzly-like deputy gets out. He's zipped into a jacket whose size must have multiple Xs before its L. He stomps his way through new snow over to Maggie and Hank.

The two men lean in for a one-shouldered guy-hug, clapping each other on the back and making small talk about family and football.

Hank turns to Maggie. "Travis and I have known each other since he was a little squirt hanging out watching the big boys ride bulls."

Of course. Hank and his family trace their Wyoming roots back to the late 1800s, when their ancestors homesteaded their land. Deep roots mean something here, and from what Maggie has seen, Hank knows and is respected by most of the people in northern Wyoming and southeastern Montana, even east into the Black Hills of South Dakota.

Travis grips Maggie's hand with his cold, dry one and shakes. "Ms. Killian. Good to see you again." They'd met the month before when there was a series of burglaries at the guest cabin Maggie was staying in, and later when Rudy Simon, a spurned fan of Maggie's, attacked Hank.

"Deputy Travis. I'm not sure about good. At least not for Paco."

"Yeah, Mr. Lopez. Bad business." Travis nods. "Sorry I had to come alone. We're shorthanded."

"You'll do, buddy." Hank steps onto the road back to the outbuildings. "Come on. We can talk on the way. We've got a Ranger gassed up and waiting."

Maggie takes a step and immediately feels her foot slide, so she slips her hand through Hank's arm for balance. Hank's changed his footwear from cowboy boots to tactical boots that look like they're waterproof.

Travis is wearing snow boots. "Tell me what you saw, then."

Maggie looks down at her feet and has a sharp and sudden case of boot envy.

"Maggie'd never seen our dead pile. When she got close, her dog brought out a boot. One of Paco's. He was buried in the pile. But the dog excavated enough that we saw his legs and the back of his belt."

"You didn't see his face?"

"No. We didn't want to disturb anything, so we backed away, and I called 911."

"Good. When was the last time you saw him? Alive, that is."

Hank cocks his head at Maggie. "Two, three days ago?"

Maggie counts it on her fingers. "Three. At breakfast on Friday. He was taking a long weekend."

Travis says, "So today is Monday. Wouldn't you have expected him back by now?"

"Sort of. Maybe." Hank shrugs. "If he hadn't come back by midweek, I would have worried. Otherwise, I would have just assumed it was Paco blowing off steam."

Travis's forehead crinkles. "Did he say where he was going?"

Hank stops at the gate to a paddock. He puts his foot on the bottom rail and leans a forearm on the top. "Actually, no. He said he was following the fun."

Maggie glances at the northern sky and sees a dark gray wall of clouds advancing like a steamroller. The mountains block the view of northern fronts until they're bearing down on the ranch.

Travis crosses his arms, surveying the ranch in a one-hundred-eighty-degree arc. "What did he mean by that?"

Hank smiles, but his eyes are sad. "Paco liked cards, women, and whiskey. When he came back from time off, he was usually dropped here by an angry woman squealing tires out of the place, and looking like he'd been mule-kicked all the way back from Lynchburg, Tennessee."

"You'd suspect a woman, then?"

"Maybe. But I've never seen one mad enough to kill him and leave him on our dead pile."

"Who would be?"

"Personally, I wouldn't know. Someone he beat at cards, stiffed when he lost, or ran out on when they caught him cheating? A boyfriend or husband who didn't like to share?"

"Any you know?"

"Like I said, none personally. Just his legend."

"What about family, friends, a steady girl?"

"His family's in South Texas. I guess we were his friends, although he also palled around with some of the hands on the area ranches. And I've never known him to tie himself down to one woman."

"Who benefits from his death?"

Hank rubs his chin. "I don't rightly know. He had a little bit of life insurance through Double S. Not enough to kill over, I wouldn't think, but maybe to someone. I don't know who gets it or if he had anything else worth much. He had a real nice roping saddle. That's about it." His face darkens. "And, well, he had this job. If someone wanted it, I guess that's something."

"Or if someone wanted him out of it."

Hank doesn't respond.

"Kind of hard for someone to get out to that dead pile without anyone here noticing."

"There's miles and miles of unmonitored fence line on this place."

"Inhospitable fence line."

"Unwelcoming. But not inhospitable."

Travis changes tacks. "You said Paco was your top hand. Will someone get bumped up with him gone?"

"We only have one other full-time hand. Andy. An Amish kid."

"He'll be promoted, then."

"Maybe. That isn't a sure thing. But the Amish are nonviolent, and Andy wouldn't hurt a fly." Hank resumes walking to the barn, Travis behind him and Maggie beside him.

"Did you have any relationship with Paco, Maggie?"

Maggie feels icy snowflakes pelting her face as the gray clouds close in on them. "He helped fix my truck once. But really, nothing other than small talk at meals. I've been teaching Andy to read music and play the guitar, but Paco wasn't interested."

Travis says. "Really? I read online that you'd given up music."

Maggie stops, and Travis bumps into her. She just loves all the media attention lately. *Not.* "I gave up performing music professionally a long time ago. I didn't forget how to make it."

Hank snorts. He wants her to play more. Since he reentered her life, the music is coming back to her, but it owned her once before, and she's not going through that again for anyone. This time, music is on her terms or not at all.

The wind picks up as they reach the stable yard, where Travis greets Gene and Andy. Travis barely glances at Andy's homemade blue pants and oilcloth coat, distinctive wide-brimmed hat, and blousy work shirt.

Travis takes Gene and Andy through the same type of questions he'd already gone over with Hank and Maggie, making occasional notes in a spiral pad. Gene confirms most of what Hank said, although he expresses more consternation about Paco extending his vacations. The only new information comes from Andy.

"He had a girl. Back in Texas. Her father was none too happy with Paco because the time had come for him to go back for her and marry. Paco was dragging his feet. He hasn't been faithful to her. He's something of a ladies' man."

Maggie isn't surprised about the ladies' man part, although the fiancée is a shock. Paco is—was—a charmer who loved to recite raunchy cowboy poetry. He had mischievous eyes, a compact, muscular build, thick, wavy dark hair, a black mustache, and a square jaw. He wasn't her type, but he was definitely attractive.

Travis's eyebrows rise. "Have you met her?"

"No. I've seen a picture. He keeps it under his mattress. One time he showed it to me when he'd been drinking."

"What's her name?"

"He called her Maribel."

"Last name?"

"He didn't say."

"Why was he dragging his feet?"

Andy looks around like he's the stray dog and Travis the dogcatcher. There's nowhere for him to run. "He liked his freedom."

Travis closes his notepad. "I'll need to search his quarters."

Gene says, "He has a room in the bunkhouse."

"I'll swing by after we go see the body. Could we get that room locked up in the meantime?"

Gene nods. "No problem."

Andy and Gene wave as Hank, Maggie, and Travis pile into a four-seat Ranger, with Hank at the wheel. They stop at the house for Travis's crime scene bag, then continue into the white pasture. The wind has picked up, and Maggie wishes she'd brought a scarf. She dons the gloves she keeps stuffed in her pockets. It's slowgoing. The two-tracks are rough and starting to drift. Twice the Ranger bogs down and they have to dig it out with a folding shovel from the storage compartment.

The second time, Hank taps the gas gauge. It doesn't move. "Andy gave us the one with the broken gas gauge, dammit. But it should be almost full."

When they reach the dead pile, they park and walk closer, up the hill. Maggie is glad when she hears the others breathing as hard as she is. Travis surveys the scene as he catches his breath. Maggie huddles into Hank's chest. The snow feels pelletized and the wind is lashing it against her face, where it then slides down her neck.

After walking a complete circuit around the dead pile, Travis retrieves crime scene tape and stakes from his bag in the Ranger. The wind whips the tape as he cordons off the area, then begins taking pictures. Several times he brushes snow aside to expose items for photographs, but Maggie is too far away to identify them. Occasionally Travis slips things into plastic baggies that he stuffs down the front of his bulky coat.

Just as suddenly as they began, the snow and wind stop and the gray clouds move south. Even with the sun coming out, though, it feels far colder now than it had when Maggie and Hank were out here earlier. Maggie is grateful for the temperature in one respect: the dead pile is frozen and odor-free. Travis works his way carefully up the pile to Paco's body, about ten feet off the ground. She wouldn't want to be in Travis's shoes, climbing and digging through dead bodies, however stiff they are. She watches as Travis excavates around Paco until his torso is visible. Hank turns away.

"What a waste," Hank says. He shakes his head.

"How could he even have ended up in there like that?" Maggie asks.

"We use the tractor to dump livestock there."

"You think someone used a Double S tractor?"

Hank is facing the pile again. His voice is like sandpaper. "It's possible. If not, it sure would have been difficult for someone to get a tractor on our land without us knowing about it. But hell, maybe he climbed up there himself. He could have been drunk and sleeping it off. Or hiding out."

She remembers his terse exchange with Travis earlier, when he'd insisted Piney Bottoms was easily accessible. He's contradicting himself a little now, but she gets it. If he admits his fears to Travis, he's pointing a finger at his own people. Protecting his own might mean failing to defend Paco. He's in a tough spot. Either way he leans goes against the type of man he is.

Suddenly, Paco breaks free from the space he's wedged into, between the remains of what looks like a steer and a young heifer. Travis scrambles out of the way as the body tumbles down the pile and lands face-first in front of Hank and Maggie, his body making snapping and cracking sounds on the way down.

Maggie gasps.

"Son of a bitch," Hank says.

There's a knife lodged in the base of Paco's skull, its white handle sticking out like an accusatory finger pointing at Hank.

Maggie says, "I'm guessing he didn't climb up there himself after all."

FOUR

Dinner that night is a somber affair. At the far end of the table, Gene and Andy are in deep conversation with the two day hands—they get three squares with their paychecks, although they don't live onsite—when Mrs. Sibley arrives, quarreling with Laura. Seated by Hank across the enormous table from mother and daughter, Maggie has a front-row seat.

The old woman sniffs. "All I'm saying is I left my batteries in the bathroom, and they're gone now."

"Mom, they were used batteries. They didn't work anymore."

"They were mine. Someone stole them."

"No one stole them. They were trash. I threw them away."

"I didn't raise you to steal."

Laura squeezes her eyes shut. Maggie notices dark circles underneath them, with skin that seems transparent. When they open, they're fixed on Hank. "I couldn't get her to nap. How do you and Tom do it?" she says, referring to Mrs. Sibley's caretaker, who's taking vacation while Laura visits.

"I feel ya, sis."

Trudy hollers from the kitchen. "Sorry, you guys. Just a few more minutes." Her red hair spills from its low bun. Her normally serene face is smudged with flour.

"It's okay," Hank tells her.

"Thanks, boss," she calls.

"Mickey's not going to let me come anymore. I'm worn to a frazzle when I get home, every time." Laura smiles to show she's joking. Her husband, Mickey, doesn't make it up to Wyoming much, Hank says. Maggie has never met him, but she's heard good things. She figures he's a saint if he's survived marriage to feisty Laura.

Hank pours himself and Maggie iced teas. Maggie thinks how much better her sweet tea would be with Koltiska liqueur in it. A sweet TKO, as it's known locally, since the liqueur goes by the KO family ranch brand.

Hank says, "You're earning your spot in heaven. How are things back at home?"

"Where's my dinner?" Mrs. Sibley demands.

"Soon, Mom." Laura puts a hand on her mother's. "Things are crazy right now. Farrah wants to quit the University of New Mexico and go to Amarillo College. To be closer to Greg, her boyfriend. He's working in a dance club, with the lofty aspiration of being an EDM DJ."

"Electronic dance music? Wow. So they're into rave culture," Maggie says.

"Maybe. I've gotten too old to get it."

Hank guffaws. "You were probably always too old, sis."

"Bite me, Hank. But I am tired all the time. I'm just thankful the equine therapy camps are over until next summer. Ever since we let Farrah go to Bonnaroo with Greg and his friends last spring, she's been sliding off the deep end. Now she says Greg is a ghost producer for some famous DJ. All I know is he stays up all night and dropped out of school." She laughs, a harsh sound. "I suck as a mother. I've never been able to nurture anything, not even a plant. The only thing I've ever even kept alive was a succulent from Walmart, but after I congratulated myself for my green thumb, Mickey showed me the damn plant was fake. God knew what he was doing when he made me barren after all."

Hank shakes his head at her. "Don't say that. You're a great mother to Farrah."

Maggie remembers Hank telling her that Mickey and Laura had fostered Farrah and only adopted her as a teenager. She's been in Farrah's shoes herself—she was obsessed with music at her age—so she tries to reassure Laura. "I've been there. I'm sure she'll be fine."

"Really? And how did that go for you?"

Trudy whisks in with an enormous covered platter, which she sets beside the butter plate. A bag of Cheetos is on top of the platter. She tosses the bag to Gene and winks. He catches it. His cheeks redden.

Hank squeezes Maggie's knee.

She's seething. Laura has taken the gloves off, referring—Maggie is sure

—to her famous rehab stints and the undeniable reality that she is no longer in the business. She musters a sweet smile and purrs musically. "A number one album, a Grammy, and international fame."

Trudy reappears with a covered pot and ladle. "Keeping it simple tonight, everyone. Cornbread and chili."

Gene smiles at her. "Thanks, Trudy. Are you joining us?"

"I'm busier than a one-armed paperhanger. Y'all dig in."

Gene seems lost in thought, watching her walk back into the kitchen.

Laura nods at Maggie. "How wonderful for you. I'm not into your kind of music, so you'll have to excuse me."

A backhanded compliment at best. Maggie's hackles rise and she tries to formulate a retort about the obscurity of quarter-horse jockeys compared to alt-country rockers.

Luckily, Mrs. Sibley interrupts before the two women put their backs into it. "Isn't it about time for grace, Henry?"

The table goes silent. It's a clear sign that Mrs. Sibley is having a bad day when she thinks Hank is her deceased husband, Henry.

"I'm Hank, Mom. Will everyone bow their heads, please?" Hank clears his throat. "Dear Lord, thank you for your many blessings, the nourishment of the food on this table, and the hands that prepared it. We ask for your grace and peace as we mourn the loss of your son Paco. Please welcome him into your kingdom and help us find justice on earth for whoever did this horrible thing to him. In Jesus's name we pray, amen."

A chorus of amens echoes his.

Everyone remains quiet as they pass around platters of cornbread, then bowls for the chili that Hank ladles. Trudy pops her head in to check that everyone has what they need. She wipes her hands on a ruffled pink-and-green gingham apron that's far more old-fashioned than she is, then brings another pitcher of iced tea. Sweat beads on the pale skin at her hairline.

"Thank you, Trudy," Gene says.

She curtsies, holding out one side of her apron over her Wranglers and the snap-front Western shirt with a feminine cut that shows off her curves.

After she disappears back into the kitchen, Gene and Hank share a glance. Hank nods.

Gene says, "Thank you all for cooperating with law enforcement today." Crime scene techs, an additional detective, and the county coroner had joined Travis soon after he examined the dead pile, and the group had only packed up and left half an hour before dinner. "We're real broken-up about Paco. I know you are, too."

"Who's Paco?" Mrs. Sibley says, her voice reverberating.

Laura distracts her with a discussion about honey for her cornbread.

"We've been in touch with his family. They've agreed we can have a memorial service for him here. We were thinking Prairie Dog Community Church. Unfortunately, though, I'm going to be in Oklahoma with some buckers, but Hank will have that covered."

The service conflicts with the Duncan rodeo? Maggie's disappointment is deep. Does this mean she and Hank won't be going? But it's not the time to ask.

"Will they be coming to collect him?" Andy asks.

Gene nods. "Soon. But we'll have time for the memorial first. Unfortunately, this is a busy time for us. We're defending our NFR Stock Contractor of the Year title, with NFR only a few weeks away." Gene doesn't mention that they'd only reclaimed their NFR contract a few weeks before, after the murder of their neighbor and competitor, Patrick Rhodes. Everyone has been in a mad scramble to get ready since then. "We're going to have to bring on another full-time hand, immediately."

Andy studies the wooden slats in the tabletop.

"We have a good candidate. I've called him to come in tomorrow morning, to have him try us on for size and vice versa."

Pink creeps over Andy's ears.

"Andy, we'd be much obliged if you'd accept a promotion to top hand for us."

Andy's head lifts. His beard covers most of the blush on his face. "Th-th-thank you. I'm honored."

"Congratulations, Andy," Hank says, lifting his iced tea glass to salute him. "I'm sorry it's under these circumstances, but you've earned it."

The day hands, Maggie, Laura, and Trudy join in the congratulations.

Gene smiles at him. "I'm leaving on a scouting trip tomorrow. Hank and I will be counting on you to bring the new hand on right."

"Yes, sir. Absolutely, sir."

Maggie's phone vibrates in her pocket. She sneaks it out and glances at the screen just as it notifies her that the caller—Charlotte, her mother—left a voicemail. She suppresses a groan. There's only one reason Charlotte is calling, and that is to pressure her to come back to Texas. She already feels enough of that pressure from inside herself. She doesn't need it from her mother, too.

When Maggie left the music industry, she was in a death spiral. She'd lost her contract, been through rehab twice, and alienated everyone she'd ever worked with. Then her record company went belly-up, and she'd accepted her little antique shop and house in lieu of payment for her albums and songs. It had been a slow climb back from dead busted to self-sufficient. A few years ago, she discovered she was adopted and had a secretly rich birth mother—Gidget—and a politician birth father—Boyd. She inherited everything when Gidget died. But she's only rich on paper. She can't bear the thought of selling off treasures like the Andy Warhol or the vintage Jaguar, much less Gidget's farm, especially after she lost everything else in the fires. So she's rudderless, between careers, and cashless. The only place it seems she can solve these problems is back in Texas, but the thought of leaving Hank in Wyoming is like a death sentence.

As if she's reading her mind, Mrs. Sibley says, "What does that woman do to support herself? Lord knows she isn't doing a lick of work here, and she's eating up our food and sleeping under our roof."

Maggie chokes on the cornbread that is suddenly dry in her throat. She can't argue with the accuracy of Mrs. Sibley's complaint. She only hopes Hank's mother doesn't realize exactly where under their roof she's sleeping.

Hank slaps Maggie's back until she recovers. "Mom, that's uncalled for. Maggie is my guest."

Laura smirks. "It *would* be nice to hear Maggie's plans."

Maggie feels like there's a knife sticking out of her back, and she gets an uncomfortable rush of imagery. Paco in the dead pile, stiff, the knife in his neck. It makes her think of the knife Hank lent her. She'd left it on the nightstand earlier when she changed into dry clothes.

Hank glowers. "Laura, please."

"What? You told me she doesn't have a home or business back in Texas. I'm interested."

His voice grows even louder. "Laura. Stop it. Now."

Maggie clears her throat. "It's okay, Hank. Laura, I'm trying to figure that out right now. I'll have to go back to Texas soon one way or the other, once I get some figures back from my insurance company and some quotes from contractors. The adjuster was headed out to my place today."

Mrs. Sibley sniffs. "Take the goats with you when you go. This isn't a goat ranch."

"Ignore her. And don't be in a rush." Hank squeezes her knee. "You just got here."

She looks at him, and she's shocked to see his eyes are damp and emotional.

"Yeah," Andy says, his voice cracking. "We've just started my guitar lessons."

Maggie scoops chili into her mouth so she doesn't have to answer anyone, especially not Hank, not in front of the group. She hasn't told him that what she really wants is for him to move the Double S to Texas and come south with her. Piney Bottoms belongs to his mother. Gene is from Texas, where there are more rodeos anyway. Running the Double S from Giddings makes good sense to her. There's a long-term tenant at Gidget's old place now, but when the lease is up, there'd be plenty of room for the bucking stock. Especially if they leased the neighbor's place, too, and that old coot Lumpy would love the income. It wouldn't hurt to contact a realtor and see what's available in the area, either. That way when she brings it up with Hank, she'll have complete information on the possibilities to wow him with. She's just worried it won't strike the same chord with Hank.

Into the strained silence, Gene says, "Have you told your family you're learning the guitar, Andy?"

"No. Some of them feel that playing instruments is a show of vanity. Not all of them."

"But you're on Rumspringa, aren't you?" Gene asks. He's referring to the time before baptism into the church when Amish youth are allowed to go out into the English—non-Amish—world, before they decide whether to make a commitment to formally join their church and community.

"Yes."

Maggie says, "Do you still live by Amish rules while you're on Rumspringa?"

"To the extent you want to. I do, mostly. It's important to my father."

Gene smiles. "And Andy's father, Reggie, has been known to show up here without warning to check on him."

Maggie remembers seeing Andy talking to Reggie earlier. "I thought your family was in Montana?" Maggie says.

"They are. He rides into Sheridan with a former Amish several times a week to work."

Gene helps himself to a second bowl of chili. "What will Reggie and the rest of your family think about your promotion?" He grins at Maggie. "Andy has nine younger siblings."

"They'll be proud of me."

Maggie pushes her bowl back. The spicy chili was good, but she's not very hungry. "Are you going back when Rumspringa is over?"

Andy mumbles something.

"What?"

"I'm not sure."

Mrs. Sibley interjects again. "At least that young man works, like what *she* should be doing instead of freeloading off my husband while she tries to take him from me."

Hank puts a hand on her arm. "I'm Hank, Mom. Your son. And Maggie isn't trying to take anyone."

She glares at him, her eyes deep, dark, and round, like she's been possessed by a demon.

Laura stands. "That's our cue." She wheels her mother away from the table. "Good night, everyone."

Mrs. Sibley drags her heels on the plank floor. "She's trying to steal everything from me."

"Come on, Mom."

"No, you can't make me. No, goddammit, no."

Laura prevails, and the two disappear, although Mrs. Sibley's strident voice echoes into the dining room. Maggie has never heard the old woman use the Lord's name in vain before.

"I'm sorry," Hank whispers to Maggie.

She stares into his sad eyes. Her own father had Alzheimer's. Her memories of him in his last years aren't pretty. She covers Hank's hand with hers. "No. I am."

FIVE

THE DINNER GROUP breaks up slowly after apple cobbler and ice cream and gathers in the great room at the front of the house. Mrs. Sibley's wing downstairs and Hank's suite upstairs are family-only, but the common areas are set up for everyone at the ranch to enjoy, with computers, a television, games, a beer refrigerator, and books. Maggie pulls Hank away to his rooms, stopping first to take a bouncy, happy Louise from the mudroom to a sabbatical outside.

"Are you ready for bed?" Hank asks when they reach the top of the stairs.

"Maybe." Maggie picks up a vintage wooden mortar and pestle from the sofa table behind a leather couch in Hank's private living area. "I love this."

"You and old things. That's a family heirloom. Come to bed with me, and I'll show you another."

"Oh?" She sets them back down. "More old junk?"

"Bite your tongue. The family jewels."

She rolls her eyes. "Like I said."

"Just meet me in there."

"You going somewhere else first?"

"Trust me."

Maggie slips into his bedroom suite and strips down to her bra and panties. The emotions of the day rush over her—Hank's revelation about his brain health issues, Paco's death, the exhausting reality of Mrs. Sibley's condition, Laura's disapproval of Maggie—and mix with her lingering sadness over her lost home and business. She retrieves her Martin acoustic guitar from its battered case. As she stands in a stream of moonlight from the window, something melancholy forms in her mind, and her fingers translate it into a melody on the strings. Words emerge from deep inside her. Maggie sings softly as she picks to an appreciative audience of one black-and-white dog curled up on a pillow under the window.

"Lost. What once was here now is gone. Lost. Will it ever be found? It's lost. Lost."

"What's that?"

Her fingers still. She turns toward Hank, setting the Martin back in its case. "Nothing. Randomness."

"Don't stop, music girl."

Her eyes take him in, head to toe, lingering on the triangle of his strong neck and shoulders. Muscles honed through hard work, not on machines in a gym. She strolls to him, her music-warmed fingers outstretched. She traces his collarbone and manages a shirt button before the rest of her reaches him. Rocking and humming to the slow melody that plays on in her brain, she finishes the buttons and stops with her fingers on his belt. "You want me to play for you some more now?"

His eyes glint in the same moonlight she'd bathed in while playing her guitar. "Don't stop."

She laughs. "Fickle man."

"I'm not, actually."

She drops her forehead to his chest and kisses the contours there. "I know."

"I can't believe we had to wait fifteen years for this."

"Did you? Wait?" She leaves her lips on his chest, breathing him in, waiting for his answer.

"I've been with other women since. As have you. Men, I mean."

Maggie laughs. "That wasn't what I meant."

Hank whistles and his hand slides down her back to her ass. "Liar."

Maggie draws in a deep breath. She's been holding something back that Gene told her, waiting for the right time to talk about it. Now. Now is that time. "When were you going to tell me you came after me?"

The room is quiet except for the sounds of their breathing.

Finally, Hank says, "So you knew?"

"Not back then. Gene told me a few weeks ago. That you came to one of my shows in Denver and got turned away. And that you showed up for me at rehab."

Hank's hand slides around her waist. "I also tried calling. Your publicist and manager were real assholes."

"I'm sorry. They never told me."

"That's a relief. At the time, I thought they were following your orders."

Maggie tilts her head back so she can see his eyes in the dimly lit room. "Not on your life. There's a million reasons I couldn't take that life. Everyone thinking they could control me for their own reasons was a big one. I wish they'd told me."

"Water under the bridge."

"I don't think I completely trusted you until Gene said you'd tried to reach me." She kisses his chest again, this time in the center, high.

"At least one of us reached out."

"Believe me, I followed you as best I could. I wrote a whole album trying to draw you out." She moves down an inch, drops another kiss.

He laughs.

"Then you kind of fell off the face of the earth, while I got sucked further and further into that crazy world." Another inch, another kiss.

"I heard you on the radio once. A big national show. Aaron Cryor." He pulls her up, kisses her lips hard, then nips them. "You really kicked his ass."

Maggie remembers and groans. "What a jerk. Pretending he was all sanctimonious, then the things he did to me in that studio. The things he expected me to do to him. Total asswipe."

"You got him fired, didn't you?"

"And that got me national attention, which was the beginning of the insanity that shot me like a rocket to the bad ending." She rubs her cheek against his.

"I think it all turned out okay. But maybe that's just because you're in my arms now."

"I kind of like being here. And I believe there's rising evidence that you like it, too." She unbuckles his belt, then pulls it off and drops it to the floor.

"We could test the theory."

Backing away toward the bed, she pulls him by the belt loops to follow her.

"Wait. I have a question for you." He resists. "Why are you in such a hurry to go? When you just got here."

"You mean to the bed?" She unfastens his jeans, then tugs them and his briefs down at the same time. "We can do this wherever you want."

He kicks them off. "No." His jaw bunches. His Adam's apple bulges. "From Wyoming. From me. Back to Texas. When we've just found each other after all this time."

Maggie puts her hands around his waist and pulls, bumping him into her, and together they tumble onto the four-poster bed. Another heirloom. She gathers her courage for the words she's been scared to say to him. "Why don't you come with me?"

His body stiffens on top of her, and not in the good way that leads to fun and games. "I've got the ranch here. Your home, your business in Texas, they're gone."

"But I have family, friends, and a brand. Horses and bulls can live anywhere."

"I'm here, Maggie. I'm tied to here."

She cuts him off with a kiss. Now isn't the time to debate this. She'll make another run at the topic later, when she can be rational and persuasive. When emotions aren't so charged. "So am I. We're together. Nothing is going to change that."

"Together. Or *together*?"

"*Together*. Through the good and the bad and the worse. Together. Let me show you how very much together, cowboy."

A surge of wanting him consumes her, and she flips him onto his back. She grabs him, taking charge, rough and urgent. He responds in kind. They're wild, reckless, and lost. In the midst of their passion, there's a loud crack under the bed. It falls to the floor, mattress, box spring, and all. Louise yelps and scrambles to the door.

"Shit." She's so close, so close to something bigger and better than she's ever felt before. She thrusts against him.

He pulls back.

She presses her forehead into his. "Don't be a quitter, Hank."

Hank yells. "Argh."

"Yes, baby." Maggie sinks her teeth into his chest. "Yes."

"No." He pushes her off of him. "No."

She lands on her back beside him. He rolls into a fetal position, clutching himself.

"Hank? Are you okay?"

He groans. "I think we broke it."

"The bed? I know. I'm sorry."

"No. It. My, um . . ."

She finally gets it. Sees what he's holding on to. Understands why he stopped. "OH. The family jewels?"

"Yes."

"Let me see."

He covers himself with both hands. "Give me a minute."

A sharp knock at the door jerks them both upright. Hank still holds his hand like an athletic cup over his personal parts.

Maggie scrambles for a sheet and whispers, "Did you lock it?"

Laura's voice is so distinct it feels like she's in bed between them. "Hank? Are you in there? I need help with Mom."

"Son of a bitch," he mutters. Then, louder, "Be right down."

"Your . . . jewels." Maggie reaches for him. "What can I do?"

He finally manages a grin. "Don't give up on me. I've had worse injuries in my rodeo days, and I recover fast." He crawls to the edge of the bed, wincing, then walks gingerly to his pile of clothing. He looks down. "Damn, I think it's changing colors."

"Seriously, do I need to take you to the emergency room?"

"Nah. I'll get ibuprofen and an ice pack on my way back up." He zips and buttons his jeans and pulls on a T-shirt from a chest of drawers. He stops at the door. "I love you, Maggie."

He's out before she can tell him that she loves him, too, in a crazy way that scares her. But who's she kidding? He's told her he loves her over and over now, and she always finds a way not to utter the three little words.

SIX

MAGGIE SLIDES down the broken bed like it's a ski slope and hops over the frame to the floor. On her hands and knees, she peers under. Even in the dark, she can see that one of the support slats is broken. The mattress and box spring are tipped inside the frame. Naked from her romp with Hank, she uses her legs and back to take the weight off the remaining slats while she redistributes them inside the frame, then jerks the mattress and box spring back into position. It's a temporary fix, at best.

She's broken a lot of things in her life, but never a bed. Or a penis. Poor Hank.

She crawls out as her phone chimes with a new voicemail notification. The room feels colder. Where is her phone? She finds it in the pocket of her jeans. She scurries back to bed and burrows under the covers. She reads the screen. The notification is new, but the two messages from her mother are from earlier. Her T-Mobile coverage here and throughout Wyoming is hit-or-miss at best.

The first message: "You didn't return my call yesterday. Some reporter contacted me about you. A new one. Amos something-or-other. I told him no comment. Call me."

The second: "Are you mad at me for getting married without telling you? Because I can't think of any other reason you'd move to Wyoming and cut me out of your life. Call me."

Oh, Mother, Mother. She's not ducking her. Life has just been hectic. And this thing, this beautiful thing she has with Hank, has been all-consuming. Surely her newlywed mom can understand that, a woman so in love she eloped without telling her only child. Listening to the squeaky chirp of a night bird, she decides to call Charlotte back in the morning. An owl screeches, raising hackles on her skin. *It will be going after the little bird,* she thinks.

She wraps herself in the comforter and pads over to the window. Louise whines, and Maggie reaches down to pet her head. She doesn't find an owl, but in the beam of the outdoor lights, she sees a man running toward the bunkhouse. *Odd.* She leans all the way to the cold glass. He's short, with dark hair and dark skin. And bright red knee-high boots.

Like Paco.

But that can't be—Paco's dead. She shuts her eyes to clear her vision and tries again. It has to be someone else. It could be Gene. Gene is short and dark. He shouldn't be running to the hired hands' cabin, though. He lives in the opposite direction. And he doesn't have red boots. At least she doesn't think he does. Maybe she's just wrong about the boots. Can she even see red in the low light?

But there's no way to know for sure, because when she opens her eyes again, the man is gone. The landscape is night-bare and lonely. A gust of wind rattles the window and pushes snow through the ranch grounds like a schoolyard bully.

The door to the bedroom opens, and she turns away from the window. It's Hank, and the hall behind him is pitch dark. He moves into the relative light of the room. His shoulders are slumped—more of an inverted U than a V now—and he walks like a man thirty years older than he is.

"Is your mom okay?"

He collapses onto the bed and lets out a short bark.

"What?" Maggie stands in front of him.

"Ice pack. Frozen peas and carrots to the junk."

"It's like you're making a stew. Sausage and veggies."

"God, I hope not." He laughs, then shakes his head. "And about my mom—she's not really okay tonight."

"What's the matter?"

"She's sundowning."

Maggie sits beside him and runs her fingers through his hair. Even though Maggie's father had Alzheimer's, her parents had kept his diagnosis from her as a teenager. She'd never heard the term *sundowning.* "What's that?"

"She has trouble functioning at bedtime, then can't fall asleep and gets up over and over during the night, each time more irrational than the last."

"Does it happen often?"

"More than it used to. Laura hasn't dealt with it before. She's going to have a tough night, I think, but she says she can handle it."

"God, Hank. I'm sorry."

He throws the bag of vegetables toward the bathroom. They hit the tile floor and skid out of sight. "To hell with icing. What I need is your arms around me."

Maggie puts her head on his shoulder, careful to keep her weight off his injured spots. "How's this?"

He doesn't answer, but his breathing speeds up and his chest heaves.

She touches his cheek, and her fingers come away wet. Tears. "Hank?"

"Damn, Paco. I never knew he had a fiancée. I thought of him like a little brother. Or the son I'd never have." A sob breaks free, but he reels it back in quickly. "How could someone do that to him? And why put him in our dead pile like an animal?"

Maggie strokes the tears dry on his cheek.

"And my mother, suffering. So young. Both my parents. They're good people. They didn't deserve this."

"Of course not."

"Thank you for being here, Maggie. I never get a chance . . ." He stops, holding his breath.

"To have feelings?" she says, and kisses the place where she'd dried his tears.

Again his chest shakes, and when he doesn't answer, she stays quiet, listening as his breathing settles into a rhythm and soft snores escape his lips. Then she drops her own lids and lets herself fall asleep in his arms, with her cheek pressed against his big, aching heart.

SEVEN

Mrs. Sibley is absent from breakfast, but Laura shows up to fill two plates.

"Did you get any sleep?" Hank stands, holding out the skillet of his mother's favorite cowboy biscuits.

Laura takes two, scoops strawberry jam, and slices a large pat of butter. "I'm okay."

"It usually takes her a day or two to recover from a bad episode. Hopefully she'll start a resting cycle today." Hank puts two slices of bacon on each plate.

"Want me to pour you coffee?" Maggie is already up, grabbing cups off the sideboard.

"Thanks." Laura adds a generous helping of scrambled eggs to one plate, none to the other.

"Black?"

"That's fine."

Maggie pours, then walks the cups to Laura. "I can carry them for you."

Laura and Hank exchange a look. Laura exhales extra breath, a sort of sigh. "Probably not the best time for an encounter. But thank you. Let's just make room for them on the plates."

Hank crouches at the sideboard and comes up with a tray. "Here."

He arranges the plates and cups on the tray. When she's set, Laura leaves without another word. What was already a quiet breakfast with the absence of Paco turns maudlin. Andy mumbles something about prepping the horses for transport and leaves with a bacon biscuit in each big paw and the day hands trailing him. Maggie picks at her food, head down.

Gene breaks the silence. "I've got to get on the road. Sorry to leave you with all this and dealing with transport."

The haulers are coming for the rodeo livestock today. The animals have a long drive and need plenty of rest before performance time, which starts for them on Thursday.

Hank puts his napkin on his plate. "It's fine."

"Michael should be here any time. I haven't had time to finish his background check, but we'll make this probationary, and I'll have it done by the end of the week. You're okay putting the service for Paco together for Thursday?"

"Trudy is helping me. Doing most of it, actually."

"Well, if there's one thing I know, it's that we can count on Trudy." Gene stands. "See you later, new sis."

Hank's chair clatters back. "All right."

Maggie jumps up, too. "Have a safe trip."

As Gene leaves, Hank heads for the door as well.

Maggie touches his elbow. "You okay?"

Hank's eyes are flat, his cheeks without his smile dimples. "I'll be fine." He steps away from her. "Sorry about last night."

"Why?"

"Dumping all that on you."

"Dump all you need to. Do you, um, need any ice or ibuprofen, for your injury?"

The trace of a smile flickers, teasing, then fades. "I think it will survive."

"Phew. And your head?"

"Maggie, I'm fine. Don't fuss."

Andy pokes his head back in the dining room. "The new hand is here."

Hank turns to Maggie. "See you later." He follows Andy out.

Maggie lifts her fingers and waves at his retreating back. "Mm-hmm."

Alone, Maggie contemplates her options. Today she'll call her mother, maybe run some online searches for potential property for Hank near Giddings, and she'll connect with Franklin, her insurance adjuster. It's past time for some answers. She's mired down in indecision without information. Not that she's complaining. Wyoming is a lovely place, and being with Hank is a dream come true.

But first she heads outside, where she's met with a surprise: except for patches in the shade, the snow has melted. It's colder in the house than it is outdoors. She shucks her jacket immediately and hangs it on a peg inside the door. As soon as the door swings closed behind her, Louise is at her side.

"Hey, girl." Maggie leans down to fondle the dog's ears and sees something sticking to her muzzle. She puts her hand under Louise's chin, tilting it up to get a better look. It's something white, and—when she touches one—soft. She rubs it between fingers, then groans. It's down. As in feathers-from-a-baby-bird down.

Louise wags her tail, which rocks her head and sets her long, patchy black-and-white-freckled ears swaying. Maggie straightens, looking for the source of the down. Louise, reading her mood change, ducks and turns. Maggie's eyes follow the dog. Ten feet from the entry steps, she sees it.

"Oh, Fucker, no." Maggie uses the nickname the dog earned almost immediately after she'd adopted Maggie as her person.

Maggie walks briskly to the little mound of feathers, looking around to be sure no one is watching. Louise slinks a few steps away. Blood-spotted white-and-brown feathers are camouflaged into the dead grass and snow in the shade thrown by the house. Using the toe of her boot, Maggie tilts the creature up and over. It's head flops, neck broken. Staring at her from round, sightless eyes is a dead baby owl. On either side of its head, tufts of feathers stick up in horns. Like a tiny devil, only cuter.

She uses her firmest voice, but quietly, knowing that killing animals can get Louise in a lot of trouble on a ranch. "Bad, bad dog."

Louise lowers her head.

Maggie's phone rings. She looks around. No one is watching her. The owl is her secret. She glances at her screen. It's her insurance adjuster—she has to take this call. "Bad," she says again to Louise for good measure. She answers. "Hello?"

"Maggie Killian, please."

"Speaking." Maggie moves back into the sun and sits on the stoop. The sun is delicious.

"Hi, Maggie. This is Franklin Best."

"Do you have good news for me, Franklin?"

Louise noses Maggie's hand. Maggie glares at her and moves her hand away. It's too soon. She can't pet the head that just murdered a baby owl.

"I wish I did."

"What's the matter?"

"I was at your place yesterday, but I couldn't get into the barn. It was padlocked. Looked like one of those kinds of locks law enforcement uses when they're done with a scene."

"Shit."

"I can't finish without getting in there to inventory the condition of what you have left."

"Can't you just cut the lock?"

"No, ma'am. It's against policy."

Maggie shoves her thick hair back. She needs a hat or a headband. "Fine. I'll have someone go out and do it."

"I'd recommend you call the sheriff's department first."

"Oh, you can count on that."

"Well, let me know when I can get in. Sorry."

They hang up.

Maggie fetches a hat, pondering. On the way back downstairs, she speed-dials a number she wishes wasn't in her Recents.

"Lee County Sheriff's Department," a female voice says.

"Junior, please."

"The deputy isn't available right now. Can someone else help you?"

"Tell him Maggie Killian called. I'm having the padlock on my barn cut. And I'm pretty pissed he didn't tell me it was there."

"Is there a number where he can reach you?"

"Oh, he has it."

When she ends that call, she's standing in the common room. Maggie doesn't hesitate. She hits a number in her Favorites.

"Michele Lopez Hanson."

"I hope you're having a better day than me."

"Maggie! How are you? How's Wyoming?"

"It's fine." Michele is a worrier. There's no reason to burden her with the whole truth. "I need a favor, though."

"Anything. Well, almost."

She says that, but she's already done too much lately. The scale between them is way out of balance. "Junior padlocked my barn shut, and the adjuster couldn't get in to finish my claim. Can you or Rashidi cut it for me?"

Michele's voice changes as she speaks away from the phone. "Rashidi—do we have anything that will cut a padlock?"

"A big one," Maggie adds, walking into the kitchen for a cup of tea.

She hears Michele's boyfriend's lilting island accent. "Yah mon."

Trudy is coming in the back door, an empty garbage can in hand. Maggie smiles at her and lifts a hand in greeting. She returns both. Suddenly, Maggie forgets about the tea. She knows how to dispose of her owl problem. She grabs two trash bags from the pantry and waves to Trudy again as she exits.

Michele continues talking to Rashidi. "Can you drop by Maggie's and cut one off her barn?"

"Soon," Maggie says. She winces, hating to push when she's imposing already. She opens the front door and squints in the bright sun.

Rashidi says, "I leaving now for College Station. I do it on the way."

Michele puts her mouth back to the phone. "Consider it done."

"Thank you both. Very much. I promise I'll be back soon and won't be asking any favors again for a very long time. Anything up with you?"

Michele hesitates. Maggie hears rattling keys and something that sounds like a kiss, then seconds later, a door closing.

"Oh, just a few little things. Rashidi's got a new contract with an organic grocer. Belle is in love again, although I haven't met him. Sam and Charlie are good, and his girlfriend Rachel is around a lot more again. I've finished *Baby's Breath* and my agent is on me to start a new book."

"Isn't it enough that you've got a *New York Times* bestseller and blockbuster movie out at the same time?"

"Alas, no. But I wasn't done with my update. There's a new shrine up to Gary in Round Top. Garish. It's like a mecca for the trailer-park crowd. You'll hate it. He'd love it."

"Great."

"Your mom and my dad are grossing out everyone in town with their PDA. She wants you to call."

"Tell me something I don't know."

"And . . ."

"And what?"

"Ava wants your number. Can I give it to her?"

Maggie walks over to the owl and crouches, giving herself time to think about how to answer the question. Ava. Her onetime nemesis. Michele's friend. Currently the indie darling of the pop charts. She puts her hand in one of the trash bags, then pulls it inside out to cover her hand. She uses the bag like a glove to pick up the owl, gently, then turns the bag right side out again and releases the bird inside. She ties the bag shut.

"What does she want? I don't need any bullshit."

Michele laughs. "No bullshit. I think she has a proposition for you."

"What kind?"

"Work stuff."

"I'm a junker. Does she want to stake me in my new store?"

"Don't play dumb. *Music* work stuff."

"I'm a retired Texana singer. She's a pop superstar. And she's wasting her breath."

"A Grammy winner, which is more than she can say. And it's her breath to waste."

Louise approaches Maggie and sniffs the bag.

"Bad."

"What did I do?"

"Not you. The dog. Long story."

"So I'm giving her your number."

"You already did, didn't you?"

Maggie hears a smile in Michele's voice. "Nice talking to you. Tell Hank and Gene I said hey."

EIGHT

Carrying her grim package and trailing one hangdog mutt, Maggie walks to Lily's paddock. The black horse spares her a glance, then pretends to ignore her. Using the rope halter hanging on the gate, Maggie catches her and leads her to the barn. She fastens her to the hitching post, then sets the bag of baby bird against the side of the barn.

A tall blond man she's seen at the ranch a time or two before is with Andy and the two day hands, examining horses lined up in a loading chute. At the other end of the chute is the trailer already half-full.

Maggie fetches her gear from the tack room. On her way back out to the mare, Hank and the new hand, Michael, appear.

"Hi. I'm Maggie. We met yesterday, Michael. Welcome to the Double S."

Glittering black eyes fasten on her. "Thank you. I'm glad to be here."

"We didn't expect it to be so soon, but we're lucky you came along." Hank claps him on the back.

"Who's that?" Maggie points at the man working with the hands.

"Doc Billy. The vet. Doing wellness checks on the stock for Duncan."

"Gotcha."

To Maggie he says, "You riding out?"

"Yeah. Pretty weather."

"You got your phone?"

"Yes. And your knife." She pats the scabbard on her hip. Her load is getting heavy, so she hoists the saddle, blanket, and bridle higher.

"I'd feel better if you weren't alone."

She grins over her shoulder at him. "I won't be. I have nearly a ton of horse and my superhero dog." Louise had caught the arsonist last month in Texas. She couldn't ask for a better protector.

Hank grunts. "At least tell me where you're headed."

"Um." Maggie knows safety should be her first priority, but if she tells him, he'll raise a stink. "Out toward Rudy's old house. I'll stick to the fence lines and be back before lunch. Have a good first day, Michael."

Maggie grooms and saddles Lily, then ties the trash bag and its contents behind the cantle of the saddle. The men depart in a Ranger. Just as she's about to mount, Andy rides over on Tatonka. He ties up at the space Lily and Maggie vacate.

"Hey, Andy. Want to work on your guitar later?"

"If I can break free. I have a lot to do with Paco gone. And that new guy here."

Something about his voice stops her from putting her foot in the stirrup. "You don't like Michael?"

Andy blushes. He turns to Tatonka and starts unsaddling him. "It's not that I don't like him. I just grew up on the edge of the Cheyenne reservation. My father hates them all. Some of them are okay. But a lot of them expect something for nothing, like life is all a big government handout. And they drink a lot of alcohol. Take a lot of drugs. Michael's not from a good family."

Maggie has never heard Andy say a negative word about anyone before, so his words are a shock. "I'm sure it will be fine."

"Yes. Hank and Gene are counting on me. I won't let them down."

"I know you won't." Maggie mounts Lily and whistles for Louise, who, from the sound of the squeak, is chasing something small and furry in the barn.

Maggie makes good time, despite gates and Lily begging to graze the brown grass every few yards. Maggie urges the heavy mare into a low trot. She doesn't want Lily to overdo it, but it's the only way she knows to keep the mama-to-be's nose out of the grass. Louise runs circles around them, literally. Huge circles as she hunts and digs.

The phone rings in Maggie's pocket. Lily is calm, so she checks the caller ID. It's a 615 area code phone number. Her stomach flips. It's been years since she's taken calls from Nashville, so she picks up.

"Maggie Killian."

"Maggie, this is Jeff Franke with Goliad Records. How are you today?" The voice is young and energetic.

Goliad Records. She's not familiar with the name. "I'm fine. What's this about?"

"Um, right down to business—okay. We bought your albums—*Throwback*, *Texana*, and *Buckle Bunny*—when your prior record company went out of business. I believe you'd already sold the royalty rights in the music to them, and we have those as well."

Louise flushes a jackrabbit, who bounds across the field between patches of white and brown.

"Good for you."

The man laughs with an ironic edge. "Recently you've been getting a lot of publicity, which has been great for our revenue from your music. We —Goliad—is wondering if you'd like to cut another record. With us."

"You're offering me a record deal?"

"With contingencies, of course."

"Contingencies?"

"For, er, behavior. Morality clauses, if you will."

"Moral behavior."

Lily clomps onward, but Maggie feels the horse tense. She's not oblivious to the drama unfolding from her back.

"Yes."

"Like the Ten Commandments type of behavior?"

"More like drugs. No substance abuse. Or addictions."

"Addictions. So if I'm addicted to, say, sex, then you're saying no fucking."

"No, I mean, I don't know, I—Shit. People warned me that talking to you is like cuddling a hedgehog. Well, they were right."

Riding the fence line against a dirt road off property, Maggie sees a beat-up truck pass. Something about the driver makes her double-take. She could swear he was wearing an Amish beard and hat. But hadn't Andy said the Amish don't drive? She has to have been mistaken.

"What was your name again?"

"Jeff Franke."

"Jeff, you realize I am a recovered drug addict. I can't erase the addict part. So by the very nature of your morality clause, I can't enter a valid contract with you. Or if I get desperate enough to do so, you'd have grounds to screw me anytime you want to. I may have a checkered past, but I'm not brain-damaged. Still got all my marbles."

"I wasn't suggesting that—"

"What's in it for me, then?"

"Money, of course, and redemption. Another shot."

She thinks of the new songs she's been working on. Goliad isn't getting them, that's for sure. "I suspect you don't know a thing about me, Jeff, or you'd know that I don't give a shit about redemption or another shot, and if I did, I could finance those without your help."

Lily snorts. The big horse lowers her head and shakes it.

"Label backing would legitimize—"

"I'm a Grammy winner. I don't need a two-bit label fleecing me back to legitimacy. Fuck off, Jeff. And tell your buddies at Goliad to fuck off, too."

Maggie hangs up the phone. "Patronizing asshole. User. Millennial."

It's a small leap from her irritation about the record company to her irritation with the insurance company. She needs to let the adjuster know the lock has been cut. She texts Michele: *Confirm Rashidi cut padlock? Adjuster waiting to hear.* Then she takes a chance, texting Franklin: *Padlock cut. When can you go back out?*

The phone rings in her hand. Lily snorts and dances. She tosses her nose, pulling the reins looser. She half trots, half walks in an arc back toward the ranch headquarters. Maggie pulls up the slack in the reins and uses firm legs to set the horse back on course. "Whoa." Lily huffs. There's no doubt how she feels about Maggie's level of attention.

Maggie squeezes the phone tight, not wanting to talk to Jeff again. But the call is from Charlotte. All her good intentions to call her mom back disintegrate. She presses DECLINE and thrusts the phone into her pocket. She's had enough aggravation for now. Who did that little weasel think he was, calling up and acting like he was doing her a favor? Like cutting an album with an unknown would give her legitimacy. She'd be the one giving them legitimacy, at the cost of her pride, privacy, and peace. And leading with morality clauses. They'd never worked with her before. All they were doing was piggybacking on the conclusions drawn in lazy journalism.

After traversing a gulch where Louise spooks a whitetail doe with a fawn minus most of its spots, Maggie is still fighting mad, but she spies vultures. Her destination is close. Five minutes later, she crests a rise and sees the pile of dead livestock, complete with yellow crime scene tape. She'd forgotten about the tape. She dismounts outside the perimeter and drops Lily's lead rope to the ground.

"Don't you run off."

Lily mows grass and swishes her tail.

Maggie unties her cargo. The place feels spooky and unsettled. If she stands at the edge of the tape closest to the pile, she thinks she can heave the bird onto its final resting place. It's not the dignified ending she'd envisioned, but she can do it without violating the crime scene. Well, without violating it with anything other than the baby owl.

"Sorry, baby owl. My dog is an asshole." She grasps the limp bird and turns the bag inside out. The animal looks worse for the transport, and it makes her sad. She throws it like a football toward the pile. It lands with a soft thud.

Louise sprints after it, like it's the ball in a game of fetch.

"No, Fucker."

Louise turns to her, wagging her tail.

"I wonder if I've just broken any Game and Fish laws?"

Lily nickers, low and rumbly. Maggie turns to see Deputy Travis, this time on a gray horse half Lily's size with big dapples on his rear end. She doesn't recognize the animal or the brand, which looks like a T intersection.

"What do you think you're doing, Ms. Killian?"

Maggie lifts her hands and flexes her palms up and out with a shrug. "Shit. I'm sorry. My dog killed an owl. I didn't want her to get in trouble, so I brought it out here where no one would know she'd done it."

Travis's squinty eyes and wrinkled brow tell her he's not buying it. "Out of thousands of acres, the only hiding place you can find for it is in the middle of my crime scene?"

"When you put it that way, it does seem crazy, but I promise it made perfect sense to me."

Travis stares at the owl. "So this has nothing to do with Paco?"

"Nothing. How could it?"

He turns his horse so that he's facing her. "Have you seen anyone out this direction in the last few days?"

Maggie frowns. "I haven't been out here. I see Hank, Gene, and the hands headed out from the ranch buildings all the time."

"Did any of their movements seem out of the ordinary?"

"Um, no, I don't think so. The only odd movement I've seen around here was today."

"Odd in what way?"

"Just that I saw an Amish man driving a truck on the road, as I was riding out here."

"So not odd in relation to Paco or this pile?"

"No."

"What about at night?"

For an instant, she remembers seeing someone running to the bunkhouse the night before. Someone in red boots. But her gut tells her not to mention it, so she doesn't. "I can only speak for Hank. And he spends the nights with me."

Travis's horse spins in a circle, but Travis quiets and reorients him. "Last time we met, he was with Sheila." His tone suggests he's Team Sheila. He's local, so chances are he knows her or is related to her, but that doesn't numb the sting.

She drills him with laser eyes. "What's your point?"

"None. Sorry."

"If there's nothing else, then?"

"We're waiting on the conclusions about manner and time of death. When we get that, I may be back."

"Fine. Do I have to remove the owl?"

"Hand me your bag."

Maggie gives the bag to him. Travis dismounts, gives her his reins, and walks carefully to the pile. He rebags the owl and ties the bag closed. He hands it back to her.

"Thanks." Her voice mocks the word.

He grunts. "Have a good day, then, Ms. Killian."

She wheels Lily, whistles for Louise, and sets off at a trot for home. Halfway back to the ranch, she stops in a patch of grass that doesn't seem too rocky. Using her borrowed knife, she digs a hole just deep enough for the little owl and buries it, bag and all.

NINE

BACK AT THE RANCH HEADQUARTERS, Maggie unsaddles Lily. As she's walking into the barn to put up the saddle and tack, a man is hurrying out, and runs into her.

"Oh, sorry." He grabs her by both arms to keep from knocking her down. "The sun was in my eyes."

"That's okay." She remembers the blond man. "Hey, are you the vet who was checking out the horses this morning?"

"Yes. Folks call me Doc Billy. Or just Doc." He releases her arms and clasps her hand instead. They're standing too close to shake.

"I'm Maggie Killian. I'm a friend of Hank's. Do you have a moment to look at my mare?"

"Um—" His eyes dart to his truck, parked on the other side of the driveway to the barn.

"She's just tied to the hitching post right there. The black Percheron. She got caught out in the storm yesterday, out by the dead pile, and she's really pregnant. Just a once-over."

He sighs and looks at the hitching post. "Oh, Lily. A Double S mare." Then he smiles. "A quick look. All the way out by the dead pile, huh?"

"Yes." Maggie leads him to her. "Normally, I'd have just asked Paco to doctor her up. He was my go-to for that kind of thing. Did you know him?"

Doc Billy stiffens, then shakes it off and runs a hand along Lily's neck, back, and rump. "Yes."

"What do you think?"

"I think he had a way of intruding on other people's territory." His voice is icy cold, but he doesn't look at Maggie, just continues examining Lily, looking at her gums, her eyes, pinching her skin, prodding at her udder, and lifting her tail.

She's taken aback. "He was just trying to help the ranch."

"I wasn't talking about—oh, never mind. Yes, he was good with the horses." Doc Billy stands and pats Lily. "She isn't scratched up, and she doesn't seem stressed or dehydrated. But I do think she's going to have this foal early. I was around for her first few, and she hasn't gone to term once. Her udder and teats are filling, her pelvic area is relaxing, and she's starting to wax a little. Keep a close eye on her. Call me if she looks like she's having any trouble."

"Can I still ride her?"

"Pleasure riding, sure. Exercise is good for her."

"Thank you, Doc."

"I'm late for lunch with my wife. Nice to meet you."

"You, too."

Maggie returns Lily to her paddock with some sweet feed, then hustles into the main house just in time to catch the end of lunch.

Hank's eyebrows lift when he sees her. "You ever think about checking your cellphone?"

Maggie checks. There's no missed calls. Her phone also claims she has no service. "T-Mobile, remember? I don't always get them. Sorry I'm late."

"Well, Laura and I are leaving now to take Mom to a doctor's appointment. If you eat fast, you can meet us at the truck after we get her loaded up."

Laura shakes her head. "No, Hank."

"What?"

"I said no."

Mrs. Sibley, who is clutching her sandwich like it will run away if she relaxes her grip, sets it down. Her expression is reptilian. "I don't want that woman with me at the doctor." Then she attacks her sandwich again, chewing as if her life depends on it.

Maggie ignores the bite of the words. She wishes she'd known Hank's mother before Alzheimer's. She concentrates on building her sloppy joe. She adds salad and chips to her plate. "I can sit in the waiting room while she's in with the doctor."

Laura gives Maggie the side-eye. "I'm sorry, but I get practically zero time with my brother, and we have things we need to talk about."

Hank's voice is deadly. "You're being a b—"

"No problem. I have things to do anyway." Maggie cuts him off before he can escalate the awkwardness in front of the hands, who already look like they wish they'd eaten at the dead pile or manure dump. Anywhere but here.

Laura nods. "Thank you. Hank, I'll meet you and Mom at the truck." She pushes her jet hair behind one ear as she leaves.

Hank says, "I'm sorry about that. Laura hasn't had any sleep."

Mrs. Sibley speaks through a mouthful of food. "Don't talk about your sister behind her back."

Hank sighs. "And neither has my mother. Andy, the place is yours. I'll be back before dinner. Maggie . . ."

"I already told you. I have things to do. Including a guitar lesson for Andy, if he's done in time." She lifts her sandwich. Filling falls to her plate. She takes a bite and more gushes out.

Andy wipes his mouth. "I'm taking Michael to check the herds, ride fence, and trade out some pastures. Probably best after dinner."

Maggie smiles at him, finishes chewing, and swallows. "That's best for me, too."

Maggie knows Hank stood up for her to Laura, as much as she let him, anyway. But Laura's words still hurt her. It's not rational, but even though she's not choosing Andy over him, she wants Hank to feel her pain, too.

A hurt look flickers in Hank's eyes. "All right. Well then, we're off. Mom, let's go."

Mrs. Sibley jerks her sandwich toward her shoulder, like Hank is trying to pry it from her hands. "I'm not finished. The portions that new cook serves are far too big. Wasteful."

"Can you wrap it up for her?" he asks Trudy, then mouths, "Sorry."

She winks at him. "Let me save this for you, Mrs. S."

Mrs. Sibley relinquishes her sandwich and her plate to Trudy, who disappears into the kitchen.

"Laura served your plate, and Trudy isn't new here, Mom. It wasn't nice to talk like that in front of her."

"Are you saying I'm not nice? I was just being truthful."

He pulls her wheelchair back from the table. "I'm not saying anything."

They're still arguing over whether or not she was nice as they exit. When the door slams shut behind them, the room grows even more tense. The hands are evenly divided on each side of the table, with Andy and Michael stark contrasts across from each other. Andy is blond and self-contained, with a full beard and homemade clothes. Michael is clean-shaven, dark, and bristling with energy.

Trudy brings in a platter and lifts a dish towel from it. "Too bad the Sibleys had to miss dessert."

Maggie tries to lighten things up. "Yum, apple strudel. Thanks, Trudy." She helps herself to a slice and passes it to Andy.

He takes one and slides it to the middle of the table. The day hands grab pieces. So does Michael.

There's a knock at the front door.

"I'll get it," Trudy says, and cuts through the dining room.

Maggie and the hands eat apple strudel in silence heavy as a down comforter.

Trudy comes back in, shivering, and points at Andy. "Deputy Travis is here. He wants to talk to you, Andy. But take a coat. I can't believe this weather. There's another storm blowing up."

Andy says, "M-m-me?"

"Yes."

"I don't understand."

Maggie knows what it's like to have the cops up in your grill for no reason. "Want me to come with you?"

"If you don't mind."

"Lunch was great, Trudy." Maggie walks ahead of Andy into the common room.

"Thanks." She watches them with concern in her eyes.

In the great room, Deputy Travis is staring out the window. He speaks without looking at them. "Yesterday was a dusting of powder. Today's storm is supposed to get wicked. Winter is coming early."

In the last half hour, frost has crept from the edges of the windows, working its way to the centers, but thick gray clouds are still visible through the center of the panes. The house groans and creaks as the wind batters it. The trees struggle to stay upright. Maggie can't believe she was out riding comfortably an hour before.

Travis turns to Andy. "What's your full name again?"

Andy catches the back of a couch and grips it. "Andrew Reginald Yoder, sir."

"What's this about?" Maggie asks. She walks all the way up to Travis and crosses her arms.

Travis ignores her. "So your initials are A-R-Y?"

"Yes, sir."

"Do you own a folding knife with a bone handle?"

"Yes, sir. I bought it for myself after I took this job."

"Are your initials, A-R-Y, etched into the blade?"

"Yes, sir."

"Can you get it for me and show it to me?"

Andy clears his throat. He starts to speak but only a croak comes out. On his second attempt, he says, "No, sir."

"Why is that?"

"Because I haven't seen it in a week."

"That's convenient."

"I'm not trying to smear your eyes. I left it in the barn, and I haven't been able to find it."

Travis rubs his chin. His five-o'clock shadow looks closer to two days old. "I'm sorry, but I'm going to need you to come in with me for some more questions."

Maggie bristles. "Whoa. You've been watching too much *Amish Mafia*. Why can't you just ask him what you need to here?"

Andy's eyes are terrified, but now his voice is steady. "No. It's okay. I don't have anything to be afraid of, because I ain't done nothing wrong."

"Is he under arrest?" Maggie demands.

Travis inspects his nails. "If he was, I'd be reading him his rights."

She gets between Travis and Andy, facing her friend. With all the protection Michele has showered on her recently every time the cops have harassed Maggie, it's time to pay it forward. "I'm driving you, then."

Travis talks to her back. "I'd prefer he ride with me."

She doesn't turn to face him. "I'm sure you would. Andy, you're with me."

TEN

THE BLIZZARD HITS full force from the north while Andy and Maggie are on the road to Sheridan. Visibility is shit, and Maggie creeps along the interstate in Bess, her vintage magenta Ford pickup. Not the best vehicle for the conditions, and without chains. Hank had encouraged her to get snow tires a few days before, but she'd put it off, not understanding why it was important when she was just visiting. Now she gets it.

"Should we go back?" Andy asks.

"We're over halfway. Maybe we'll drive through the storm and out the north edge. If we turn for home, we'll be in the thick of it. I think we should keep going. We made a commitment to get you in for an interview, anyway." What she doesn't say, since it's pessimistic, is that she wants to be as close to Sheridan as she can get in case they end up on the side of the road. She glances at her phone. Especially since there's no cell service where they are.

"Okay. I hope Michael got the animals taken care of."

Before they left, Andy had overcome his issues with Michael enough to have an urgent conversation with him about bringing in the expectant mares. Most had foaled in the spring. It's not ideal for them to give birth in the winter, and usually doesn't happen unless by accident. Lily the escape artist had managed to get herself knocked up at the wrong time of year when she let herself into a pasture with a stallion while she was in heat. So she's on the short list of mares that need to be stabled, which is why she's being kept in a paddock near the barn. The cows are all pregnant but not due until spring.

"He seemed to have it under control. And the day hands will be doing their part."

"It's his first day."

"Gene and Hank wouldn't have hired him if they didn't believe he's capable." Although Gene hadn't gotten around to Michael's background check yet.

"Then it's on them, because I wouldn't have picked him."

"He'll get it done."

"If he doesn't knock off at the dinner bell." His eyes are blazing. "A cowboy works until he gets it done. The animals come first."

Andy seems more upset about Michael and the animals than he is about being under suspicion and questioning for a friend's murder. Something about it gives Maggie pause.

"Is all this distrust about Michael just because he's Cheyenne?"

Andy's face clouds. "It's funny timing. Him showing up asking for work on the day Paco is found dead."

"Did they know each other?"

"I don't know."

Doc Billy's reaction to the mention of Paco flashes through her mind. "I'll tell you who didn't seem to like Paco, and that's the vet. What's that all about?"

An eighteen-wheeler suddenly bears down on them, driving far too fast for road conditions. It honks, then whips around them, fishtailing as it passes them. Maggie gasps as her own truck veers to the right. She fights to keep it under control and lets off the gas. The deeper snow on the shoulder grabs the tires and moves the steering wheel of its own accord. She taps the brakes once, twice, three times, and the truck straightens. She steers it gently back into the right lane.

"Idiot," she says, her voice squeaky. She shakes a fist after the truck.

Andy's face is pale and his eyes wide. "Good job."

When her heart slows, she quickly checks her cell again for service. There's none. Not only does she wonder what would happen to them if they went off the road here, it kills her that she can't call Hank, Gene, Michele—who is an attorney in addition to being a successful author—or John Fortney, the only lawyer she knows in Wyoming, to get help for Andy.

And Maggie is very sure Andy needs help.

She'd left a message with Trudy to tell Hank where she and Andy have gone, but by the time he gets it, it will be too late. She slows the truck more as they encounter more traffic. Only a few miles to go to the first exit into Sheridan now. She keeps one eye on the rearview mirror for more tractor-trailers, and the other on the road, where she can barely tell where the pavement edge is under the swirling snow—it's hard to even tell up from down. Thank God for the hazard bumps on the side of the road that alert her when she loses her way.

Her tension eases a little when they reach the Fifth Street exit. Bess takes the ramp like a champ, and they do well on the city street, too, thanks to the snowplows already at work.

As they near their destination, she says, "If they had more evidence, you'd be under arrest."

"What do you mean by *evidence?*"

A snowplow flings snow and road debris onto her windshield.

She slows down to a crawl. "Fingerprints. DNA. A witness."

"They won't find any evidence."

"Have you been fingerprinted before?" She takes a right on Main. There's road construction ahead, but she can't see the hazards through the snow. Her stomach tightens. She remembers a section of this road where she'd seen a three-foot drop the week before.

"No."

"They're going to ask to do that today, then."

"Fine."

"Not fine. I don't think you have to unless you're charged."

"But I didn't kill Paco."

"It doesn't matter. They need a suspect. If they focus on you, they'll lose any interest in finding another one. No fingerprints unless charged."

"What about justice?"

She sighs. How sheltered his life in the Amish community has been from the "English" ways of justice. "Oh, Andy. I wish we could trust in justice. Even more, I wish I could have reached an attorney to meet us there."

"Hiring a lawyer's mighty spendy, ain't it?" He pounds his fist in his hand, his first outward sign of intense emotion over his situation. "I really had the bull by the tail, moving along. And now this."

"Let me worry about how much it costs."

"I don't take handouts."

"I know you'll work it off in trade if you have to, and that's fine with me."

Maggie parks Bess, sure that she'll never make it out of the already drifted lot when they're done. She's also sure that she needs a pair of winter boots. Andy catches her by the arm and prevents her from going down on the slick sidewalk. Just as they're entering a tan brick building that looks like any other government structure built in the 1970s, her phone chimes. She has cell service.

"You go on in. I've got signal. I need to call to get you some help."

"Out here?"

"I don't want people in there hearing your business."

"Can you call and leave a message at my father's country store phone? I want him to know what's going on."

"I don't see how he could get here in this weather."

"Father often works here in Sheridan."

Maggie takes the number from him and makes the call. After she leaves the message, she says, "Good luck. I'll be waiting for you when you're done. If I'm able to get an attorney, I'll send them in. And Andy, say as little as possible. Don't explain. Just yes, no, or I don't know, if you can."

The look he gives her is defiant, and she knows his ethics dictate cooperation and create an expectation in him that others will operate by a strict code, too. Maybe he's morally right, but in her experience, the code in the actual justice system is so different from his.

He disappears into the lobby. A blonde woman exits through the interior vestibule door he holds open for her. She's bundled up in a puffy jacket, scarf, and furry boots. Her ponytail cascades through a hole in her wool cap like Maggie's from the day before. She looks Wyoming-winter fashion-forward, if there is such a thing.

Her blue eyes meet Maggie's when she gets to the front steps, and she stops in her tracks. "You."

Maggie's finger is poised to speed-dial Hank when she realizes who the woman with the unlined face is. Sheila. His sort-of fiancée, until Hank ditched her to come after Maggie in Texas. But only sort of, since Sheila did the asking while Hank was medically incapable of operating heavy machinery or making matrimonial decisions.

Maggie's voice would curdle milk. "Sheila."

"What are you doing here?"

"You mean in Wyoming, or here at the Sheriff's Department in particular?"

"Never mind." Sheila starts to push past her.

"What are *you* doing here? A little trouble with the law?"

Sheila stops, eyes blazing. "As if. I'm renewing my concealed carry permit."

That doesn't give Maggie a peaceful, easy feeling. She frowns.

Sheila smirks. "Don't like guns? I'm an instructor. Why don't you take a class from me? We rarely have fatal accidents. I could make an exception for you, though."

"Pass."

Sheila starts to walk on, then flounces to a stop. "Have you ever heard the expression 'Live by the sword, die by the sword?'"

"Excuse me?"

"In this case it means if you have to steal a man to get him, expect to lose him the same way."

"I didn't *steal* Hank. He was mine long before he was yours. And I didn't have to trick him into an engagement while he was sedated, either."

"You're engaged?"

Maggie hadn't anticipated that interpretation. "What *we* are is together. What *you* are is not." Maggie shoos her with her fingers. "Now move along. Hank's waiting on my call."

"Is he, now? I just saw him in the bar at the Rib and Chop. With some woman that wasn't you."

"Don't you have young minds to brainwash?"

"They let out before lunch because of the storm. And don't you even want to know who he was drinking with?"

"No, because I already know."

Sheila smirks. "You're looking at her."

Maggie controls her reaction, unwilling to give Sheila satisfaction.

"Yeah. So you have a nice day thinking about him having a drink with me without telling you." She waggles her fingers in a goodbye gesture that mocks Maggie's earlier shooing motion.

Maggie turns her back on Sheila and presses Hank's number. The message Maggie leaves for Hank is less lovey-dovey than it would have been before running into his ex.

"I'm at the Sheridan County Sheriff's Department with Andy, who was strong-armed into coming in for questioning. I'm also worried about how we're going to get home in this blizzard. If you're still in town, can you come here? I hope your time with Laura was good and that your mother is okay. Oh, and how was that drink with Sheila?"

She tries Michele. No answer. Gene. No answer, but not surprising since he's on the road in a state not known for excellent rural cell signal. She calls John Fortney, the attorney in Buffalo. An outgoing message announces his offices are closed for the day due to the blizzard. And she'd heard how Wyomingites are so weather-tough. What is this, the storm of the century?

She texts Michele: *Need legal advice. Hank's top hand being questioned in a murder. Big storm. I can't find anyone to help me. Call if you can.*

The snow has worked its way into her coat. In Texas, what she has on would be considered severe-weather wear, good for anything except rain. Her heavy brocade coat is lined with fleece and flares over her hips. But it's yet another thing for her list of items that need a Wyoming upgrade. She hurries into the lobby and takes a seat, grateful for the double doors of the vestibule that are keeping most of the cold out where it belongs.

Minutes tick slowly away. She asks the receptionist for an update and gets nothing. She checks her phone and ringer obsessively, to no avail. To pass the time, she surfs property for sale near hers in Giddings, focusing on acreage. A three-hundred-acre ranch seems promising, so she emails the realtor for more information. After about half an hour, the inside door opens to let in an Amish man with brilliant blue eyes and a long beard. He looks familiar. Her mind offers up an image of the Amish man she'd seen earlier talking to Andy at the ranch. Could this be the same man? Whether he is or not, he can only be here because of Andy. Before Maggie can intercept him, he approaches the receptionist.

The man's voice booms. "I'm here for Andrew Yoder."

"And you are who, sir?"

"His father. Reggie Yoder."

ELEVEN

THE RECEPTIONIST CONFERS WITH A COLLEAGUE, then returns to the glowering man. He slowly turns a round-brimmed hat between his fingers.

"Sir, he's in an interview. You're welcome to take a seat."

"How long will he be?"

"There's no way to know at this point."

"But he will be free to leave with me when the deputies are through with him?"

"That's my understanding, sir. Subject to change if they find a reason to hold him over."

"Such as?"

"Well, if they arrest him."

Anger hangs over Reggie like a dark cloud. He wheels and stalks stiff-legged to a chair several feet away from where Maggie sits.

"Sir?" Maggie says.

At first he doesn't register she's addressing him.

"Mr. Yoder?"

His head jerks in her direction. "You speaking to me?"

Reggie has a medicinal odor to him. She wonders if it's cough syrup, but he's not coughing. "Yes, sir. My name is Maggie Killian. I understand you're Andy's father?"

"That conversation was not for your ears."

Maggie grinds her teeth. "Andy asked me to be on the lookout for you."

"Who are you to my son?"

How to explain this? "My boyfriend, Hank, is one of the owners of the Double S, where Andy works. I gave Andy a ride to town today."

"This is a family matter. Your services are no longer needed. He'll be coming with me."

Heat consumes her ears. She'd expected politeness, if not gratitude. "I'm not sure I understand."

Maggie hears the door from the interior of the station open. She looks up to see a visibly distressed Andy. He notices his father immediately, and she sees a mask of self-control slip over his features.

"Ms. Killian. Father."

Reggie snatches his hat from his knees and stands. "Old Mr. Gregory is waiting with the truck. I'll meet you out there."

"For what?"

"Our ride back to the community."

"Father, I can't go with you. I have a job. They need me at the Double S."

"This is not a discussion."

As they're leaving, the receptionist calls out, "Need a shovel?"

Maggie stops. "What?"

Andy says, "No, we've got one."

To Andy, Maggie says, "What was that about?"

"Digging out."

The three of them move outside. In the parking lot, Maggie sees why the receptionist offered them the shovel. The snow has piled up even higher while they've been inside. Plows are out clearing the roads, but not the parking lot.

Andy stands taller, his wool scarf flapping, his back like a flagpole. "Thank you for coming, Father. I sure am sorry to shame you like this, although I ain't done nothing wrong. But I've got livestock to tend to, and this weather puts them at risk. You always taught me about responsibility and hard work. Those animals and that ranch are my responsibility as top hand, and I can't just leave them."

Reggie stomps away, seeming not to even notice Andy's mention of his promotion, however subtle. Maggie's eyes follow him and she watches the profile of his beard and hat in a beat-up Chevy truck parked just a few feet away. The truck backs up. The wheels spin, then grip. It reverses course, fishtails for a moment, then disappears within seconds.

Andy's voice is strangled. "Let's go."

He pulls a snow shovel out of the truck bed.

Maggie asks, "Where did that come from?"

"I threw it in before we left. Due to the weather. There's an ice scraper in the glove box." He shovels, clearing a path.

"Oh."

She feels worthless—and worse, naïve—as she scrapes snow from the windshields. It hadn't occurred to her to check for snow tools before driving to town. Being stuck in a parking lot is one thing—a minor irritant. But if they go off a road, there could be no help for hours. Or days. She ticks off things it would be a good idea to have in the future. Not just a shovel and ice scraper, but a satellite phone. Blankets. A bag of kitty litter or sand for traction. Chains. Water. Nutrition bars. Flares. Taking things for granted here could be deadly.

She and Andy get in the truck. He doesn't look at her.

She exits the parking lot. "Are you okay?"

"It's humiliating to accept help from a woman in front of my father."

Maggie tries to stifle the offense that rises in her. Now is not the time to fight a gender battle. "Don't be ridiculous. We all need help sometimes. No shame in taking it."

They ride in silence through town. Maggie hopes he'll open up, but he doesn't.

Finally, she can't hold back any longer. "How did it go in there?"

"Fine."

"Did you learn anything new?"

"My knife killed Paco."

"Andy, I'm so sorry."

"They'll be contacting everyone at the ranch about the knife and my alibi."

"They have a time of death?"

"Not exactly. But I gave them my whereabouts ever since Paco left."

"Did they fingerprint you?"

"Yes. And I gave them hair for a DNA sample, too."

Maggie bites her tongue. She wants so badly to chastise him for giving law enforcement things they have no right to yet, but it won't change anything now. And she understands Andy's reasons, even if they're different from her own.

The worst of the storm has passed, so the visibility is far better than on the way into town. Maggie lets the ride pass in silence. When they reach the ranch, she drops Andy at the barn—per his request to go make sure Michael took care of things right—then parks at the ranch house. The snow is soft and powdery under her feet as she walks to the front door. Just as she touches the knob, her phone starts issuing notifications rapid-fire. Messages, voicemails, emails. Just inside the door, she stops to check them. Apparently her signal hadn't been good enough to receive anything while she was driving back from Sheridan. Everyone she'd contacted had reached back out to her, although a fat lot of good it did Andy now. She even had a return call from Franklin.

Before she has time to read or listen to a word of them, she sees headlights creeping toward the ranch house. The battered truck she'd seen earlier stops by the front door, and Reggie Yoder covers the ground in a few long strides, a large satchel in his hand. His knock is forceful and continues until she opens the door.

"You again," he says.

"Mr. Yoder." She nods.

"I want to speak to Andy's employer."

Maggie steps back, once again getting a whiff of something astringent. She ushers him into the common room.

Hank calls to her from upstairs, his voice a raised whisper. "Bring Mr. Yoder to my sitting room up here, please. I'd like to keep it quiet downstairs so Mom and Laura can get some rest."

"After you, sir." Maggie beckons Reggie ahead of her on the stairs. In the second-floor sitting room, Hank is nowhere to be seen. "Please, have a seat. I'm sure Mr. Sibley will be with you any moment."

Reggie sets his satchel down and stands at attention.

Maggie goes back downstairs to shuck her boots and outerwear at the rack and pegs by the door. When she returns, Reggie is holding the Sibley mortar and pestle.

"Family heirloom," Maggie tells him.

He doesn't reply or make eye contact, so she continues on to the room she shares with Hank. Louise meets her at the door.

Maggie goes inside and closes the door with a soft click. "You let the dog in. Thanks."

Hank's buttoning a flannel shirt. "I was just getting in the shower. How come you never called me back?" His voice is stiff, and he doesn't make a move toward her.

She approaches him and kisses the cheek he doesn't offer. What's he doing mad at her when he was the one having a drink with Sheila when he was supposedly at the doctor with his mother? She backs away, her temper starting to flare, but she holds it in, for now. There's a visitor on the other side of the wall. "My phone wasn't working for incoming calls. I just got a ton of voicemails and stuff when I came inside the house. I haven't had a chance to listen to them yet."

His eyes flick to hers. "Is Andy okay?"

"As much as he can be. They didn't arrest him, anyway."

"What's up with Reggie?"

"Andy left word for him about what was going on, and Reggie showed up at the sheriff's department. He demanded Andy go back to Montana with him, and Andy refused. Told him he had work to do here. Reggie followed us home. That's about it."

"Anything else I need to know before I talk to him?"

Before she consciously thinks it, Maggie says, "That he smells like rotgut."

"Booze?"

"To my nose."

"The Amish don't drink."

"Maybe it's bad cough syrup. Or something."

"Has to be."

Hank leaves the room. Maggie's slow burn turns into a boil. It's been a shitty day, and Hank doesn't have to make it worse. For a moment she wonders if he's having a head episode. Or if maybe things went badly with Laura and his mother. But that just makes her angrier. Tough times are for working out with her, not with his ex over drinks. Otherwise, there's no future for Hank and her. And if there's no future for the two of them, then that just makes it even more important that she figure out what to do about her ruined home and business. She balls her fists and closes her eyes. To think she'd been searching for a ranch for him in Texas earlier. Louise sidles up to her and nuzzles her hand. Maggie strokes the dog's long, furry ears.

Raised voices from the sitting room draw her closer to the door. She can't make out what they're saying. Hank had shut the door on his way out, but Maggie turns the knob silently and creates a crack of several inches. Immediately she's able to hear their words.

"—English corruption. It's the wrong place for my son. If he was home, none of this would be happening."

Hank sounds placating. "This is a safe place. We've done nothing to corrupt him."

"I disagree. He's a suspect in a murder because of you."

"Andy's innocent. He was only in for questioning."

"You're exposing him to murder and immoral relationships."

Maggie puts her hand over her mouth.

Hank's voice hardens. "We didn't cause Paco's death. And what do you mean about immoral relationships?"

Louise whines.

"You, and that . . . woman . . . that drove him to town."

He's talking about her. She's the immoral relationship. Her blood boils.

"You're out of line, Mr. Yoder."

"And you're a heathen. I want my son released immediately."

Hank's laugh is a snort. "He's not our prisoner."

"Then send him home with me."

"If he wants to go, he'll go. I won't be assisting you in kidnapping a grown man."

Downstairs, the front door opens and closes.

Andy's voice calls out so softly that Maggie barely hears it. "Hank?"

"Up here, Andy. With your father."

Booted feet ascend the stairs with a soft clomp-clomp-clomping. The sounds grow more distinct, then stop. "Father."

"Pack your things, Andrew. We're leaving tonight."

"I already told you, I'm staying here."

"You're risking your eternal soul."

"Father—"

"And shunning by our community."

"I ain't broken no church rules. I'm not even baptized, Father."

"Come and confess your sins, and all will be forgiven."

Andy's voice is firm. "You're embarrassing me. I work here. You need to leave."

Maggie feels her lips turn up with a smile she hadn't expected. Andy's standing up for himself.

Hank chimes in, and she hears the smile in his voice, too. "You heard the man, Mr. Yoder. Time for you to go."

The boots on the stairs recede. These clomps are far louder. At the bottom, they stop, but the door doesn't open. Maggie steps out into the hall, curious, and Louise bolts ahead of her to sniff Hank, giving him a thorough going-over. Andy and Hank are both inspecting their feet. After a few more long seconds, the door slams, and moments later, she hears a truck drive away.

TWELVE

MAGGIE TRIPS over a dead mole on the front steps as she's leaving the house the next morning. "Gross, Louise!"

Hearing her name, the dog bounds toward Maggie. Maggie kicks the mole off the porch with her hard-toed cowboy boots, as far as she can. It lands ten feet away, partially hidden in the snow.

"This one is going over the fence. I'm pretty sure you won't get in trouble for killing a pasture nuisance."

And Maggie sure doesn't want any more trouble. Mrs. Sibley is on the warpath this morning, irrational and angry. After two nights without sleep, Laura didn't show up for breakfast, which was probably for the best. Mrs. Sibley is convinced Hank is her husband. Nothing he says or does persuades her otherwise. That makes Maggie her rival, out to steal her husband from her, so she threw a biscuit that missed Maggie's head by inches. Trudy covertly made Maggie a to-go plate, and Maggie snuck out the back door with it, then around front to eat alone in the great room.

Trouble isn't limited to Mrs. Sibley, either. Maggie and Hank went to bed without talking. Not about the handful of ibuprofen he dry-swallowed for his broken man parts, the migraine meds she saw him take, Paco, Andy, or Maggie's lack of progress in Texas. And especially not about his drink with Sheila. Hank tossed and turned in his sleep, muttering and occasionally flailing and crying out, which means Maggie is exhausted and on the ragged edge this morning.

Now she's got a bloody varmint to deal with, too.

Sighing, she opens the door to go back for a garbage bag to cart it off in. The door gives too easily, and she falls forward into Gene on the other side.

"Whoa there." He catches her and boosts her back upright.

"Hey, Gene. I thought you were on the road?"

"I was. But I was headed south, where it's even worse than here, on my way to Oklahoma. So instead, I'm on my way north, to fly out of Billings." He grins. "And decided to drop in here for a few things. What has you exploding into the house?"

"You don't want to know."

"I heard I missed some excitement."

"Yeah, poor Andy. I don't know which is worse—his father or the deputies. Andy really doesn't like Michael, by the way."

Gene shakes his head. "They need to get over it. The Cheyenne don't like the Amish, the Amish don't like the Indians. They're Double S employees now."

"Did you get a chance to look into Michael's background? Andy is convinced he's from a family of drug-abusing drunkards on the federal dole."

"No, but I'll call around from the road."

Hank clomps down the stairs. "Ready, Gene?"

For the first time, Maggie notices the overnight bag at Gene's feet.

He throws it over his shoulder. "Off to Billings."

Maggie's brow creases as she looks at Hank. "Both of you?"

Gene grins. "He's my chauffeur."

Hank doesn't smile at her. "I'll be back tonight."

Maggie chafes at his lack of communication. She hates the coldness between them. "Is that extra tank of gas really cheaper than parking?"

Hank shrugs. "Gives me a chance to pick up a few things, meet with a few people."

Under her breath, Maggie's voice is seething. "And you were going to tell me about this when?"

He looks past her and doesn't stop. "All in a day's work. Here for breakfast, here before bed. What does it matter where in between?"

Gene raises his eyebrows at her. "What's up your ass, Sibley?"

Hank hops in the truck. "Ask her." He slams the door.

Maggie growls. "Ask him why I had to hear it from Sheila that he had a drink with her yesterday."

"Oh shit." Gene puts his hand on the truck door. "I think I'll leave this to the two of you. Other than to warn you that trust is a big deal to Hank."

"Then he should be trustworthy."

Gene steps back to get closer to her and drops his voice. "No. *Being* trusted. He considers himself an honorable guy."

"He shouldn't have gone out with her."

"Who's to say he did?"

"What?" Maggie is confused for a moment, then it hits her. She doesn't know who asked who or if there was any asking at all. She's so accustomed to the man-whoring ways of her old boyfriend Gary, she'd just assumed. Still, hearing it from Sheila instead of Hank? Although, her phone wasn't working yesterday. And she still hasn't listened to all her messages.

Gene nudges her with a shoulder. "Listen, I'll talk to him, but consider *asking* him when he gets back."

Her face prickles, a sure sign she's blushing. "Thanks."

Maggie salutes him and waves to Hank, who lifts his hand. A dead fish has more life than him. Gene has a point, but Hank needs to quit acting like an oversensitive teenage girl and just talk to her. The truck pulls away, and immediately she feels a ferocious tug on her heart. She runs after them, wanting another chance to get goodbye right. But she's too late, and the truck bounces down the snowy dirt road toward the gate.

"Shit. That didn't go well."

Louise licks her fingers. Maggie jerks them away, not wanting dead-mole tongue on her skin. Louise wags her tail.

"Come on, Fucker. Let's get rid of the evidence of your latest crime."

THIRTEEN

AFTER THROWING the mole over the fence and then taking an apple to Lily, Maggie returns to the warmth of the house to check her messages. Before she can even access her voicemail, though, her phone rings. It's Boyd Herrington, her birth father.

"Hey, Boyd."

"Maggie! How's the great white north treating my daughter? Have you managed to get up to the Crow reservation to learn about our ancestors?"

"White and cold. And yes, I have. You need to come see it sometime. Maybe next summer for the Crow Fair. It's a big powwow."

"That would be great. Are you serious about white and cold?"

"Big blizzard yesterday."

"Wow. It's eighty-five degrees in Round Top right now. I believe I'll make my visit in the summer."

"I'm not sure which weather is worse."

"Listen, I have some exciting news."

"What's up?"

"My campaign is a go."

Boyd had withdrawn from a run at the presidency during the last election cycle when news broke that his sister Julie murdered Maggie's birth mother, and a few other people along the way. That was bad, but what made it worse was that she was Boyd's campaign manager, and that she'd committed the crimes to cover up Maggie's parentage. The truth had come out anyway, and when Maggie learned his identity, she was horrified to remember that he'd hit on her the year before. Her new father was a notorious horndog. What could be worse than learning you'd slept with your own daddy? Ugh. Thank God she'd turned him down. But to Boyd's great credit, he celebrated the news that he had a daughter from the moment he learned who Maggie really was to him.

"That's great. I wish you success." She wonders for a moment what office he's campaigning for, but she assumes he'll just be trying to regain his senate seat.

"Michele's book and movie have really neutralized any attempt to paint me in a bad light about you and Julie." *The Love Child and Murder That Toppled the Herrington Dynasty* was a bestseller and blockbuster hit. "And they've been great for name recognition. Better than a reality show."

Knowing Boyd as Maggie now does, she realizes he's probably trying to get one. Maggie shudders. *Please, God, no.* "Yeah, I'll bet."

"But my publicist wants us to push the ball a little further down the field. That's where you come in."

"Oh?" Maggie slips off her boots and flops onto the bed with her hand over her eyes. She braces. The other shoe is about to drop.

"Joint interviews. What do you think?"

"You and who?"

"Me and *you*, of course."

Maggie would rather crawl through snow naked carrying dead baby owls in her bare teeth than submit to interviews. She's had bloggers on her tail for the last few months, ever since her latest rise in notoriety in a "How the Mighty Maggie Killian Has Fallen" piece. It had the horrible timing of raising interest in her just as she was accused of murder. That led to her former bandmate Celinda finding her and exacting revenge for their disastrous past through arson, murder, and identity theft, which only added fuel to the flame of Maggie's notoriety. Her music plays on the radio regularly now. Reporters stalk her friends and family. So why would she offer herself up for more public humiliation?

Boyd fills the silence. "We could set any ground rules you want."

She knows that never works. "It's a bad idea, Boyd."

"Just one? It would really help me."

It's not that she owes him anything. He'd never been there for her, but then again, he'd never been given the chance. Maybe blood is thicker than water, because she hears herself saying, "One and done."

"Thank you. I'll owe you."

"Big-time."

"When are you coming home? We can do it in person, together."

"I don't know. I'm working on it."

"I miss you. We just found each other, and now you're gone. Maybe I should just come visit you in Wyoming after all, and we can do the interview there."

"Don't bring reporters here."

"I didn't—"

"I'm serious, Boyd."

"Okay, okay. I'll call you when the plans start to firm up. Email me if you want to set some topics off-limits. Or if you have any broadcast journalists you prefer to work with. Or not."

She agrees and they end the call.

Lying on the bed, she listens to her voicemail.

Hank: "I just got home. Call me as soon as you know anything about Andy. And give me a break about Sheila. Laura and I had lunch there with Mom after her appointment. They sat us at a table in the bar. Sheila came in and invited herself to sit down. She had a drink, then we left. I can't believe you don't trust me."

Maggie feels sick to her stomach. She wishes she'd listened to her messages the day before. Sunlight streams through the window and across her face. She's not used to being in a grown-up relationship with a good man. Or being the good woman in a grown-up relationship herself.

She texts Hank: *Finally had time to listen to your voicemail. I'm sorry. Sheila manipulated me. I shouldn't have let her. I trust you. I miss you. Let me make it up to you later? xxox*

Michele had texted back general advice that agreed with Maggie's inclinations. Andy had defied most of it, but Maggie felt relieved she'd been right in giving it. To Michele she sent a *Thanks, love you* text.

And finally she listened to the voicemail from Franklin, the adjuster. "I went by your place this afternoon and have what I need. I think you'll be pleased with the amount. I'll call you when it's final—probably tomorrow."

Maggie's heart flutters. She has to figure out a course of action that will protect her finances without having to sell off Gidget's two remaining treasures or the little farm. It's bad enough that all Gidget's paintings burned up. Maggie loved the paintings, her house, and her store. She has goodwill and a brand remaining from the Coop, not just a piece of land.

Surely if she rebuilds the shop, the land will be more valuable. She'll have time to acquire new stock while the contractors are at work. Then, whether she returns to run it or sells it, she'll be in good shape to make a decision. Maybe Hank will develop a hankering to raise bucking stock in Texas. It could happen.

Or maybe the house would be the more important thing to rebuild. More people are in the market for a house then an antique shop. But would they prefer to build their own, if they were buying new construction? Ugh. Why are the decisions so complicated?

What she needs is some estimates so she can compare her options. And a number from Franklin, so she'll know her parameters. She decides to reach out to some of the contractors she's been in touch with already, back when the project was nothing more than repairs from vandalism. When she opens her email, she has one from the realtor she emailed yesterday about the ranch. She reads it after she sends messages to the contractors about getting quotes.

> *Ms. Killian:*
>
> *I hope you don't mind me saying, but I know who you are and about your nice property outside Giddings. I am very sorry to hear you lost your house and shop in fires. If you're interested in selling—or even just talking about the possibility—I'd be happy to get together. I drove by the place, and it looks like your barn is still standing. County property records show you own twelve acres. I could list it for you. Maybe $95,000 or $100,000? As for the ranch, let me give you a tour. It's a turnkey cattle ranch, with a three-bedroom farmhouse."*

Only ninety-five thousand for her place? Maggie's heart drops. She has a small savings account and an even smaller checking account. Franklin's claim estimate better come back big bucks, or Maggie's in a bigger pickle financially than she'd thought.

FOURTEEN

MAGGIE WAKES WITH A START. Someone is calling her name. A woman. The voice is coming closer.

She stretches and wipes drool from her face. "I'm in here."

Laura appears in her doorway. "We missed you at lunch. I just wanted to be sure you're all right."

Maggie sits up and shuts her laptop. "I was working. I must have dozed off."

Laura turns to go. "Trudy said she was putting a plate aside for you."

"Thank you. For checking on me." Maggie smiles. "I would have thought you'd be relieved if I went missing."

Laura puts her hand on the door frame and looks back at her. "I don't *dislike* you, you know."

Maggie laughs. "You do a great imitation of it."

"You broke my brother's heart. He's never lived a normal life, because of you. Just when he has it together, you show up again and break up his first mature relationship. I hate where this is going for him."

"Wait, what? He broke *my* heart."

"Whatever. I lived through it with him. Dad's illness. Hank's injury and depression. His loneliness. Between Mom and my own problems, I don't have the bandwidth right now to go through that again with him."

"Laura, I care about Hank. I want the best for him."

"That may be true. But you're not exactly the poster child for stability. Or sobriety. Hell, I used to be a fan."

"I thought you said you weren't into my kind of music."

"I said I *used to* be a fan. I actually saw you perform in Waco, at a dinner theater. You were wasted. When did you quit smoking, by the way?"

"What?"

"I saw you talking to the cops, smoking like a chimney."

"Rehab. I quit at rehab."

Laura nods. "Anyway, you were a real letdown. I don't think I ever listened to you again after that. And this was before Hank had even told us about you. He didn't confess until years later. I guess he was afraid of disappointing me."

Maggie bristles. "That wasn't a good time in my life." She's remained calm, but Laura's getting personal, whether she's right or not. "But I've been a business owner and pillar of my community for ten years. You're out of line and unfair."

"Once an addict, always an addict."

Maggie advances on her. "For the sake of your relationship with your brother, I think this conversation should be over."

Laura stares at Maggie, deep into her eyes. "I'll be in his life long after you're gone." Then, before Maggie can answer, she leaves.

Fuming, Maggie jerks on her boots, then goes to the bathroom and wipes the sleep from her eyes. She stomps down the stairs to the kitchen. Trudy is gone, but on the counter are two plates of food covered with plastic wrap.

"I hear Trudy left me a plate."

She turns to see Michael. "You missed lunch, too, huh?" She points at the covered meals.

"Yeah. I got an ATV stuck in a drift." He smiles, showing perfect white teeth, except for one that's missing. An eyetooth. "I'm taking a horse out this afternoon. They're a little more reliable in these conditions."

"How's the weather?"

"Cold, but clear and sunny. The sky looks like the Caribbean Sea. Not that I've ever seen it, except on TV."

Maggie eats her beef stroganoff and rice with a spoon, standing at the counter. Michael follows her lead.

"It would have been nice to ride out in twos, but we're kind of slammed with Hank and Gene gone, and Andy, um, missing part of yesterday. And then tomorrow people will be gone for Paco's service."

"I'll bet."

"Although I'm not sure Andy would ride with me anyway, even if he could."

Maggie rinses her plate and avoids eye contact. "Oh?"

"I think he has a thing against the Cheyenne."

"Why do you say that?"

"The Amish are our neighbors, but we're not neighborly."

It sounds like an admission, so Maggie follows up on it. "So do you have a thing against the Amish?"

"No more than anyone else I know back home. I don't like how they treat their animals, but maybe Andy will be different."

"What do you mean?"

"The Amish I know ride their horses into the ground and starve them. I was pushing cows with some Amish this summer, and I had to take my saddle off my horse and walk him back—he was that beat. The Amish just whipped theirs up and ran them home. Their feet were awful, cracked, turned up. Most of them were half-lame." He snorts. "Not their teams, though. They treat their teams real good. But then again, if they're your transportation and your tractor, you better keep 'em running."

"Andy's been nothing but good to the animals here."

"He moved away. That says something. And the best farrier I ever saw was Amish. Or ex-Amish. I do some blacksmithing myself, and he won every competition I ever saw."

"Are you from the reservation?"

"Yeah. But I left a few years ago. I'm trying to stay out of the res scene. There's nothing for me there. But it's hard. I'm pretty broke."

Maggie remembers leaving home younger than him, a lifetime ago. Broke, too. Everything had been so much simpler, until it wasn't. If what Andy says is true, things aren't simple at all for Michael back on the res. "Well, I hope the two of you will get along. Since he'll be your supervisor."

"I'll be fine."

She looks out the kitchen window. Not a cloud in the sky. She has decisions to make, and there's nothing like wide-open Wyoming to clear her head. "I make a pretty good second. Or at least I can dial 911 in an emergency. If there's signal."

He laughs. "You beat out all the competition, but it won't get me in trouble with Hank, will it?"

She scoffs and checks for a text back from Hank. There's none. "Of course not."

FIFTEEN

Lily is sassy after twenty-four hours in a stall, where the hands had put her when the weather went to crap the day before. She dips her head and shakes it as she canters along behind Michael and his horse.

"Who are you and what have you done with my lazy pregnant mare?" But Maggie understands. She likes her freedom, too.

Ahead of them, Michael is doing a post-storm welfare check. He counts heads of cows and calves. It's easier said than done, because they don't stand still for it. When he's done, he turns back and frowns. "I'm short two head. Can you see what count you get?"

"Whoa, Lily." Maggie counts, keeping track by fives on one hand. Lily fidgets in a circle. Maggie uses leg pressure to push her back. "I got thirty-two."

"Shit. That's what I got. And after I've been lucky all day."

"Do you know which tags are missing?" All the Double S bovines wear numbered, colored ear tags.

"Nope. If we have to, I can ride back and get them. But I need to check the fence and break up some ice, too, so let's start by riding it."

"Break ice?"

They take off, riding single-file along the fence. The cold makes her breathing stuffy. She rubs some Mentholatum under her nose and coughs, then returns the little tube to her pocket.

"In the tubs."

"Aren't they automatic?" Maggie thinks about all the ranchers she knows in south central Texas. Their tanks have floats for refilling. Even in the coldest weather, the water usually replenishes.

"No. We don't use floats this far north. Ice breaks floats, and broken floats kill. Animals die fast here without water. Plus a broken float can waste the water itself, spill it all out on the ground, where it doesn't do them any good."

"What about the creeks and ponds?"

"They don't freeze as fast, so we can break the ice by hand. But when it gets too cold, we'll have to bring the livestock where we can keep them fed and hydrated, I imagine. That's what most everyone up here does."

Maggie imagines the overcrowded barn conditions. "There's not room for them all in the ranch buildings."

"Oh, they're fine outside. Especially the horses. They adapt pretty well to cold forage. Better than cattle. The cows are known to hunker in ravines that fill up with ice and snow, then starve their damn selves to death. Horses move to higher ground where the wind blows the snow off the grass leftover from the growth months. Horses can even get their hydration from eating snow. Cattle don't."

"But it gets so cold here. And so windy. Won't they freeze to death?" Maggie's plenty cold now, even with the sun out. She leans back as Lily picks her way down a steep incline. The horse slides a few feet. Maggie clutches the saddle horn, but Lily seems nonplussed.

"You'd be surprised. I've heard an unclipped horse's ideal weather is twenty degrees. I don't know about that, because I haven't ever been able to get one to tell me, but I've seen our horses on the res refuse to take shelter even when we offer it, in double digits below zero."

"How do they survive?"

"They just huddle together with their butts against the wind."

"But two cows aren't enough for a huddle. I hope they didn't get loose."

"Most likely they're just over a ridge, enjoying the sun. But we'll make sure."

Lily snorts and jerks her head up. A red fox darts in front of them in a crazy zigzag pattern, then across the snow to the fence line. Maggie remembers the brown jackrabbit hopping over the grass only a day or two ago. This landscape is nothing if not constantly changing. The sky is crazy clear and the snow sparkles like diamonds. On the face of the mountain, the rustic family cabin looks like a Swiss chalet. A bald eagle swoops up and down the ridge, letting out a series of high-pitched whistles.

Maggie tents her hand to peer after the raptor. "It sure doesn't make a very powerful sound."

"Doesn't have to. The eagle knows he is mighty. We are blessed by his presence. He comes to us from heaven."

Maggie smiles. "A visitor from heaven. Really?"

"That's what my grandfather says. Maybe this one is sent by your friend Paco."

"Maybe." Maggie doesn't bother to sound convinced.

Michael's head moves slowly left to right and back as he scans the landscape, looking for signs of the missing cattle. "I only met him once. Did you know him well?"

"A little. He was full of life. A charmer. And good with mechanics. Like, things with engines. He helped me when my truck broke down."

Michael stops and stares at something for a moment, then he urges his mount forward again. "My Cheyenne name is Talks to Eagles. When I was a boy, an eagle flew through my bedroom window. He was not happy. He went crazy, flapping his wings, breaking things. I talked to him until he calmed down. I told him I was his little brother and I would help him. He finally let me pick him up. I carried him outside and released him to kiss the sky."

How different her childhood and whole life would have been if she had known about her own Native American ancestry and lived closer to that side of her family. Suddenly she really wants to find out who they are. Not just that they are part of the Crow nation, but who the people are. To meet them. She needs to ask Boyd for their names.

"Was the eagle hurt?"

"Only his pride, I think."

Maggie smiles, enjoying the thought of eagles kissing the sky as she watches the eagle continue its journey along the ridge.

"Eagles are sacred to my people. They represent truth, courage, wisdom, and freedom. So my eagle's visit was like a visit from the divine. Because of this, I was treated with the deep respect that people reserve for him."

His words are moving to Maggie, but she doesn't know how to express it. So she stays quiet and thinks about this young man and his family. He certainly isn't telling a story that sounds like it is filled with drunks and druggies.

"His visit has been the source of my strength in many hard times. I've had many visitors since then, because of him. Spirits, sometimes in the form of other animals. Even the dead."

"How do you know? I mean, when you get the visitors, how do you know?" Maggie has had visits from the dead herself. Several, in fact, from her renter, Leslie, after she was murdered, but she doesn't mention this to Michael.

"I just know. My eagle taught me to trust in my power."

Maggie warms inside. Maybe she needs to trust more in her own power. Her own wisdom. She'd doubted her visitor was a dead woman, but it had turned out she was. She looks back up at the eagle. She can barely see it now as it flies off into the distance up the mountainside, past the Sibleys' cabin. Her eyes drop, and as they do, she catches a glimpse of a man. Stooped. Hat pulled low. Not dressed for the weather. Red boots glaring out from the snow. He's headed down a ravine, and she knows it's Paco. Even though it can't be, she knows.

She draws in a sharp breath. "Paco."

Michael raises his hand for her to stop. "Hello there." His voice echoes in the stillness.

The man doesn't react.

"You see him, too?" Maggie asks, her voice thready.

"Our visitor? Yes. He could be walking the in-between world, looking for peace."

"So I'm not crazy."

"I can't say that. But this doesn't make you crazy. Just perceptive. If I didn't know better, I'd say you were Indian."

"I am. Partly. Crow." She remembers the red-booted man she'd seen the night she found Paco's body. The one running to the bunkhouse. Could that have been Paco, too?

"See that?" Michael points down a ravine at two black furry bodies. One of them moos. "That's where Paco was headed. He's still doing his job."

Maggie looks back for Paco, but he's disappeared. She shivers and pulls the collar of her coat closed tighter. "The little bastards. They can't hide from us."

"Help me push them back to the herd?"

"Do we need to do anything about Paco?"

Michael looks at her like she's crazy now. "He's not in this world anymore. There's nothing we can do for him. But we can take care of these cows."

"What do I do?"

"We'll fan out behind them, maybe five yards back."

Michael and his horse drive the cows out of the gully and past Maggie. She urges Lily after them and positions the horse to the left of their retreating backs, nose-even with Michael and his horse's rump. She barely has to guide Lily, who seems to know exactly what to do.

"You're a natural."

Maggie smiles. She's not sure about that, but she's taken to ranch life far more than she'd ever thought she would.

SIXTEEN

Maggie showers and dresses, checking her phone every five minutes. She still hasn't heard back from Hank, and she's getting worried. The weather is clear, but that doesn't mean bad things can't happen on the road between the ranch and Billings. Semitrucks with overly aggressive drivers. Ice. Deer. Sleepiness. Trouble with his head.

She texts: *Let me know you're okay. I can't wait for you to get home.*

This time she gets a reply. *Hey, sorry. Signal spotty. Driving. All good. Home by 10.*

Maggie's relief makes her giddy. She responds with a heart emoticon, feeling like a silly adolescent. She stops just short of begging him not to be mad at her. When things aren't right between them, things aren't right with her. Hell, she may not be able to say the L-word, but she knows she's a goner for this cowboy.

Dinner is quiet. Laura has taken Mrs. Sibley into Story to the Wagon Box for chicken fried steak, a tradition the older woman keeps with her caregiver. Gene is probably in Oklahoma already, and Hank won't be home for hours. It's just Trudy, Maggie, and the four hands.

Michael breaks the silence, teasing Maggie about her new cowgirl skills.

"I told you I was the right person for the job." Maggie twirls spaghetti noodles on her fork. The thick meat sauce slides off, so she scoops it back onto the fork.

Andy has a funny look on his face. "Hank is pretty protective of her. I'd be careful if I were you."

Trudy plops down at the table. She serves herself spaghetti. "He's fine, Andy."

Maggie wipes her mouth and swallows. "Hank doesn't get jealous. Besides, I'm a grown woman. If I want to push cows, I'm going to push cows."

"Michael works here. You don't. And I think you've got Hank running around a stump."

"What?"

"The man doesn't know up from down with you around. Why do you think he took off today?"

"Gene needed a ride."

Andy harrumphs. "Maybe so. But Hank is trying to worry something out. And you're the only thing he worries about. Remember, we're with him here when you're not."

Trudy stabs the air with garlic bread. "Andy, I think you need to shut it down."

"I don't want in the middle of that," Michael says, shaking his head.

Maggie squeezes the cloth napkin in her lap. "You're not in the middle of anything. It's okay. Hank doesn't mind me teaching Andy guitar." She takes a deep breath and lets it out quickly, twirls up more spaghetti and lets it hover in the air. "Speaking of which, are we on tonight, Andy? It would be a good distraction for you, I think."

"I've been thinking on that. The roads are clear. Would you be willing to take me to the Occidental tonight for the bluegrass jam instead?" Andy puts his elbows on the table and takes another bite.

Maggie wonders if his worries are more about Michael than Hank. "You go on. A saloon? On a work night?"

He blushes and ducks his head.

"I think it would be fun. And good for your own playing to watch musicians jam."

"You don't think it's disrespectful, this soon after Paco's, um, after he's gone?"

"What would Paco say?"

A grin lifts one side of Andy's beard. "He'd be the one asking me to go with him."

"Music is always appropriate in my book."

"If you don't think it will look bad to the sheriff. Like I don't care about Paco."

Or like he's guilty. But he's not. "The deputies will figure out the real killer. Listening to music isn't evidence. I'd be more worried about what your father will think."

"I'm on Rumspringa. It doesn't matter." He pushes his bowl away and scoops whipped cream onto an enormous apple dumpling, then pulls that bowl toward himself.

"I've been meaning to ask you about him."

"What?"

"I saw an Amish man that looked like him, driving a truck. Outside the ranch."

"My father doesn't drive."

"Okay. I did think it was odd."

"Are you sure he was Amish?"

"Not a hundred percent."

"All right, then."

Michael glances between the two of them. "My sister loves the jam. She's a musician."

Maggie can tell he's waiting for an invite. He and Andy need to work things out and move on to something normal. But she's not going to force it on Andy when he's already got so much to deal with. And Andy doesn't respond.

Well, so be it. Maggie considers an apple dumpling. She never thought she could get sick of apples, but she is. She stands. She'll skip dessert. "Let me change. I'll meet you out front in twenty minutes?"

Andy nods, his mouth overfull of apple dumpling and a look of bliss on his face. Michael scowls and attacks his dessert.

Upstairs, Maggie puts on heavier boots and swaps out her sweatshirt for a cable-knit sweater over a button-down. After she swipes on lipstick, she texts Hank again.

I'm taking Andy to the Ox in lieu of music lesson. Home by 9.

Andy's words replay in her head. "Hank is trying to worry something out. You're the only thing he worries about." She knows she jumped to conclusions about Sheila. She shouldn't have blamed him. Hopefully that's all he's worrying about, but she knows he's concerned about her plans. Her place in Texas. Their future. She is, too, but only because she hasn't figured out how to get him to Texas yet. Tomorrow she'll call that realtor about the ranch for sale. She needs to know about cross-fencing and facilities and set up a time to see it. A time when she can get Hank down there with her.

Forty-five minutes later, she and Andy find two seats next to each other in the Ox at a table for four with a smiling couple in matching plaid shirts who are noshing on burgers and french fries. Maggie loves the greasy-spoon smell, the jovial atmosphere, and the authentic décor. Especially the décor, from the bullet holes in the ceiling to the heavily lacquered hand-hewn tables to the wildlife mounts of every animal known to Wyoming, plus a few. A waitress with a blonde braid weaves over and takes their order. If Maggie had a dime for every blonde braid she's seen in Wyoming, she'd be a rich woman. Maggie opts for one TKO and one coffee. She's not eager to learn how good her winter driving skills are after a few drinks. She'll pace herself, very slowly.

Andy orders a ginger beer. "Will you play tonight?"

"Oh no. Not on your life."

"I really wish I could see you." He gestures at the players, who are warming up by running through snippets of songs. There are six of them. An old guy in dusty, baggy jeans with a red bandana around his neck, a pimply teenage boy, a soprano-voiced banjo player with long dark hair, a foreign-accented woman on the fiddle, and two more old guys who look like twins. "They're good, but I've listened to you play. Live, at the ranch, and on your albums."

"My albums? How?"

"Cassette tapes. Hank lent me his stash. There's a boom box in the bunkhouse."

Hank has a stash of her albums, on cassette. That means he got them back in the years they were apart. And kept them. Every piece of evidence that he really loves her is a sunburst in her chest. "Wow. I didn't know."

His brown eyes plead. "Please play."

Andy's had such a terrible week. War wages inside Maggie. How can she deny him this? It's only her ego standing in the way. She flinches. Yes, her ego. She doesn't want people to see her perform less than perfectly. Even retired, she's a professional musician. But an out-of-practice one, out of her element and playing with strangers. There's no way she's going to be perfect if she gets up there. Maybe no one but Andy will figure out who she is, though.

She sighs. "Fine. What do I do?"

SEVENTEEN

ANDY BEAMS and claps his hands once, loud and sharp, one hand going up, the other away. "Just go tell them who you are."

"Oh no. I'll play the jam, but only if it's anonymously," Maggie says.

"Well, say hello, anyway. They'll invite you in. It's how they've done it here at the Ox the times I've seen them before. When Paco brought me here."

She shakes a fist at him. "If this goes bad, I'm coming after you, Andy."

"You'll be the best they've ever heard."

"I doubt that." She turns sideways and sidles between chairs. "Excuse me. Pardon me."

People move out of her way with no grumbling. At the front of the room, the jamming musicians are between songs.

She approaches the old guy with the bandana at the vocal mic. "Hey. I hear you let musicians work in?"

"Sure do. What do you play?"

Maggie surveys the instruments. Piano. Standing bass. Banjo. Fiddles. Acoustic guitars. Tambourine. Washboard. "Everything you've got."

"Did you bring an instrument?"

"Nah. I had no idea this was an option." She takes a step back. "It's okay if I can't."

"Nope. Just checking. How about you start on the piano? We rotate up to the vocals through the instruments we each know. When you get the vocal mic, you announce your song and key and set the tempo."

"Sounds good."

"Name?"

"Maggie."

He turns to the group. "This here's Maggie. She's working in, starting on the piano."

Friendly, curious faces greet her and offer names. Penny. Brad. Donna. Hal and Cal. The old guy says his last. "And I'm Wally."

"Nice to meet you, Wally."

"Song is 'Rocky Top.' Key is G."

He's picked something she knows, which is a good start. She seats herself on the piano bench. Wally announces the song to the bar and introduces her. She waves. A few hands in the crowded bar lift. Andy's is high and vigorous. Wally counts off, and the musicians launch into a joyful noise. Maggie's chords are complementary and rhythmic. The players are all quite good and have obviously played together many times. The banjo-playing girl with the long black hair is a standout. *Penny. That's what her name is,* Maggie thinks.

It's an easy way to work in, being in the background. She can't help smiling and bobbing her head. By the end of the song, she's exhilarated and embellishing. Okay, she misses this. Not solo performance, but this. Being inside a song, even an amateurly delivered jam song. It lifts her soul and fills her with a light she hadn't realized was burned out. When they finish the song, the crowd applauds with vigor. Andy stands up and whistles with two fingers.

Wally scoots onto the piano bench. "You play this thing like you've been pounding keys all your life."

"Something like that." She moves on to the standing bass.

Piano is the least of her skills. Give her anything her fingers can pick and strum, and she's in her element. As she cycles through the bass, the banjo, the fiddle, and the tambourine, they play old standards. "Cherokee Shuffle." "Will the Circle Be Unbroken." "Old Joe Clark." "Whiskey Before Breakfast." Then it's her turn at the vocal mic, with the guitar. She ponders song choices. She needs something bluegrass that she knows all the words to, when what she really wants to play is "Kickapoo Redemption," something she heard recently from Shea Abshier and the Nighthowlers. Her choices are limited by her experience and her memory. She'd do better with a list to choose from. The other musicians huddle behind her. Just when she's about to ask them to offer up a tune, Wally nudges her.

"We voted. We want you to play 'I Hate Cowboys.' We'll bluegrass it up a little for you."

Maggie bites her lip. "Um, I . . ."

"You didn't think we wouldn't figure out who you are, did you? That face of yours is way too famous, and word's out about you and that Sibley boy. But we had a hint, too."

Maggie scans their faces. What hint? She glances at Andy, but he looks innocent and oblivious.

Wally laughs. "Ole Hal here knows all your songs by heart. He's even had us play 'em a time or two."

Hal tips his hat. Cal tips his, too.

She bows to them, then blows a kiss. "I usually hate playing my own stuff. It blows my cover."

Wally claps her on the shoulder. "You're amongst new friends. And I'm not sure you have much cover to blow. Now, give us a treat."

She makes eye contact with Andy and nods at him. Into the mic, she says, "'I Hate Cowboys,' key of E. This one is for my friend Andy."

Just as she launches into the music as familiar to her as her own breath, she sees Andy isn't looking at her. He's looking past her. She glances back and catches Penny's gaze locked on Andy. A chuckle escapes her, but she ends it in time to sing the lyrics Hank inspired so many years ago. She strums and sings along to the accompaniment of the bluegrass musicians. The music feels different on a strange guitar, and she misses her Martin back at the ranch. She becomes aware a buzz is growing in the room. How long has it been since she sang this song in front of humans? Ten years? Twelve? When she reaches the ending, she sings the chorus one last time.

I hate cowboys—especially bull riders—
I hate cowboys.
Their buckles look funny,
And they call their girls bunnies.
I hate cowboys. I hate bull-riding cowboys.

She shakes the guitar gently, drawing out the sound of the last note. The saloon patrons are on their feet, cheering. Calling her name. Her secret is definitely out. Andy basks in the glow and nods at her. Wally claps her on the back so hard she falls forward from the stool.

He catches her. "Sorry! Just a little excited. That was real special for us."

The rest of the musicians surround her. She accepts hugs and handshakes. Penny holds out a Sharpie and asks her to sign the back of her banjo.

"Oh no. Anything but your beautiful instrument. How about the case instead?"

The girl agrees and returns with a beat-up case covered in bumper stickers. Maggie signs and tries to hand the marker back.

"You're going to need it." Penny points.

A line has formed.

Wally takes the mic. "We're going to take a break to let you folks thank Ms. Killian for gracing us with her talent. Back in a few."

Maggie signs autographs and chats while keeping one eye on Andy. He beelines toward Penny. She barely meets his eyes, but she nods. The girl is shy, that's for sure. After they exchange a few words, she joins him at the bar. A few minutes later, Maggie sees fresh ginger beers in their hands. Maggie finally begs off from the patrons wanting to talk about her music to join them.

"Hey, you two. Penny, you have a great sound. What did you think, Andy?"

"I think she is wonderful."

The two stare at each other like there's no one else in the room.

Maggie laughs. "I meant about the music, Andy. You're here as my student."

Penny breaks eye contact and swivels to Maggie. "You teach? I'd love to take lessons from you."

"Well, Andy's my first student. Ever."

"I can be your second."

"She could take lessons *with* me," Andy suggests. His voice quivers a little, like he's not used to being this forward with girls. A non-Amish girl, at that.

Maggie shrugs. "We could do that." She recites her number, and Penny types it into her phone.

Andy says, "There's the woman Paco was sparking."

He doesn't point, but he nods at a curvy brunette in her late twenties or early thirties standing near the pool table in the back room. She's sipping her drink through a straw, then stirring the ice cubes. There's a cluster of women around her. One looks familiar to Maggie. Had she seen her out on a date with Gene a few months before?

"Maggie. Didn't you just bring down the house?" A female voice drips sarcasm to Maggie's left, even as it slurs.

Maggie looks over. Sheila. She's way, way drunk, and probably carrying concealed under her puffy lavender vest. "Time to scat, Andy."

"But . . ."

"What, Maggie, are you running away from me?" Sheila says.

Maggie turns away from Sheila, imagining a bullet through the back. She ignores Sheila and answers Andy. "You can meet me outside, then."

"No! I mean, I can't let you go out there alone." He shoots a glance at the glowering, staggering Sheila, then turns his attention back to Penny. His brow furrows. "I, um, I don't have a phone, Penny." Maggie knows this is an Amish thing, and she aches for him for a moment. Dating outside his community in Montana is a challenging thing. "But I'd like to see you again."

"We're going to take music lessons together."

"How about I get the two of you together Monday night?" Maggie suggests.

Sheila stares daggers through her. "Hello?"

Penny looks down. "Sounds good."

"I'll see you then." Andy's face relaxes.

Penny smiles sweetly. "Thanks for the drink. Nice to meet you, Maggie."

Sheila's voice elevates to a screech. "I'm talking to you, Maggie Killian. You can't ignore me just because you think you're some big hotshot."

The curvy brunette and the familiar-looking friend appear beside Sheila, and now Maggie is sure it's the same girl she saw out with Gene.

She narrows her eyes at Maggie. "You."

Andy takes Maggie's elbow. He's never touched her before. "Let's go."

"Definitely."

Andy hustles her ahead of him toward the door. Maggie is really glad she's sober, or she'd be ending this night in a public catfight.

Sheila's voice isn't far behind them. "Run like a little bitch."

"What did Hank ever see in that beast?" Maggie mutters.

The cold slaps her in the face when they hit the sidewalk, but it's not nearly as shocking as what she sees. Hank is standing there, arms crossed and legs slightly apart, looking like a Remington bronze.

"Hank!" She throws her arms around him, but stops short of climbing him and biting his neck like she wants to. "You're here." Their noses bump, and his is icy cold.

"I decided to come straight here instead of stopping at home."

She nuzzles into his neck. "I'm so glad. I missed you. I'm sorry I was jealous yesterday." She cranes her head back and catches a sight of the dimples. Something inside her chest flutters.

He presses his lips to her ear. "I missed you, too. Let's get your boy home and crawl into bed."

She shivers. "I'll race you."

EIGHTEEN

Before Maggie, Hank, and Andy can leave, the door to the Ox flies open. Sheila barrels out with her two sidekicks.

"There she is," Sheila says. Then, "Oh. With you."

Maggie and Hank lock eyes.

"Unprovoked, I promise," Maggie says.

"She tried to cause a problem yesterday. Why should today be any different?" He kisses her, his warm lips all the reassurance she needs. "Let me see if I can stop this."

They break apart. Sheila is still bristly, but starting to deflate.

"Enough, Sheila. I told you yesterday. You're a great woman. But I'm not the guy for you."

Her eyes glisten. "You were. You could be again."

"Come on, Sheila." The brunette tugs on Sheila's arm. Then to Hank, she says, "Sorry."

"Thanks, Mary." To Maggie he says, "This is Mary Marton. You already know June, I think?"

Sheila jerks her arm away from her friend. "Get her away from me, June."

Maggie says, "Nice to meet you, Mary. Hello, June."

Mary says, "Nice to meet you."

June scowls and moves between Mary and Sheila.

Two men a few years older than Andy walk out. One says, "Hey, thanks for playing, Maggie!"

She waves. "You're welcome."

Hank shoots Maggie a questioning look, but then turns back to Sheila. His voice is rock solid. "No, I never will be again. My heart belongs to Maggie."

"You said she's moving back to Texas."

Maggie's mouth flies open.

Hank holds out an arm, stopping Maggie before she can advance on Sheila. Or him. "You asked me about her place in Texas. I told you she's going back to take care of things. And that's all I said. You need to stop this. Get on with your life." He turns to her friends. "We're leaving. Get her back inside. Better yet, get her home to sober up. She's got to teach in the morning."

The women nod. Sheila crosses her arms and plants her feet.

Hank takes Maggie's arm and starts walking her away. "I want you and Andy to drive ahead of me. Andy, you're on duty."

Andy falls in step with them and pats his ribs. "Don't worry, Hank. I'm carrying."

Maggie smiles. "That's not very Amish of you."

"Hank left me in charge of you."

"Is that why you were upset that I rode out with Michael?"

"Not exactly."

"What?" Hank asks.

She looks over her shoulder. Sheila and her friends are still arguing. The temperature is falling, and the cold is seeping into Maggie. She wraps her arms around her midsection. "I'll tell you at home, babe. I've got to get Bess's heater on."

They walk a little farther and reach Maggie's magenta truck behind the courthouse.

"I'm back on the street out front. Come around and wait for me so I can follow you."

Five minutes later, Andy and Maggie chug off with Hank behind them. Bess finally heats up five minutes before they reach the ranch.

Andy says, "I'll walk from the main house."

"Are you sure?"

"Yeah. It's not far."

"Okay. Thanks, Andy."

They get out. Hank parks beside Bess. All the lights are off, inside and outside the house. Andy waves and slips away into the darkness.

A hard body crashes into Maggie. Her squeal is cut off by warm lips, her fall arrested by strong arms around her. They lean into the cold metal of her truck. She hooks a leg around Hank's hip, pulls herself up, then wraps the other around him and locks her ankles, all without breaking their intense kiss. But then she pulls her lips away and sinks her teeth gently into the base of his neck.

Hank groans. "Don't let go of me."

She doesn't.

Somehow they make it in the door, up the stairs, and to the bedroom without Hank crashing or Maggie falling. He kicks the door shut behind them, then staggers to the bed, where they topple.

Maggie laughs as it crashes to the floor. "Whoops. I think we need a permanent fix."

"I'm on it. Just not right now." He grabs her face and holds it between his hands, his pressure possessive and just the right side of rough. "I fucking love you. It's driving me crazy. I thought it was bad before. When we were younger. But I feel like a kid again."

"Oh God. Me, too."

His lips rove across her face to her ear, then down her neck. He stops suddenly. "It's not always a good thing, but it's always amazing."

Maggie knows exactly what he means. "Less telling. More showing. If you can. With your broken unit and all."

"My unit is fully functional." He laughs. "Did I mention I fucking love you?" Then he rips off his shirt, and all telling stops.

NINETEEN

"I CAN'T DECIDE what I like best about sex with you. Wanting you, having you, or the afterglow." Maggie traces her finger across and around his sculpted chest.

"Stop. You're going to kill me."

"Is it hurting you?"

"Is what hurting me?"

"Well, you're, um, looking ready to go again. And you did injure yourself, after all."

He smiles. "The bruising is bad, and it's crooked. I look like I got the worst of it with a bull hoof to the crotch."

"But it's treatable, right?"

"Bull injuries?"

"No. Sex injuries."

"What the hell kind of nonsense is that?"

"If it hurts, then you should get it looked at."

"It will only hurt if you laugh at it."

"I won't. But if it does."

"Maggie, I didn't see a doctor for a broken back. I'm sure not going to see him for a crooked penis."

"Let me see."

"No."

"Seriously, just stand up."

He sighs, but stands naked in the moonlight.

Maggie tilts her head. "It's black and blue. Mostly black."

"I told you so."

"And you look like you're signaling a right turn." She scoots to the right on the bed. "You want me to keep going? I feel like I should run a lap around the room. To the right, to the right."

"Didn't we just discuss you not laughing at it?"

She makes a zipping motion over her lips. "Not laughing. But I don't think you should run around naked in public anytime soon."

He takes the left side of the bed and pulls the covers up over them. "No public nakedness. Unless I tie my horse to sagebrush."

"You lost me, cowboy."

"Have I never told you that story?"

"Um, obviously, no."

Hank puts his arms around her and pulls her against him, a little spoon to his bigger fork. "I was working for an outfitter to make extra cash during hunting season."

"Before you met me?"

"Yep, but not long before. I was moving our camp while he took the clients out. It was Indian summer, perfect weather, and after I finished setting up the new camp, I took my favorite horse from the string—Dollar— down to the creek"—which he pronounces *crick* in the Wyoming fashion —"where there was a hot spring. The only thing near the water was sagebrush, but Dollar was a good old horse, so I looped his reins around it. I took off everything but my hat, and I got in the hot spring and relaxed the dust off. All of a sudden, I saw a big gray horse running by me back to the old camp, dragging the sagebrush. I jumped out and into my boots and started after him, walking slow so as not to spook him."

"In nothing but your hat and boots?"

"Nothing but."

"Did you catch him?"

"I sure did. But not until after I scared the bejeezus out of two women hikers, who couldn't quite look me in the eye. One of them pointed behind her and said, 'Your horse went thataway.' So I tipped my hat and said, 'Yes, ma'am. Thank you. You ladies have a nice day,' and skedaddled after him."

Maggie starts to chortle. Her laugh builds to a hee-haw. "Oh, Hank. I'm going to pee."

"Not on me." He tickles her, and she rolls away, screaming and clutching her sides, with tears running down her face. "Someone is ticklish."

Tickling turns to kissing, and kissing into round two. When they're back to the afterglow stage, she pokes him.

"You're a mess. I can just picture you in the boots and hat. You know, you could have taken the hat off and covered yourself."

"There was a lot going on. It didn't occur to me until too late." He smiles at her. "I've matured. And now I have stable income, so I don't need to go running off naked after horses into the mountains."

His words jiggle loose a thought. She should update him. About her day. Her altercation with Laura. The ride with Michael. The email from the realtor. She stalls. "How was Billings?"

"Makes me as glad as ever that I live here and not there. I spent a lot of money. Met with a few ranchers and a rodeo organizer. Made it without hitting a deer in both directions. About as good as it gets. How was your day?"

"Laura and I had . . . words."

"Oh no."

"She doesn't like me."

"I like you."

"Thank God for that. I also napped. Michael got an ATV stuck, so after lunch I rode Lily out with him to count cows and got to cowgirl up and help him herd in two strays."

"Michael doesn't need your help for that," Hank says in a grumbly voice.

"It was fun."

"You could get hurt."

"Stop. There's more. We saw an eagle."

"Not uncommon around here, but nice."

"Yes. Oh, and I got a call from a record label. The ones that bought my music when my label went under."

"You're a rock star. What did they want?"

She snorts. "They wanted me to record a new album. To capitalize on my current notoriety. But they insisted on a morality clause since I'm such a live wire."

"You're shitting me."

"Nope. So I told them to fuck off."

"Good for you. Although I do wish you'd play again, music girl. But you don't need it like that."

She summons up her courage for the tougher topic. "I also contacted a real estate agent."

He squeezes her. "You're putting your place on the market?"

She hears the smile in his words and feels guilty because she knows she's going to burst his bubble. "Well, not exactly."

"What, then, exactly?"

"I might. Eventually. Honestly, I've been waffling back and forth about what to do. Selling my place is a consideration. Even fixing it up and selling it. But also fixing it up and working it." She turns to face him and puts her hands on his cheeks. "Just listen for a second, okay?"

"I'm not liking this."

"Shh." She touches a finger to his lips. "I've got Gidget's farm. It's a hundred acres. There's a place next to it, about the same size, that we could lease. And I made an inquiry on a few hundred more acres nearby. Just to see what it would cost to set up down there."

"Set up what?"

"Double S." She gnaws the inside of her lip.

"I already told you, I can't do that."

Can't or won't? His words are stinging nettle, but she covers up her hurt. "Okay. Well, I still need to figure out how to compare apples to apples on my options. I've contacted some contractors for estimates. What would I make rebuilding and running it versus selling it as is versus fixing it up and selling it." She withholds one option: selling off her inheritance of Gidget's farm, the Warhol, and the antique Jaguar. She doesn't want to let them go. Plus, it just seems dilettante. Not like her. She wants to support herself, and the inheritance is a last resort.

Hank is so quiet he seems to be soaking in sound like a black hole in space.

It eats at her until she blurts out, "I'd think you could trust me and be happy for me. I'm trying to follow my heart."

"Follow your *heart*? I thought you followed your *heart* to Wyoming. To me."

"You know what I mean."

"Honestly, Maggie, I'm not a hundred percent sure I do. Last time we ended with you running off to work in Nashville. Now it sounds like you're gearing up to run back to work in Texas. I can tell you one thing. I've spent fifteen years apart from you, wanting you. I'm not spending another fifteen that way." He turns his back on her and hauls the covers up in one swift move.

"Hank."

"Good night, Maggie."

"Don't be this way."

He flips over, his mouth inches from hers as he speaks. "Funny, that's exactly what I was trying to say to you." Then he rolls back over, leaving her alone and shivering on her side of the bed in the dark.

TWENTY

HANK IS GONE before Maggie wakes the next morning. She sits up. He must have left early, because he didn't let Louise out. The dog is whining like she does when bacon's frying on the stove and she isn't getting any. *Spoiled mutt.* Maggie only let her in after Hank fell asleep the night before, so it's not like she's been trapped inside for long.

Maggie feels like whining, too. She can't figure out whether their rift is her fault for bringing up Texas or Hank's for being stubborn and sensitive, but she knows she doesn't want to fight. Her heart hurts. *Damn, love is hard.* Love, or whatever this is called. There may be a reason she's never succeeded in a real relationship before.

She checks the time on her phone. It's after seven. So much for breakfast. She throws on sweatpants and one of Hank's extra-large Wyoming Cowboys sweatshirts with some Uggs. As she's dressing, she sees Hank's suitcase by the door. For a moment, she panics. Why is he leaving? Then she remembers they're leaving today for Oklahoma and the rodeo. She puts her hand on the suitcase, then walks to his chest of drawers. She's not sure why, but she opens his top drawer. Snooping isn't her thing, usually, but this up and down with Hank has her outside herself. She doesn't even know what she's looking for, but she looks anyway. Feeling around, she shoves her hands under his stack of folded underwear. Folded? She doesn't even fold hers, and she's a woman. She finds a flat box and pulls it out. Opens it. Holds her breath.

Inside is a piece of folded paper, like the kind torn from a hotel memo pad. Unfolding it, she sees the logo for the Buffalo Lodge and the address in Chugwater, Wyoming. Her heart hitches in her chest. She reads her own words in her scribbled writing:

Best night of my life, cowboy. I hate missing breakfast, but Nashville called and I have to go. The truck will be at the airport. Come get your belt buckle.

It's signed with a big heart, an *xxox*, her name, and her old phone number back in Nashville, so many years ago.

Hank had kept her note. The one she'd left him fifteen years ago. Tears well in her eyes. She wipes them, chagrined at her emotionality. What does it matter if he keeps romantic notes if they can't get along for more than a few days at a time?

She stomps to the front door and lets Louise out. Louise scampers toward the barn for breakfast with the ranch dogs, nose to the ground and tail up the whole way. Maggie shuffles into the kitchen in search of scraps. She'll pack after she eats. Trudy is there, the eye of a tornado. Around her in the kitchen are baked goods and casseroles of every description. The whole place smells like powdered sugar and angel kisses. The obligatory apple pie —*God, let that be the last of the apples for the season*, Maggie prays—and a basket of icebox rolls. A glazed pound cake. Potato salad. A steaming pot of baked beans.

"You're killing it in here. What's the occasion?"

Trudy squints at her. "Paco's memorial."

"Oh shit. I forgot. Can I help?"

"Don't you need to eat breakfast and get ready? We have to leave here in half an hour." Under her voluminous white chef's apron, Trudy is in ironed jeans, a purple snap-front shirt, and black boots. Her hair—normally scraped into something that's half falling apart from hard work—is in a neat French twist with strawberry-blonde tendrils framing her perfectly oval face. Gold earrings in the shape of feathers dangle nearly to her shoulders.

"Good idea. Have you seen Hank?"

"He grabbed coffee while I was making breakfast. He was doing his grizzly bear impression." Trudy glances at Maggie, like she's checking for a reaction, but Maggie doesn't give away her emotional state. Closing the oven with her hip, Trudy holds another apple pie aloft. "There are apple cinnamon muffins in the bread box. Coffee on the stove." She keeps a percolator hot and full all day.

Maggie rolls up the lid and snatches a muffin, even though she would have sold her soul for blueberry. Banana nut. Carrot. Anything but more apple. "Thanks. I'll be back down to help as fast as I can."

"No bother. I have Andy and Michael loading the truck for me. We're in good shape."

Maggie stuffs half the muffin into her mouth on the way up the stairs and regrets not pouring herself coffee. Or a glass of water. She struggles to swallow, but follows up with the other half before she turns on the shower in the bathroom. Dry shampoo will have to work for her hair, since she's out of time before she's even getting started today. She's in and out in five minutes. Taking her cue from Trudy, she opts for country Sunday attire. She's sliding a black sweater over her head to go with her jeans when Hank comes in.

Without a word, he turns the shower back on.

"Hank."

He shuts the bathroom door.

She opens it and then closes it again, leaning against the inside for support. "Don't do this."

He shucks his clothes. Dammit, she can't help admiring the view, even when things are like this between them. She loves every scar and indentation on his beautiful body.

"My head hurts. I can't talk right now."

She flows across the floor and takes his hand. "Let me help you."

He looks at her. His eyes are glazed with pain or medication or both. "Let me be okay, like I am."

"I can do that." She turns on cold water and holds her hands under it, then places one on his forehead. "Feel good?"

He moans. "Do that again."

She puts the other hand in its place, then kisses his temple. "You take your meds?"

"No."

"What am I going to do with you?" She tears open a packet and hands it to him.

He closes his eyes and dry-swallows. "Love me forever."

"Oh, Hank." The image of the note he keeps in his top drawer flashes in her mind. She wraps herself gently around his naked body and puts her head on his chest. "I have. I will. I just wish it was easier. Were we always this up and down?"

His voice is a rumbly vibration against her cheek. "We were together less than twenty-four hours."

One snort-laugh escapes her. "It was a lifetime ago. We were so young. I remember it as so much longer. So much more."

He rocks her. "It was. It was everything."

A loud knocking on the bathroom door makes them both jump. Laura hollers at them. "Are you guys riding with Mom and me? Because we're leaving."

Hank winces. "Meet you there?"

"So I don't get your help because you have to sneak a shower quickie when we have things to do? It's not enough that I'm taking care of Mom while you play with your horses and girlfriend the rest of the time?"

"Whoa there, sis. Who do you think gets up with her nights and covers Tom's days off when you're in New Mexico?"

Maggie's rage is instantaneous. She throws open the door, revealing Hank's nude body.

"If you don't mind, your brother is having a horrible headache. You're not helping. I'm trying to. I don't think he'll be able to drive. You can either wait for us, or I can bring him to the church. Your choice. We'll be downstairs in ten."

She enjoys a glimpse of Laura's round eyes and mouth before she slams the door in her face. Then she points at the shower and raises her eyebrows at Hank.

"There's the girl I love. You're so damn cute when you're fierce."

She winks. "I'll pick you out some clothes while I pack a bag for our trip. Want the lights out?" It sometimes helps him.

"Sure."

She flicks the switch.

Hank's head peeks out from the curtained shower. "And Maggie?"

"Yes?"

"I'm sorry."

"I'm sorry, too."

TWENTY-ONE

THE ONE-ROOM white clapboard church is packed tight, humid with humanity as the pastor finishes a short service for Paco and announces the hymn. Frost on the windows partially obscures the white landscape surrounding the building. The tables in the back are groaning under the offerings of food. The front of the nave looks like an ad for a florist. Maggie wishes Paco's blood family could have been here to see his church family show up en masse to wish him farewell. Fifty voices offer up "Amazing Grace" slightly off-key while the Danish musician Maggie met at the Ox plays the fiddle and Wally the keyboard.

Deputy Travis is in the row behind her, not singing. Maggie is sandwiched between Hank, who is holding her hand, and Andy, who's shifting uneasily. Beside Andy, Trudy warbles in a pure soprano. Next to her, Laura has her arm around Mrs. Sibley and is whispering in her ear. The older woman is growing increasingly agitated, turning her whole body in her chair to look back at the door.

The song ends. The pastor opens the mic to the congregation, and people offer brief eulogies. Hank goes last. He gets choked up at the podium, but manages to bid Paco Godspeed and give Gene's regrets for not being able to be there. Maggie knows Paco would have understood and agreed with Gene's decision to get on the road to meet the bucking stock in Duncan. Livestock comes first on a ranch, that much she has already learned.

The pastor releases everyone to eat and visit. Folding chairs scrape the floor as people move from them and form a line for the food.

"I've got to get Mom home," Laura announces, wheeling Mrs. Sibley in front of Hank.

Mrs. Sibley lets loose a string of curse words that impress Maggie with their crudeness and creativity. Where had Mrs. Sibley picked up "dick smack" and "asswipe?"

Hank pulls at his bolo tie. It's black with a bronze bull rider on a silver oval. "I'll help you load up, but I can't go yet." Since Laura had waited for Maggie and Hank to ride over together from Piney Bottoms, they only have one vehicle now. "Want to drive around and come back for us, or should we cram in with Trudy and Andy and the dishes?"

Laura pushes her short hair back. She looks haggard. Maggie almost feels sorry for her, but after earlier, not quite. "I'll drive into town and get her a hamburger, then come back for you. Maybe she'll fall asleep on the way."

Hank turns to Maggie. "I'll be back in a minute."

"Of course."

People part to make way as Hank and Laura walk out together with their mother.

Andy appears beside Maggie and whispers to her. "Is the deputy here to keep an eye on me?"

"I think it's pretty standard for law enforcement to come to the funerals of murder victims."

"Why?"

"What I've heard is that often the murderer will be there."

"Like me. Great."

"Come on. He's not here for you."

"Then why do I feel like he's spying on me?"

"I'm feeling a little spied on myself." Maggie glances pointedly at Sheila and her girlfriend on the other side of the room. They're staring at her and whispering.

"Why don't we get some food? It might make us both feel better."

"Lead the way."

At the buffet line, she and Andy converse across the tables with Wally and the fiddler, who she is relieved to hear Wally call by name. Donna. Maggie steers the conversation to their instrumental backgrounds and away from herself. Suddenly, Penny is in line with them, too, her long black hair shining and hanging in a curtain down her back.

"Hey, everyone." Her eyes are red like she's been crying.

"Penny. Good to see you." Maggie grabs a paper plate and rolled napkin full of plastic cutlery.

Andy turns red to the roots of his sandy hair. "P-p-penny."

"Hi, Andy."

"I didn't know you knew Paco." Maggie skips the apple pie and takes a big slice of pound cake instead.

"We hung out a few times."

Andy looks away.

Penny was another of Paco's admirers? "I'm sorry for your loss."

Penny inclines her head. "Well, I just wanted to say hi. My ride is here. I'll call you about the lesson Monday, Maggie." She glances at Andy. "Bye, Andy."

"Goodbye." He watches her go.

Maggie adds a slice of ham and a link of Basque sausage to her already heaping plate. "Did you know she was friends with Paco?"

Andy concentrates on ladling potato salad. "Uh-huh."

Nothing is making much sense to Maggie. "So you knew her before last night?"

A tap on her shoulder saves Andy. Maggie nearly dumps her plate against the stomach of Deputy Travis's bomber jacket. Andy backs away and disappears into the crowd.

TWENTY-TWO

TRAVIS JUMPS BACK, one eye on Maggie's load of food. "Can I have a word, Ms. Killian?"

Maggie tilts her head at her plate. "Kinda occupied here."

"There are two empty chairs over there." He nods. "You eat. I talk."

Maggie's sigh is long and dramatic. "Really. At a funeral."

Travis takes her free elbow. She jerks it away but walks to the two chairs near the window. It isn't until she takes a seat that she notices Sheila and her friends standing next to the chairs. Today Sheila's puffy vest is black and matches boots with fur lining peeking out, which Maggie guesses is in deference to Paco. Her hair is down in a blonde cloud. She snorts and pokes Mary, the brunette from the Ox. Mary doesn't react. Her eyes look as red as Penny's. More. She's staring out the window.

Maggie scooches her chair until its back is to them. She ignores Travis, too, by digging into the sausage, even though her mouth is dry and the meat tastes like dirt.

"I have some follow-up questions for you."

With her mouth full, Maggie tries to say, "I thought you said I'd eat and you'd talk." It comes out as, "I taught you said I eat and you tock."

Travis seems to understand her anyway. "You can drag this out if you want. I've got all day."

Suddenly, Sheila is in front of them. She bends over nearly into Travis's lap. "Trav, how are you? I missed you at homecoming."

A flash of irritation crosses his face. He pulls back from Sheila as far as he can in his chair. "Work. You know."

"Oh, hi, Maggie." She shows all her teeth in a fake smile.

Maggie hadn't realized Sheila looked so much like a beaver. It makes her happy.

Sheila uses a conspiratorial tone with Travis. "I ran into Maggie and Andy last night at the Ox. And the day before when, um, they were at your office."

Travis lifts an arm and uses it to guide Sheila away from his personal space. "All right, Sheila, we were in the middle of something. I'll be seeing you."

She pouts prettily. "Travvers. All right. Don't be a stranger." She drops the pretense and gives Maggie a death mask, but keeps her voice sugary sweet. "Maggie."

Maggie tests the baked beans without responding, and Sheila rejoins her friends. Funny how talking to Sheila makes Travis slightly more palatable.

Travis lowers his voice. "I've heard a few new details about Paco that disturb me."

Maggie dips a carrot in ranch dip and nibbles.

"One of Paco's buddies, a guy named Emile, said Paco was concerned before his disappearance."

"About what?"

"About Hank."

Maggie puts her carrot down. "Hank? Why?"

"Hank warned him off you, apparently."

"That's crazy."

"Is it?" Travis looks at Hank, who's standing in the doorway, red-cheeked and staring at the two of them. "He's a volatile guy with a reputation for solving his problems physically."

Maggie swallows a big lump. This isn't the first time the Sheridan County Sheriff's Department has targeted Hank because of fighting. She'd had a front-row seat to the fight with Patrick Rhodes that made Hank a suspect in the man's murder, until Maggie handed Travis the real killer. Plus Hank's told her stories. Confessed to using his fists, when he maybe should have walked away. And then there's his head injury and headaches. Volatile? With her, at least lately. She won't win a debate on this issue with Travis, so she won't go there.

"And you think I'm his problem?"

"Or Paco was. What was your relationship with him?"

Maggie's eyes lock on Hank's. He starts walking toward her. "Nothing special. He worked for Hank and Gene. We ate meals as a group. He'd saddle my horse sometimes. He worked on my truck. He was a nice guy, but he was younger, and he was always going on about some woman or other. I was nothing to him but his boss's woman." She stands and puts her plate in the chair. What she doesn't say is that Hank had warned her that Paco thought she was "hot." But that was before she got back together with Hank. When he was dating Sheila. There was nothing wrong with Paco noticing her, or even Hank telling her. Hank just didn't want her to make a mistake and get hurt. *Right?*

"So Emile is lying?"

"Or he misunderstood. Or Paco distorted the truth."

"Can you account for Hank's whereabouts in the two days before you found Paco—every single hour?"

Of course she can't. Hank works on a very big ranch, and she doesn't follow him around like a dopey teenage girl with a crush. Before she can think of a way to answer Travis, Hank puts his hand on her shoulder and squeezes. She reaches up and catches his hand, squeezes back, and holds on.

"Harassing my girl, deputy?"

Travis reaches for Hank's other hand and shakes it at the same time that he rises from his chair. "Just finished. You two have a good day."

Hank holds Travis's hand a second longer than necessary. "You, too."

Travis grimaces, and Maggie knows Hank just crushed the bones in his hand. *Bad timing, Hank.*

Travis shakes his fingers. "Nice grip, Sibley."

Hank guides Maggie away. She looks up at his profile. He's smiling, but there's not a dimple in sight.

TWENTY-THREE

MAGGIE AND HANK drop Laura and Mrs. Sibley back at Piney Bottoms, hitch a trailer to Hank's truck, load Louise, and hit the road for Duncan, Oklahoma. The roads are clear and the sun is out. The temperature is a balmy fifty. The seasons here are so short. The window is open again on summer, but it will slam shut for the rest of the winter soon enough.

The winds, however, are hurricane strength—a year-round phenomenon—and they buffet them all over the interstate. Louise whines from the back seat of the extended cab.

Hank winks at Maggie. "Relax. I'm used to this. I've never flipped a trailer."

She's gripping the armrest so hard she leaves nail imprints. "There's always a first time. Why are we bringing the big windsail anyway? We aren't towing any animals."

"You never know what we'll want to bring back. Plus, we need a place to sleep."

"What's wrong with a hotel?" The truck veers from a gust, and Maggie pushes both feet into the floorboard.

He shoots her a disbelieving look. "I'd lose all credibility if I paid good money for a hotel when I could sleep in my rig on the grounds. Plus, I might miss something. It's a big networking thing, hanging out in lawn chairs, drinking, and telling stories."

Maggie surfs the radio until she finds a country station out of Laramie. "I hate missing day one of this thing."

"If we don't make good time, we'll miss another day. It's a sixteen-hour-or-more drive."

Suddenly, Maggie hears her name on the radio. It used to be a common occurrence, but in the last few years, less so. And lately it makes her blood run cold, because no one ever has anything good to say about her. Hank hears it, too, because he lets go of the steering wheel with one hand and turns it up. The truck swerves, and he double-grips the wheel again.

"According to Amos Hardy, a reporter out of Denver, the Black Widow has spun her web south of Sheridan and caught Wyoming's own Hank Sibley in it. You remember Hank, folks. The 2002 bull riding champ at Frontier Days. He had a helluva career before he was sidelined permanently with a wicked back and head injury. Nowadays he and a partner run Double S Bucking Stock. Pretty successfully, too. A former NFR Stock Contractor of the Year, even. Death seems to follow Maggie everywhere these days, with the most recent man down being the top hand from the Double S, right on the heels of her ex, country star Gary Fuller, rival stock contractor Patrick Rhodes, one of her renters in Texas, and a Wyoming electrician. We're not ones to gossip, but these two have a history, with Maggie ending up in rehab twice in the wake of their previous breakup. Will they make their eight seconds this time, or will one of the popular duo get thrown? Only time will tell. And, yes, she wrote this song about him."

"I Hate Cowboys" starts to play. Maggie releases a breath she hadn't known she'd been holding.

Hank turns off the radio. "So, what did you and Travis talk about back at the church?"

The abrupt change of subject would have been welcome if it were to any other topic. Maggie had hoped Hank would forget about Travis's interrogation. She needs to mull it over more before talking to Hank about it. He's feeling so much better—she doesn't want to be the reason for a setback.

"He wanted to go over the timeline of my whereabouts since the last time I'd seen Paco." It isn't a lie. It isn't the complete truth either. She hopes it's enough.

"At the funeral. Come on, man."

"I know, right?"

"Anything else about Andy?"

Now she relaxes. On this point she can tell the whole truth and nothing but. "Not a word." She glances at him. In profile, he is stalwart, strong, and achingly gorgeous. She swallows. "I need to tell you something."

He grunts, and she takes it as "Go ahead."

"I found the note you kept. The one I left for you in Chugwater."

"Found it. In my drawer. In a box." He dimples up.

"I, um . . ."

His dimples are deep and sweet. "I don't care, Maggie. I don't have anything to hide from you. If you need to look around to satisfy yourself on that, be my guest."

She hesitates. Does he expect her to return the offer? She doesn't own anything to hide. Not after the fires. But she's not sure how she'd feel about him snooping if the tables were turned. Not that she's hiding anything, just the general concept. "You kept it."

"Of course I did."

Maggie picks up her hobo bag from the floorboard. From her wallet, she retrieves the note he'd left her from a secret compartment in her wallet. She reads it aloud to him. "Best night of my life, music girl. Between you and Big Sky, I'm walking off the stiff and sore. Back in an hour with coffee and breakfast. Don't get dressed, gorgeous. Hank."

He reaches for her hand. "So you kept yours, too."

"I've had it with me ever since."

"Big Sky was one lucky draw."

"So that's your reaction to me sharing that with you?" She punches him.

"If I hadn't drawn him, I might not have won, and we might not have ended up together."

"I'll let you in on some late-breaking news: I was yours whether you won or not."

He chuckles, and she leans over the console and puts her head on his shoulder. She wakes up with a sore ribcage and crick in her neck on the south side of Casper. Hank smiles at her. "Wake up, sleepyhead." He gets out of the truck.

She sits up and stretches. By the time she has her bearings and looks outside, Hank is working his credit card at the gas pump.

Maggie comes around to stand beside him. "Time to trade off drivers after I'm back from the loo?"

Louise barks.

"And take Louise to pee?"

Hank sets the automatic pumping switch on the nozzle. "Sure. But I'll take her."

Maggie peers into the back window. Plastic sandwich bags and newspaper are shredded all over the seat. "Oh my God."

"What is it?"

"Louise got into the bag of treats Trudy sent with us."

Hank shakes his head. "Bad dog. Buy me some venison jerky, then?"

"Got it." Maggie heads inside.

After the stop is over, Hank falls asleep before Maggie wrestles the truck and trailer back onto the interstate. "Right in Time" by Lucinda Williams plays on the radio, drawing a smile from Maggie as she looks over at Hank. Louise snuffles daintily in the back seat. The miles fly by, with more stops, more trading off driving duties, and more naps. The scenery is monotonous this time of year. Tan, brown, and beige, broken up every half hour by small towns. But Maggie has eyes only for Hank beside her, and no complaints.

They make it safely to Duncan in the wee hours, with Maggie finishing her book, *Plenty-coups*, about the great Crow chief during one of her riding shifts. Hank is driving when they get there, so he parks their rig and they settle in for a few hours' sleep in the living quarters of the trailer. Maggie wakes, disoriented, when it's barely light outside, troubled but unsure why.

"Hank." She rolls over and puts her head on his chest.

He groans. "Too early." Then he goes rigid. "What's that smell?"

That's it, Maggie realizes. A noxious odor is what woke her. Then she hears the thump-thump-thumping of a tail. "Oh, Fucker."

"She didn't."

"I'm pretty sure she did. Five feet away from us. Rock, paper, scissors for who cleans it up?"

"I got it." Hank levers himself up on an elbow. "But tomorrow night, she sleeps back in the stalls."

Maggie gags and doesn't argue.

TWENTY-FOUR

HANK LEAVES with Gene to check on their hooved athletes not many hours later, with a promise to text and catch up with her soon. Maggie sleepily trolls the grounds, after walking Louise and leaving her to nap in the trailer. On the outside of the covered arena, colorful banners tout the Prairie Rim Circuit Finals Rodeo. Prairie Rim isn't a nationally known rodeo, but it's a Professional Rodeo Cowboy Association event that draws contestants from Kansas, Nebraska, and Oklahoma, so it's plenty big. Food trucks line a crowded parking lot, and the aroma of funnel cake is making Maggie salivate. Vendors are hawking wares ranging from Western wear and rodeo gear to jewelry, farm equipment, and—Maggie's favorite—home décor, not unlike the things she salvages and repurposes at her store in Texas. Or did, anyway.

As she weighs out whether to give in to funnel cake for lunch, her phone sounds its tone for voicemail. She pulls it from her jeans pocket. She has three voicemails from yesterday that only just appeared on her phone. The coverage had been spotty on the drive, which she is used to in Wyoming, but she'd expected better of eastern Colorado and the Texas Panhandle. One is from Charlotte, another from Franklin, and a third from a Colorado number. The Colorado call is the most recent, so she plays that message first.

"My name is Amos. I'm a freelance reporter, and I've written a few pieces on you. I saw you online in a video from the Occidental Saloon in Buffalo, Wyoming. Wait, did I get that right?" There's a pause. "Yeah, The

Occidental. Anyway, I'm swinging up that way and hope I can interview you. Please give me a call so we can arrange a time to get together."

Amos. The name is familiar, but she doesn't think she knows one. Was he the reporter being quoted on the air yesterday, talking about her? He sounded so smug it makes her itch to punch him. She hates reporters automatically, but she's sure she'll hate him specifically, too. And video? She should have known someone would post it from the Ox and mention her. She considers deleting his message without calling him back, but experience tells her if she does, he'll show up anyway, pester her, and interview everyone she's ever pissed off in Buffalo and Sheridan. Starting with Sheila.

She calls him back.

"Amos speaking. Hit me."

His voice sounds too old to be a hipster wannabe–cool cat. She shudders. "Absolutely not."

There's a silence. Is he there? "Sorry, I had to look at the incoming number. Is this Maggie Killian?"

"Unfortunately it is. I'm sorry, but I can't meet with you. I'm just passing through the Buffalo area."

"That's not what I heard."

Now she feels certain he's the reporter quoted on the air yesterday. "I can't control what you hear. Or the rumors you spread. Buh-bye."

She hangs up. Hopefully the call will be enough to keep Amos south.

She listens to Franklin's message next. It's a hang-up. She growls and calls him back, but the call fails to connect. She tries twice more. Same result both times. She moves on to Charlotte. Before she can play her mother's message, a text comes in.

Where's my woman?

She grins, stops, and types. *Looking for her man.*

Ready for the nickel tour of the Double S setup, then some grub?

A big, warm paw lands on her shoulder.

She startles, then smiles, matching the dimples winking down at her. "Hey, cowboy."

"Someone told me, once upon a time, that you hate cowboys. Especially bull riders."

"I'm experiencing a change of heart."

"You're having a flashback. You pretend not to like them, but I think rodeos turn you on."

Maggie laughs. "Or something."

"Behind the chutes we go, then."

"Aren't the chutes inside and your animals outside?"

"Details."

Together they stroll through the pens outside the arena. Hank can't walk five steps without someone hailing him up, slapping his back, and asking about how the Double S buckers look for the event. Nearly everyone talks about his storied past as a bull rider. Many mention what a blessing and miracle it is to see him hale and hearty, referencing his spectacular career-ending injury. Maggie is in the presence of rodeo royalty, and she revels in the respect shown Hank, and her own anonymity. He introduces her by her first name only, which she appreciates. People are nice. But Hank is the star. She feels a flash of irritation as she remembers Travis's insinuations at Paco's funeral. Hank isn't a jealous killer. Not the Hank she knows, that all these people revere, not even in the throes of the worst of one of his brain trauma episodes. It's preposterous.

Hank stops her at a pen of muscular horses in a rainbow of colors. She recognizes some of them from the ranch. They're a little jacked, milling about, lifting their heads over the metal rails and bumping into them with loud clangs.

"Every one of these beauties traces back to Sassafrass, our original broodmare."

"The one you bought with your Frontier Days winnings?"

"Yep."

"And losings."

He shrugs. "It's true. I'm not proud of that. But it's part of the history." Hank had taken money to stay out of the winner's list each day, until he met Maggie and she'd convinced him she only dated winners. He'd incurred the wrath of his Argentinean "employer" then by winning it all. Mafia thugs had chased Maggie and him over half of Wyoming, but here they were as a result.

"The man, the myth, the legend." Maggie bumps him with her hip. "Do you ever see Christiano Valdez?" He was the bull rider the mafia family had backed.

Hank bumps her back. "You're not going to believe this. Paco worked for him a few years ago. Small world."

"What did he do for Christiano?"

"Shovel shit, mostly. But I haven't seen Christiano in many years. Last I heard he was back in Argentina, fat and rich."

"Good." For many reasons, Maggie thinks. Her thoughts return to the buckers. "Don't you risk genetic issues with so much of one bloodline in your horses?"

"Lots of other bloodlines in the mix, too. We've been careful to keep it diverse. There are incredible champions in all their parentage."

"You sound like a proud papa."

"I am. We are. It's very rewarding. And exciting." He waves at the pen. "This here is a crop of youngsters. You remember we hold inside events at the ranch for up-and-coming cowboys, to evaluate our three-year-olds?"

"Yes, and I can't wait to see one."

"They're a party." Hank nods. "These horses passed that test and are working their way up to bigger venues."

"Will any of these be bucking at the National Finals Rodeo next month?"

"Nah. They'll have to earn that later. Only the best of our best, the seasoned warriors, buck at NFR."

Maggie remembers Hank explaining before that they cross draft horses into the herd to keep them hearty, and colder-blooded horses for their athletic ability and fight. "Are any of these horses related to Lily?"

He rubs his chin, then points. "That big mare, the blue-roan. This is her first season on the road. She's draftier than we usually see in our successful buckers. But nobody told her that. She's like nitroglycerin in a brick house."

"She's my favorite."

Hank smiles. "Of course. Want to go see the bulls? Gene's over there."

Maggie climbs on the rail, looking for bulls. The humped backs give them away. She spots Gene outside a pen. While her attention is off the horses, the blue-roan mare charges at her, snorting, then ducks away.

Maggie jumps down, startled. "She's feisty."

"Her blood is up. She knows it's almost showtime. If you approached her in the pasture back home, she'd ignore you."

They amble to the bulls through a repeat of the glad-handing and introductions.

One old-timer breaks away from a group. "Mr. Sibley, the first time I met you, you was wandering through the parking lot of the fairgrounds in Mandan, South Dakota. It was the middle of the night, and you wasn't wearing nothing but a long-john top. Not a stitch." The storyteller pulls at the handlebar mustache hiding his smile.

Maggie socks Hank's arm. "Wait, you were naked?"

"I was changing clothes beside my truck after a few shots of whiskey. I accidentally locked myself out. So I was looking for a pay phone. Only I didn't have a quarter."

The geezer winks at Maggie. "I hope for your sake it was only the cold that made him so—"

"Okay, that's enough." Hank claps him on the back.

He cackles and wanders back to his friends.

Maggie raises her eyebrows. "You certainly have a colorful past."

"Mostly lies and exaggerations."

"What part of streaking around bare-assed was a lie, and what part was an exaggeration?"

"Well, that was mostly true."

She loops her arm through his, and they resume walking toward Gene. The smell of bull manure grows stronger with every step.

Maggie holds the back of her hand under her nose. "Why does bull shit smell so much worse than horse shit?"

"An age-old question. And why do bovines taste so much better than equines? There's another for you."

"You've eaten horse meat?"

"I'm speaking theoretically."

Gene spots them and doffs his hat at Maggie. "What do you think of it all?" He opens a bag of Cheetos and offers it to her.

She's hungry, but the thought of food so near the bull manure turns her stomach. She holds up a hand to decline. "That you guys have come a long way from the broke-ass bull riders I met in Cheyenne. I can't believe you even scraped up enough money to buy your fancy broodmare."

"Sassafrass?"

"Yeah. Hank spent his stake of the money for her on a getaway truck for us in Wheatland."

Gene cocks a brow. "You're right, Maggie May. And I nearly killed him for it. But everyone loves a Frontier Days winner, lucky bastard, and we had just enough that they gave us a short extension."

Hank thumps his chest. "I came up with the money."

Maggie says, "You're a better man than me not to have killed him, Gene."

He grins. "Thanks. I think. Anyway, Hank's point man on the horses, but the bulls are my babies."

"Babies? Hardly. These are monsters." Maggie leaves a five-foot buffer between herself and the bull enclosure.

"Nasty, ugly muscleheads. Just how we like 'em."

"Which make more money, the horses or the bulls?"

"Used to be the horses, hands down. With the advent of bull-only events like the Professional Bull Riding shows, we've got a growing market for the uglies. But every rodeo has two bronc riding competitions—saddle and bareback—and only one bull-riding event. So it's a toss-up."

Hank slaps his thigh with his hat, back and forth, knocking off the sod the blue-roan splattered him with earlier. "The horses are a little fussier. More prone to hurting themselves."

"At events?"

"No, at life. Horses are experts at doing stupid stuff. One time we had a hand who parked a truck across an open gate. One of the horses decided to jump out, over the hood and windshield of the truck. He almost made it too, except for a back hoof. New windshield. Lotta stitches. Three-month bucking hiatus while he recovered from his injuries."

Gene nods. "A bull would have just rammed the truck and walked away."

"But both require a lot of special care traveling to and from events. We had a harder trip here than these animals. Twelve to fourteen hours of rest for every ten spent on the road. Standing in a half foot or more of sawdust to cushion their hooves and legs. A veterinarian on call at every event. At the slightest sign of strain, we pull 'em, rehab 'em, and call in an expert if needed. Anything to keep them in tip-top shape during rodeo season. It's not cheap to run the operation."

"But it must be worth it."

The two men grin at each other and answer at the same time. "Oh yeah."

Hank slings an arm around her. "We make more money than we did rodeoing, and nothing beats this life."

Maggie loves the feel of his taut frame and strong arm. She leans in. "It's making me remember how much fun the events were back when I was touring and performing. But I'd forgotten about all the vendors. It's a pretty diverse enterprise of businesses."

"A lot of the vendors just follow the rodeos all season. Like us. And some of the rodeos dwarf Prairie Rim. Money to be made, for sure. Now, let's go to our box. Time to watch our brand in action."

The seed of an idea germinates in Maggie's mind. But hunger calls first. "And feed your woman."

Hank squeezes her to him. "And that, of course."

TWENTY-FIVE

AN ANNOUNCER'S voice reverberates through the arena. "Next up we have the saddle bronc riding competition."

He keeps talking, but it's just yammering to Maggie. She turns to Hank, accidentally kicking what's left of the nachos she got at the concession into the seat-back in front of her. She braces for an explosion, but the woman who's now wearing chips and nacho cheese on her sweatshirt is oblivious. It's not *that* bad, so Maggie isn't going to be the one to clue her in.

"What's her name?" she asks Hank.

"Who?"

"Lily's blue-roan bucking baby."

"Crazy Woman."

Like an echo, the announcer says, "First up will be Josh Cassidy on a fine young mare from Double S Bucking Stock, Crazy Woman. Josh is coming off a big win in New Braunfels, Texas at the Comal County Fair. Let's see how he handles a bona fide descendant of Sassafrass, two-time winner of the PRCA Saddle Bronc of the Year."

Maggie screams with delight. "Go, go, go, Crazy Woman!" That earns her a few looks, but she doesn't care.

The blue-roan mare explodes out of the gate. Even though Hank rode bulls in his day, saddle bronc riding has always been Maggie's favorite event. And something about Lily's high-spirited daughter has lit her fire. The young mare does not disappoint. Within two jumps, she's bucking like a catapult. The cowboy on her back is clinging with his legs to the saddle, his rein hand high and other arm flailing. Maggie sees air between his butt and the seat. That's the end of the line for him, she knows.

"Go," she shouts again. "Come on, Crazy Woman!"

Beside her, Hank joins in. "Get him, girl. Get him."

And the powerhouse mare does. Her hooves rocket upward with her head down and body fully and beautifully extended. The crowd exclaims en masse. Has a horse ever bucked this high or looked this good doing it? Maggie doesn't think so. At the height of her buck, Crazy Woman twists. Her front feet are still two feet off the ground as her back half torques sideways. Everything seems to move in slow motion to Maggie now. Like a demon-possessed toy top, the horse spins before she lands. The cowboy tumbles through the air and into the dirt. Then Maggie's slo-mo ends, and the horse bucks riderless in real time.

The buzzer sounds. The cowboy is already on his feet and picking up his hat. Meanwhile, Crazy Woman attacks likes she's trying to take down the sky. Two pick-up riders make their way to her, but when they get near her, she morphs into a heaving race horse. The three horses streak down one side of the arena. Crazy Woman pulls ahead in the curve, then the pick-up horses gain on her in the straightaway again as she continues to kick and buck. At the end of the second lap, the chasers finally get close enough to remove the sheepskin flank strap. They peel away, and she slows to a lope, tail and head high, black mane flapping, sweaty sides heaving. She's a sight to behold. The crowd stands and cheers.

The announcer says, "That round goes to Crazy Woman. I can't decide if she's named right or if they should have called her Blue Lightning. Better luck next time, Josh."

After they sit, Maggie leans to Hank. "How often do horses get standing ovations?"

One corner of his lip quirks. "It's rare."

"So she really is special?"

"It appears she may be."

"I love her."

He laughs. "I know you do."

The rest of the rodeo flies by in a blur for Maggie. She cheers for the Double S stock, drinks a few beers, and eats a cool hot dog with too-sweet relish. When it's over, she's jazzed like Crazy Woman. She holds Hank's hand as they wait in line to exit.

"What now?" she asks.

"We circulate."

"Where?"

"In the parking lot. From trailer to trailer. It's a progressive party out there."

"Sounds good. Where's Gene?"

"One of the bulls was pulled because he's got a cut or something. He's going to find out what happened."

They swing hands and joke around until Maggie's phone rings.

Hank drops her hand. "It's okay if you want to get it."

"Thanks." She pulls it from her pocket and checks the screen. It's a Giddings number. "Hello?"

"Maggie Killian, please."

She doesn't recognize the woman's voice. "Who's calling?"

"This is Trish Jasper. I'm a real estate agent in Lee County, Texas. If this is Maggie, you contacted me about one of my listings."

Maggie shoots a glance at Hank. He's waving like a pageant queen. She lowers her voice. "Now's not a good time."

"Okay, can we talk quickly about you listing your place, then? I think I have a buyer who'd pay cash and promise a quick close."

Irritation burns through Maggie. *How presumptuous.* She whispers, "How can you have a buyer when I don't have it for sale?"

"Based on comparables, I have a fair idea of the value. Assuming you'd accept an offer in that ballpark, this buyer is ready."

"Ballpark as in the numbers you emailed me?"

"Yes."

"Not interested."

"Okay, then. What number would you be interested in?"

Hank stops, striking up a conversation with some really dusty cowboys. Maggie realizes they are competitors from the night's rodeo.

She holds up one finger at Hank and mouths, "Just a minute."

He nods and keeps talking.

"I'm not," Maggie says.

"I have an idea. How about we list your place at a number above what you're interested in, and just see what you get? You don't have to accept an offer. Your property is safe and remains yours if you'd like, but you get an idea of its worth on the current market."

"How about not."

"Okay, well, if you change your mind, please let me know. And if you'd like, we can talk about the ranch listing tomorrow."

"I'll call you." Maggie hangs up.

Hank is leaning against the wheel cover of a black trailer. He salutes her with a can of Bomber Mountain. "This is my girl, Maggie. Maggie, meet some of the poor saps that got their asses kicked out in the arena today."

The cowboys clustered around him are mostly a head shorter than Hank. Zero percent body fat or thereabouts with sinewy muscles and hats bigger than their rear ends. Their cheeks bulge, and one of them spits brown tobacco juice in the dirt.

"Hi, guys," she answers, to a chorus of hellos.

The dustiest of the cowboys says, "I hear your horse threw me."

"My horse?"

"Crazy Woman," Hank says. His eyes are smiling and don't leave her face.

"Does that mean you're giving her to me?"

He pops the top on another can of Bomber Mountain. "What's mine is yours, sugar."

The cowboy thrown by Crazy Woman lifts a bottle of tequila. "A toast, to Crazy Woman." He tips the bottle back. His Adam's apple bobs four times before he passes the bottle to Maggie. "She's your horse, so drink up, Miss Maggie."

"Miss Maggie? That sounds like something a chauffeur would call his elderly passenger."

"Hell no. Miss Maggie, like the smokin' hot Maggie."

"Excuse me?" Hank says.

"I'm just saying, your girlfriend is very nice-looking, Mr. Sibley."

He grumbles something that isn't a thank-you.

"Are you going to drink to your horse or not, Maggie?" the cowboy asks.

He's cute, Maggie realizes. And, while lean, he exudes strength and a cocky, self-assured manner. Like Hank. It almost makes her laugh. "Tequila makes me sad, mean, and headachy. I've outgrown self-sabotage."

Hank slides an arm around her waist and pulls her backward into him. "Have you, now?"

"Mostly. Enough that I prefer anything *but* tequila."

The cute cowboy says, "What would you like? We've got a full bar in the trailer."

"If I had my way, a sweet tea spiked with Koltiska."

He salutes. "One sweet TKO coming up." Then he disappears inside the trailer.

Hank nibbles her ear. "Just like old times. All the cowboys want my woman."

"And you won my heart, fair and square." She snuggles against him. "Now I'm just Sibley's old, worn-down nag."

"Far from it." He snorts. "Are you sure you want that drink? If not, I can think of other things to do."

"You win the prize." Maggie takes his hand and two steps toward their own trailer. "Again."

He hoots, she laughs, and they run to the trailer together.

TWENTY-SIX

SATURDAY AFTERNOON, Hank and Maggie shop the vendor booths outside the arena. Maggie is intrigued by the home décor and kitsch, but they linger in a booth with a frightening display of knives.

"Do you like these?" Hank holds up a wicked-looking knife in one hand. A leather belt scabbard with beading depicting a sunset and a pigging string knotted through a leather thong hangs from his other.

"Gorgeous." Maggie runs her fingers over the beads of the scabbard.

"And useful." He stabs over his shoulder. "In case of a mountain lion attack."

She laughs.

"I'm not kidding. We're just guests in their world up at the ranch. They stalk and attack from behind. By the time they're on you, the only thing that works is a knife. If you're lucky and fast."

"Comforting. Makes me wonder why anyone ever settled in Wyoming in the first place."

"The grizzlies and Indians were far more dangerous. And the weather."

"Case in point."

Hank hands the items to the attendant, who rings them up. "For you, my dear."

"But you already gave me a knife."

"I gave you my knife, and I want it back." He presses the bag into her hand. "Practice with it. A lot. And keep your mutt with you."

She salutes. "I will. Thank you. But you should be scared I'll use it on you when you snore."

He raises an eyebrow. "Snore? That would be you, princess."

"What? I don't snore."

"You did last night. Like a chainsaw."

"The hell you say."

"Which is exactly how I slept. Like hell." He swats her on the behind, and they walk on.

She stops to admire more home décor.

Hank holds up a barbed-wire cross. "This looks like something you'd make."

There's a good market for all things religious in Texas, and, it appears, at rodeos in general. Person after person is checking out with different sizes and types of the barbed-wire crosses. Crosses mounted on tin siding. Crosses festooned with bows and boots. Crosses accenting painted homilies on weathered barn wood.

Before she can respond to Hank, a slight guy with a hat bigger than his torso corners him. Hank listens and nods, then steps over to her.

"Maggie, give us a moment? Gotta solve an issue with a horse."

"Not Crazy Woman?"

"Yeah, but it'll be fine. She's just got more buck than we bargained for. She may be better than this rodeo. That's a good problem."

Maggie feels a warmth in her chest. Pride? "Go on. I'll be fine."

She's admiring some horseshoe art, thinking about the plentiful supply of that particular raw material at the Double S, when her phone rings. Charlotte. She never called her mother back yesterday. Hank's still occupied, so she picks up.

"Surprise!" It's Boyd's voice on her mother's line.

"It's both of us," her mother adds in a trill.

Speakerphone. Both of her living parents, birth and adoptive. "Wow." Don't the two barely know each other?

Boyd's voice holds a smile. "We joined forces over lunch, since we share a common interest."

"You," Charlotte explains.

"Yes, I got that, Mom."

Boyd continues. "We need to know when you're coming back."

Charlotte's voice is giddy. "Because I'm making a big Thanksgiving dinner. For everyone!"

"Define everyone."

"All the family. Edward. Boyd and his wife. Michele, Rashidi, Belle, Sam, and Charlie. Gene, if he can make it down. And you."

Her mom hadn't included Hank in the list. Intentional or not? "I'll be there. Hopefully with Hank. My boyfriend."

"That's great. How's it going on your house and the Coop?" Boyd asks.

"Baby steps."

Hank saunters back, looking satisfied.

"Listen, I'm at a rodeo in Oklahoma. I've gotta run."

Boyd and her mother pledge their love, and Maggie returns it before she hangs up. Maggie and Hank walk into a livestock supply booth.

"What was that about?" he asks.

"Thanksgiving. At my mom's. Wanna come?"

"Sure. We can drive up through New Mexico on the way back to Wyoming. Stop and see Mickey and Laura."

Maggie bites her tongue. She expects to be back in Texas long before Thanksgiving, hopefully with Hank, and neither of them returning to Wyoming after. And she can't think of anything worse than going to visit Laura.

Hank picks up a silver bag. "This is what we need for Crazy Woman."

Maggie reads the label. "What does Mare Magic do?"

"Makes a mare less like a hysterical woman."

"I'll give you two point five seconds to retract that explanation in favor of something that will keep you warm in bed tonight."

"It takes the hormonal edge off a difficult mare. Sometimes."

Maggie ponders. "Would it make Lily stop running off?"

"Maybe. But so would latching her gate better."

Maggie buys a bag.

"You're wasting your money."

"Mine to waste."

"There's also anecdotal evidence that an ounce per day in the last trimester is helpful for the uterus and hormones. So I guess it can't hurt."

"Good. Now buy me a funnel cake."

As they exit the booth, the cute cowboy from yesterday—the one too young to flirt with her—appears.

"Hey, you left without your drink, Miss Maggie." He whistles. "Damn, you're even more beautiful today, and twice as hot as the actress who plays you in *Love Child*."

She tenses. He figured out who she is. *Please be smart*, she thinks. But apparently he's landed on his noggin a few too many times.

"You know if you get tired of this has-been, I'm your man."

Hank moves, quick as a big cat. Suddenly, the young cowboy is dangling two inches off the ground against the side of a box trailer.

"Don't come near her ever again. Got it?" Hank's voice is lethal.

"Hey, man, I was kidding. I didn't mean nothing."

"Hank"—Maggie puts her hand on his arm—"put him down."

"He's disrespecting you, Maggie."

"I don't think it's my honor you're concerned about. Put him down, *now*."

Hank drops him.

The cowboy shakes his head. "I've always heard you were a crazy son of a bitch." He walks off, still muttering.

"I'm sorry," Maggie calls after him.

Hank growls. "Don't go apologizing to him for what he did."

"I'm not. I'm apologizing for you."

Volatile. Physical. She tries to unremember her conversation with Travis, but she can't. Neither can she hold it in any longer. "You want to know what Deputy Travis said to me at Paco's funeral?"

"I thought he was checking your alibi."

"No. He was checking yours. Because he's started hearing rumors about your jealousy, and he's been putting it together with your volatility and violence."

"Jealousy? I'm not jealous. I'm protective. Of you."

"And some guy told Travis you warned Paco to stay away from me."

"I wasn't jealous of Paco. You and I weren't even together then. I was just trying to keep him from hurting you. He's a complete womanizer."

"Well, now Travis is wondering about you. To me. Like wondering if you could have killed Paco."

"But you can't think that of me." All of a sudden, his eyes look hollow and dark, his skin pallid.

"Even though you have killed someone." She feels bad bringing it up. Sure, it was in defense of his mother, but dead is dead.

"You know what I mean."

"Honestly, I don't know what I think." She stalks away, toward their trailer. Too late, she realizes it sounded like she doesn't know whether or not he killed Paco. That's not what she meant. Or not really, anyway. She's good and pissed at him, and worrying about it a little might be good for him.

Hank doesn't follow her.

TWENTY-SEVEN

Two hours later, Maggie heads to the arena for the finals of the rodeo. Hank hasn't shown up, called, or texted. She's not going to miss seeing what she came for—the Double S stock in all their glory. But with Hank's latest explosion, Travis's words are haunting her.

Gene shouts over a line of people at the gate. "Maggie, wait up."

She waves and does.

"Have you seen Hank?" he asks.

"Not since he almost beat a guy's ass for flirting with me."

"Shit. Then he's probably half a bottle of whiskey down at a trailer somewhere out there, with an old-timer who doesn't realize he needs to send him on his way."

Maggie pulls Gene out of line, away from all the ears. "What's with him, Gene? Is he always like this? He's scaring me."

Gene sighs. "Which question do you want me to answer first?"

"Just tell me what's going on."

"Let's walk." They head inside the arena, where the sounds of the "Star-Spangled Banner" begin and swell as the crowd sings along. He raises his voice in her ear to be heard over the music. "Okay, first, he's not always like this."

Maggie exhales, loudly. "Thank God."

"He is occasionally."

"I liked your first answer better."

"You know about his brain injury? God—I hope you do, or I'll catch hell for spilling it."

"I do." Maggie shows her contractor badge to the attendant at the entrance, as does Gene.

"Good. From time to time, he needs adjustments. The headaches start again. Mood swings. Loss of control."

They head up a ramp toward the box with their reserved seats.

"But the adjustments work?"

"They always have before."

Maggie balls her fists. "So he needs to see his doctor."

"That's the challenge."

"Why?"

"By the time he needs it, he's less rational."

"Tell me about it."

The two of them swim upstream against traffic in the corridor, weaving around clusters of people like salmon in a river full of boulders. Their box is on the exact opposite side of the arena from the entrance, so it's a long swim.

"More emotional."

"Um, yeah."

"And less open to suggestion."

"Completely."

"But the jealousy—that's a new thing."

"Protectiveness."

"What?"

"Hank is just trying to protect me."

"Okay, protectiveness. That's since you. Other women just haven't mattered that much before."

"That's a backhanded compliment if I've ever heard one."

"But the point is, I think you can get him there. To the doctor. *Because* you matter to him."

"I hope so."

"Me, too."

Gene's phone rings. "It's Laura."

Fear grips Maggie, along with a little guilt. Hank doesn't need any more blows right now. Should she have gone easier on him, since she knows he's having trouble? "Take it."

Gene listens, frowns, paces, and finally says, "I'll get on it."

"Well?"

"Mrs. Sibley is threatening to slaughter your goats."

Maggie barks out a laugh.

"They got out—"

"Again."

"Again. And they left pellets all over the front steps and jumped on the hood of her car and dented it. She said to tell you, and I quote, 'They're meat, not pets.'"

Maggie enters the box. "Hopefully we can get back before she proves it."

After she's settled, Gene returns to the pens, and Maggie watches the rodeo alone, sipping a beer and dining on peanuts she buys from the beer guy roaming the stands. She tosses her shells to the floor like everyone else around her. Her mind races, and only the bucking events capture her attention. The Double S broncs and bulls are magnificent, if she does say so herself. Or if the rhinestone-bedazzled couple next to her does. They're quite taken with the bucking talent, and she's bursting to pass along their compliments to Hank, if only he'd respond. But he doesn't. Not to her five texts or two calls.

With only a few contestants to go in the last event, she bags it. She and Hank have been planning to drive through the night and be home by sundown the next day. As she sidles out, her phone buzzes with a group text with Hank from Gene. She waits to read it until she's outside, standing near the exit. The wind has picked up, pushing warm air. An ill wind. *It's a little late to blow now*, she thinks.

Gene: *If I don't see you guys before you take off, drive safe. I've got things from here. See you in Casper.*

Hank's response is immediate. *Thanks, buddy.*

Maggie wants to send a blistering text to Hank along the lines of *You sorry SOB, I know you've been getting my texts and calls.* But Gene's words still ring in her ears. She needs to get Hank in to his doctor. ASAP. So she just texts back: *Casper?*

Gene: *My return flight takes me there. You guys are picking me up tomorrow afternoon on your way home.*

Somehow she'd missed that in the planning, but it makes sense. If he returns through Billings, someone will have to drive two and a half hours each way north to get him.

She hustles to their rig through the parking lot, moving from darkness to pools of light, over and over, from light pole to light pole. The big Double S trailer is under one, and Hank is spotlit, sitting on a wheel cover, talking on his phone. His face is somber, and he has the dark circles under his eyes that tell her his story. He puts the phone down.

When he speaks to her, he blows out a bottle's worth of Jack fumes. "Before you say a word, I'm sorry." His words slur, but not as bad as she expects. "Please believe in me, Maggie. I need you to."

She grabs a finger and kisses it, then puts his hand to her chest. "I know. I do. And we can talk about it more later. For now, I'll pack while you're on your call, then we can leave."

"I think I'll be able to drive by then." His expression is serious.

She makes a sound that's a cross between a laugh and a snort. "Not on your life, cowboy." And her heart lifts like it's on wings. Something about this strong but vulnerable man does it for her like nothing and no one ever has. Or will again.

TWENTY-EIGHT

HANK AND MAGGIE MAKE DOUGLAS, Wyoming by eleven on Sunday, trading driving and napping shifts again, although Maggie's first shift was a triple while Hank slept off the previous night's excesses. Since then, Maggie has snuck in reading a few more chapters in her latest book on the Crow, *From the Heart of the Crow Country*. She must have drifted off again, though, because Hank's voice pulls her from sleep.

"Wake up, beautiful," Hank says.

Maggie yawns. Her ass hurts on the side she landed on when Lily bucked her off weeks ago. She turns her seat heater on. "How long was I out?"

"Since Cheyenne."

More than two hours. Yeah, she did more than drift off. "Are we stopping?"

Even as she's asking the question, they pass the last exit. Town gives way to farm and ranch land again. Mountains on the left. Treeless prairie on the right and in front of them northward as far as the eye can see.

"We can make Kaycee on our gas—that would be ideal, so we only have to gas up once before we get home—if you don't need a stop. And if my Excedrin holds out." He grins. "I feel like shit."

"So why'd you wake me? I could have slept another—what?—hour?" She wrinkles her nose. The truck cab is starting to smell stale, bordering on rank, after ten hours with two unshowered humans, the remains of their snacking, and one farty dog.

He offers his hand and she takes it. "I was lonely. And a little sleepy. Keep me company until we pick up Gene?"

She stretches, arching her back and rotating her neck until both pop. "Sure." She opens the lid on her mango Bai and adds. "It'll cost you, though."

"I'm good for it."

They smile at each other. Hank is clear-eyed. His phone rings from the passenger floorboard.

"Want me to get that?" she asks.

"Who is it?"

Maggie dives for the phone and reads the caller ID. "Looks like the main line from Piney Bottoms."

"Yeah, if you don't mind."

Maggie answers it. "Hank Sibley's phone."

"Uh, yes, this is Andy."

Andy doesn't have a cellphone, Maggie remembers. "Hey, Andy. It's Maggie."

"Oh, good. I was wanting to talk to you. I didn't know your number."

"What's up?"

"Deputy Travis was here."

Maggie's mouth goes dry. "What did he want?"

"He interviewed Penny."

Her mind churns his words. Why would Travis question Penny? And why would he come talk to Andy about it? "Have you talked to her?"

"I ain't got her number. She gave it to you."

Maggie's phone is plugged into the charger. She picks it up and looks up Penny in her contacts. "You ready?"

"For what?"

"Her number."

"Oh, I can't call her."

"Why not?"

"I was hoping you would."

Andy is shy and lives by a different operating manual than most people. She gets it. And she does want to know what Travis talked to Penny about. For Andy's sake, for Hank's, and for her own. "All right. But what did he want with you?"

"To go over my alibi again."

"Does he have a problem with it?"

"Only that I ain't got one for the nights Paco was gone. I was in the bunkhouse alone."

Hank looks at her and mouths, "Is everything okay?"

She shakes her head at him and mouths, "No." To Andy, she says, "Any idea why he mentioned Penny to you?"

"He thinks I'm sweet on her."

Maggie smiles. "Aren't you?"

"He thinks I was jealous of Paco. Because he dated her. And that I wanted his job."

Motive. "Oh. I'm sorry."

His voice is stricken. "Will you call her? Make sure she's all right?"

"I will. We'll be home in about five hours. Do you want me to call you back or talk to you then?"

"Then. I have to work. With Hank and Gene gone, we're mighty busy."

"Of course you are. Try not to worry about it, and I'll talk to you soon."

"Thank you."

Maggie ends the call. She briefs Hank on Andy's side of the conversation.

"That's bullshit. The last thing Andy would do is kill someone. The second to last thing he would do is try to take something from someone else. A job. A girl. Anything. The kid is moral to the core."

"He sure seems that way to me."

Maggie presses Penny's number. "Maybe Penny will have some answers." The phone rings four times and goes to voicemail. "Penny, this is Maggie Killian. We met at the Occidental and Paco's service. I hope we're still on for our music lesson tomorrow night." She is about to tell her the reason for the call, then doesn't. Something tells her the girl won't call back if she knows it's about Paco's murder. "Could you give me a call back, please? As soon as you can. Thanks." She hangs up.

They pass an exit with a Kum & Go gas station. Maggie stifles an inappropriate urge to laugh. *Whoever came up with that name had to have known how vulgar it sounds.* Hank exits the interstate. The rest of the drive to the airport is traffic lights and industrial, with a few bars sprinkled in doing brisk midday Sunday business. If Maggie was up for karaoke, they could make a detour into the Alibi Lounge. But she's not. She wants to do something, though, she realizes. She wants to feel useful.

"Hank, put me to work."

"What?" The look he gives her is one part confused, one part amused.

"On the ranch. You have plenty of work to go around. Let me do some of it."

"Where did this come from?"

"From me feeling like a freeloader." *Something not going unnoticed by your mother and sister*, she thinks.

"All right."

"Starting tomorrow."

He laughs. "All right."

"I mean it."

"So do I."

"Good. Thank you. And I want to be paid."

"Of course."

"But not in cash."

He waggles his eyebrows. "I feel so objectified."

"I already get *that*, Hank. I need something else."

"Your wish is my command."

"I want you to see your doctor. ASAP."

The temperature in the truck cab falls ten degrees.

"Hank?"

"Huh?"

"Did you hear me?"

"I heard you."

"And?"

"And tomorrow I'll call my doctor."

"With me present."

"You're killing me."

"No, and I don't want anything else to either."

He sighs. "With you present."

She leans across the console and kisses his cheek. "Thank you." She feels like a lead weight has fallen off her chest. Now all she has to do is make him follow through.

He turns into the Casper/Natrona County International Airport. Two minutes later, they see Gene. He wads up and throws away a Cheetos bag, then sticks out his thumb, hitchhiker style. It's slightly orange. Hank pulls to the curb, and Maggie throws open her door, bracing it against the wind. The last time she saw Gene, she was angsting about Hank's volatility, with Hank a rodeo-no-show. She wonders if he's thinking about it, too.

Gene is already throwing his bag into the bed. "You lovebirds want me to drive so you can canoodle in the back seat?"

There's no way Maggie is getting back there. Between the stench of Louise and the truck blowing all over the road, she'll be carsick in minutes. "My turn to drive. You get in the back and stretch out."

Maggie and Hank exchange places. He grins, in sync with her.

"If you're sure." Gene gets in the back seat. "Oh, hello, Louise."

Hank hits the locks. "I think you just got suckered, bud."

"Jesus, when was the last time you gave this dog a bath?"

Maggie passes pronghorn antelope grazing by the parking lot, then pulls out of the airport. "A month ago, maybe? When she barfed all over herself and the inside of my truck."

"That's thirty or more dead-animal rolls ago. *And* she gets carsick?"

"Not if you sing 'You Are My Sunshine' to her while rubbing her belly," Hank says.

Gene laughs. "Screw you." Then he stops abruptly. "Hey, guys, I got some news."

"About Andy's alibi?" Maggie asks.

Gene leans over the console between Maggie and Hank. "What? No. About Michael. You have news about Andy?"

Hank turns sideways in his seat. "You go first."

"The background check on Michael came back. It's not good."

TWENTY-NINE

MAGGIE CHEWS the inside of her lip. She likes Michael. Has she been wrong about him? "Bad news in what way?"

"He just got out of jail, for one thing," Gene says.

Hank cocks his head. "For what?"

"Burglary."

Maggie merges onto the interstate, heading north.

"Shit."

"Yeah. So I had a friend up in Lame Deer ask around. Apparently Michael's family is bad news. Drug dealers, big into opioids. The assumption is that they steal them to sell them."

"Was that what Michael was stealing?"

"I'm not sure. My friend said Michael's conviction came after a string of arrests that didn't stick. But he also said that burglary doesn't mean the same thing on the reservation as it does to us off of it."

Now he has Maggie's attention. "In what way?"

"It goes back centuries. Successful raids against other Indians was a respected activity. A way to prove manhood. Stay battle-ready between battles. Show superiority over an enemy. My friend says the Cheyenne considered it a sign of skill and intellect. Some still do."

Hank nods. "I've always heard that."

Maggie compares what she's learned about the Crows to what Gene is telling her about the Cheyenne. It makes sense. They crest a hilltop with large rock outcroppings and stunted evergreens, then head downhill into the sea of brown prairie again.

She asks, "What does that mean for Michael and Double S?"

Gene turns to Louise. "Get off me, mutt." In the rearview mirror, Maggie sees him push the dog to her side of the back seat. "It makes me real nervous, having a convicted thief living on the place. But we need the help. What do you think, Hank?"

"Too big a risk. I think we should cut him loose as soon as we can replace him."

"Hank!" Maggie says. "At least give him a chance. He seems like a good kid."

"A chance to steal from us? He's a grown man, Maggie."

"He's poor, Hank. Maybe now that he's away from bad influences and has a steady income and a different cultural environment, things will be better."

"Maybe. Or maybe he's a con artist who has you hornswoggled already." Hank winks. "Hand me a bag of potato chips and a water, will you?" he says to Gene.

Gene finds them in a convenience store bag and tosses them to Hank. "How about we talk to him about it and see how he responds? If he knows we know, maybe it will keep him on the straight and narrow."

Hank opens the bag, and chips erupt out the top from the release of pressure. Maggie snatches one that lands on the console. She crunches it and puts her hand out for more.

Hank deposits a handful in her palm. "I guess we could do that."

Maggie's phone rings.

Hank picks it up. "It's a 307 number."

"Put it on speaker."

He presses something on the screen, and the phone connects to the call.

"Hello?" Maggie says.

A girl's voice enters the truck with them. It's clear and bell-like. "You called me."

She smiles at Hank. "Hi, Penny. I'm driving. I have you on hands-free, okay?"

"Okay."

"Andy said the police came by to question you."

"How does he know that?"

Maggie leaves the lee of hill cover to cross a bridge. The wind roars through the creek bottoms, knocking the truck and trailer to the shoulder, near the railing. Sweat beads on her brow. She muscles the wheel left, slow and steady. Just as quickly as it rocked them, the wind disappears behind another hill as they climb back up to the prairie.

Maggie swallows hard. How many seconds have passed without her answering? "Sorry. It's really windy. Um, Deputy Travis came out to the ranch. He told Andy about it. We were all worried about you."

"I'm fine. He just wanted to know about me and Paco."

"What do you mean?"

"Like did he break up with me. Was I upset with him. When I saw him last. But I told him I was the one who broke things off. Paco dated a lot of women. I didn't want to catch a disease or something, you know?"

Oh God, how Maggie knows. She used to ask her on-and-off boyfriend Gary Fuller to bring a clean bill of health and a bottle of penicillin for her when he'd come off the road from touring. "So you hadn't seen him in a while?"

"I saw him last week. At the Ox. But we barely talked."

"And that's what you told Deputy Travis?"

"Yeah. Oh, and he wanted to know when Andy and I got together. That made me laugh. I was like, um, 'Never.' I'm used to guys who only want one thing. Not Andy. He's too shy to have a girlfriend."

"But he likes you."

"Do you think so?"

"I do. Do you like him?"

"He's cute. But kind of religious. Mary's husband is religious like that— he's Mormon, though—and he was all, 'I'm going to kill that Paco' and going on and on to Mary about how she's going to hell for committing adultery and breaking the Ten Commandments."

Hank's eyebrows shoot up, mashing his forehead like a hand organ.

Behind her, Gene whispers, "WTF?"

"Wait a second, what about Mary's husband?"

"He thought she was going to hell."

"No, he said he was going to kill Paco?"

"I think so. That's what Paco told me."

"What did Deputy Travis think about that?"

"He didn't ask me about Mary."

Another wind gust hits the trailer. If Maggie were piloting a sailboat, she'd be a contender for the America's Cup with this kind of velocity. Each creek valley is the same, but less terrifying as she becomes accustomed to cheating her steering left against the wind.

"Sounds like something he'd want to know."

"Paco didn't necessarily believe her. He said Mary had a higher-than-average need for drama."

"But the deputy could figure it out."

"Yeah."

A long, tense silence fills the truck cab. Hank rolls his hand at Maggie, like *Get on with it*. Ahead of them to the west, the silhouette of the sloping shoulder of the Bighorn Mountains appears. The rolling landscape becomes even more dramatic, with crazy tilts and drop-offs punched out of the grassland like the footprints of giants. Overhead, black and gray clouds roil. *No,* Maggie thinks. *No weather while I'm driving.*

When Penny doesn't offer anything more, Maggie looks a question at both men. Gene shakes his head. Hank shrugs.

"All right, then, Penny. I'll let Andy know you're good."

"Okay."

"Bye, then."

Maggie hears dead air through the phone. Her first reaction is happiness. Another suspect for the deputy: Mary's husband. Or even Mary herself. The more suspects there are, the less need they have to go after Andy. Or worse, Hank.

Gene says, "Well, I'll be a monkey's uncle. Paco and a Mormon wife girlfriend."

THIRTY

MAGGIE WAKES from the sleep of the dead before dawn Monday morning, still hungover from the drive and some nightmares she can't remember. Hank is stretching beside her, looking rested and happy.

"No, it's too early for today," she moans.

"Says someone who didn't grow up on a ranch. I let you sleep in."

"Stop being logical."

"I thought you'd be up with the sun this morning. It's a big day. You're my new hand. I've agreed to let you be there while I call my doctor. Light a fire under it, girlie."

Maggie huddles under the warm covers. "Who you calling girlie, boy?"

Hank spoons her and kisses her neck. Before she can snuggle into him, he's up. Cold air rushes her body as he rips the covers from the bed.

"Hank!"

"Better not be late on your first day. I hear the Double S boss is a real hard-ass."

She mumbles something about jackass, then races into the bathroom ahead of him and locks the door.

He laughs as he pounds on it. "Let me in. You're going to miss the middle of your back without me."

"You wish. You're just afraid I'm going to use all the hot water up. Which I am." She turns on the shower. "But I'll let you in if you tell me the magic word."

"What's the magic word?"

She shucks her nightgown. "If you don't know, you're not getting in."

"Please?"

"Unimaginative. Strike one."

"You need some of that Mare Magic you bought for Lily."

"Strike two."

"You're the most beautiful woman in the world."

She opens the door. "Was that so hard?"

"No, but this is."

She looks at his midsection, only a little lower. "It's so much easier to get clean that way. Come on."

He follows her in, and just as she predicted, they both end up with a cold shower, but neither one of them complains. When they're dressed and ready, Maggie straps on her new scabbard and knife.

"You can have your knife back now," she tells him.

"Hey, that looks nice." He picks up the black Double S knife. "I'll put this back in the barn."

"I can take it for you."

He hands it to her. She straps it on, too, then notices for the first time that Louise isn't in the room with them.

"Where's my dog?"

"She was whining to go out in the middle of the night."

"You let her?"

He dimples. "She didn't jump out the window."

Maggie bites her lip. She's been keeping the dog in so she won't leave dead animals on the front porch. Cute, dead baby animals. *Oh, Louise, please have been good.* "Buy me breakfast."

"Done." Hank sneezes, then looks traumatized. "I'm getting sick."

She pats him. "Take some vitamin C."

Together they walk downstairs, with Hank sniffling and clearing his throat.

Maggie says, "I'll meet you in there. I just want to check on Louise first."

She pokes her head out the door. At first she thinks she's in the clear, then she sees an adorable little lump on the landing. On closer examination, the lump is a baby porcupine. Dead, of course.

"Dammit, Louise!"

The wiggly dog comes running, pleased at Maggie's reaction to the tribute. Maggie's not sure if anyone will care about the death of the little porcupine—Louise still hasn't gone after any ranch animals—but it's painful to see it. Coatless, she wraps her arms around herself and pushes the animal off the steps with a toe. Then keeps pushing it, until it reaches the side of the house and is out of sight.

Shaking her head, Maggie walks into the dining room. "Good morning, all."

"Your cheeks are red. Been out for a morning jog?" Laura asks, straight-faced. She's pushing her mother away from the table. "Or in a knife fight?" She points at the two knives on Maggie's hips.

Maggie doesn't dignify her jibes with an answer.

Mrs. Sibley sniffs. "Decent folk have finished eating. Gene and that new hand have already left."

Maggie notices that Mrs. Sibley is mentally sharp, if as unpleasant as usual.

Hank pours Maggie a cup of coffee. "Mom, have a good day. And be nice."

"I'm always nice."

Laura mouths, "Oh my God," and she and her mother make their exit.

Maggie takes the coffee. "Thanks, Hank." She makes herself a plate and eats quickly while Hank talks her through morning chores.

"Sounds like I should have gotten started before breakfast."

"Tomorrow."

She laughs. "What have I signed up for?"

Trudy puts out a second basket of apple muffins. "Muffin? I'm trying a new recipe."

Maggie and Hank stand.

Maggie pats her tummy. *No more apples.* "You're bulking me up. Gotta say no. Thanks. That egg soufflé was delicious."

Trudy buses Maggie's plate. "I've got to master soufflés." She looks down at the toes of her boots. "Since I've been accepted to the CIA."

"The CIA?" Maggie halts at the door.

"Culinary Institute of America."

Beside her, Hank covers an anemic cough. "You're going to do great. But we're going to starve to death."

Trudy laughs. "Hardly. I'm working on finding you someone to replace me." She disappears into the kitchen.

"You knew?" Maggie asks as she and Hank walk to the front door.

"She told Gene and me last week. Wanted to keep it quiet, what with Paco and all. Gene's pretty torn up about it."

"Why?"

"You haven't noticed? He's sweet on her."

Maggie grins. "Maybe now that she won't work here he'll do something about it."

"Nah. He thinks she's too young." Hank sneezes.

"Age is just a number. Or so they say. Are you going to get a doctor's appointment today?"

"I emailed them about it last night. I have an appointment at noon."

"I'll meet you at eleven fifteen to ride together." She dons her jacket from the hook by the door.

He gives her a miserable look. "Can we leave early to stop at Walgreens? I need cold medicine."

She wonders how he went so fast from a few sneezes to this level of pitifulness. "If you don't die from the flu before then." She ducks out before he can formulate a comeback.

The snow has melted, leaving electric golden aspen and bright red and orange buckbrush behind. The wind is calm today. She's struck by the stunning beauty of the mountains. How did she get lucky enough to end up in this amazing place, with her amazing man? She's elated—relieved—to be needed, to be helping today. As she walks toward the barn, she checks her phone. There's a slew of voicemails. Several contractors wanting to talk estimates. And somehow she has another missed call from Franklin.

This voicemail has content, though. "I have your claim finished. Call me so we can talk through it."

She calls him immediately and trades voicemail. "Keep trying. I need numbers so I can get contractors started."

Disappointed, she resumes her walk to the barn. First, she unstraps her extra knife—Hank's—and hangs the scabbard from his saddle horn in the tack room. Then she starts filling dog food bowls, then water tubs.

Lily nickers, low and deep.

Maggie can't see her, but she knows her voice. "I'm coming, I'm coming."

She hustles into the barn to fill feed buckets, feeling like a badass for slicing open a bag of feed with her knife. She stacks the buckets in a box on the back of a four-wheeler. She'll do hay later.

She feeds Lily first. The mare eats like she's starving and doesn't say thank you. Maggie places her hand on the enormous belly, hoping for a kick from the foal. She gets one, and it's powerful.

"Whoa, Crazy Woman better watch out. This one is a little buckaroo."

She distributes the feed to the rest of the penned horses, then goes back for bags of cubes, which she slides across the open tailgate of a ranch truck, into the bed. One bag for each pasture, different types for bovines and

equines. And a special bag of alfalfa pellets for a pasture of retired champions, the revered senior citizens of the ranch.

She pats the phone in her pocket. Should she call the contractors back
about the estimates while she still has some cell signal? It should make her
agitated that she has all this Double S duty today when she's getting all the
calls about her life in Texas. But it doesn't. Instead, she feels a strange but
very welcome inner peace. She decides to hold off on the calls.

THIRTY-ONE

SHE'S SMILING as she gets into the driver's seat and shuts the door. She's going to relish this. The beautiful day. The gorgeous scenery. The wonderful last twenty-four hours with Hank. Feeding the amazing ranch animals, so full of life. She fires up the engine.

A knock on the truck window startles her. Michael is staring in at her. Her stomach knots. Just when everything was looking rosy. All the information Gene dumped on them yesterday about Michael—she can't help but be impacted by it. She pastes on a smile to cover it up.

She rolls the window down. "Hey, Michael, what's up?"

"You're going to want some help with the gates."

"Why?"

"Because the livestock will meet you at each one and try to push through to you."

"Oh."

"They like their chow."

"I hadn't thought of that."

"I'll come with you. I have an hour before the transport is due to arrive from Duncan."

Again, unease twists inside. Is he just using them, and her? But she wants to give him a chance. Needs to, after she advocated for it to Hank and Gene. "Thanks. Hop in."

When he's seated, Maggie guns the truck to the first gate. Michael was right. She's met by a herd of horses. He opens the gate and waves them off long enough for her to drive through and him to close up. Then he walks behind her, doing visual checks on animals while she drives slowly to the feeding area. They reach it nearly simultaneously.

"I got it," he says. "This will go really fast together." He vaults into the truck bed and opens a bag of the horse cubes, then pours them in a U on the ground around the truck bed.

Horses jostle into position. There's some kicking, biting, and squealing, but enough space for everyone once Maggie moves the truck forward, emptying the center of the U. A herd of deer vault the fence and move cautiously closer, although Maggie isn't sure whether it's the truck, the people, or the horses they're afraid of.

"Keep going. I'll meet you at the gate," Michael calls.

They repeat the process in the next few enclosures, moving in a large circle around the property. At a pasture of bulls, a big fellow with hide like a patchwork quilt refuses to budge for the truck. He paws and faces down a waving, yah-ing Michael.

"What do you want me to do?" Maggie asks through her open window.

Michael shrugs. "Push him. Just remember he's worth more than he looks. I don't want to get fired."

"Great," Maggie mutters.

She puts the truck in gear and eases off the brake. The truck moves faster than she wants, so she pushes it partway again and rides it. The truck nudges the bull. He bellows and throws his head, his horn clanging against the front hood. The nudge turns into a heave-ho and he gives way. His tail twitches angrily as he trots off to join his brethren, looking no worse for the encounter with a two-ton dualie. Maggie exhales.

Michael joins Maggie in the cab for a longer stretch of driving. The truck bounces so hard on a rock hidden in a mud puddle that Michael catches himself with a hand on the ceiling. They both laugh.

Michael points behind them. "Your dog followed us."

"Shit. That damn dog."

"What's wrong with her?"

Maggie sighs and stops the truck. "She's a stone-cold killer."

Michael opens his door, blocking muddy Louise from getting in the cab. He hoists her into the bed. Maggie resumes driving.

"What does she kill?" he asks.

"Moles. Mice. Rabbits. Today, a baby porcupine."

"Dogs will be dogs."

"Yeah. But that baby owl was so cute."

"Baby owl? What kind?"

"The adorable, innocent kind. I don't know the type. I gave it a decent burial."

"Burial? Where?"

"Out near the dead pile."

"We have to dig it up."

"Why?"

"You don't bury an owl. That's mixing the above world with the underworld, and it's bad medicine. You leave it out, so that the spirit can return to the sky."

"Bad how?"

"Bad like bad things will happen. Maybe to you. Maybe to someone you care about. I just hope it isn't too late."

"Shit, Michael. You're scaring me."

"I'm sorry. But it's important. As soon as we finish with the animals, we'll go get it."

Her mind offers up an unexpected use for her new knife. Digging up a dead baby owl from hard, cold ground. "Then what do we do with it?"

"We find a nice rock. Or build a stack of sticks. Something respectful, but open to the sky."

"Okay."

He purses his lips, staring out the window. When he turns to her, he's deadly serious. "Maybe your dog has special powers and saved you from a shapeshifter."

Somehow Maggie has not only missed owl burial but shapeshifting in her research on her heritage. God, she's a shitty Crow. "I'm not following you. Again."

"Witches and bad medicine men sometimes transform into owls. If it was a screech owl or great horned owl, that's what I would think."

"Maybe."

"When did this happen?"

"A few nights ago. I found it in the morning."

"Has your dog ever done anything like that before?"

"Well, she's killed those other animals."

"No, I mean saving people."

"As a matter of fact, yes. She tried to pull a man out of a burning house. And she chased down an arsonist and pinned her to the ground so she couldn't get to Hank and me."

"Hmm. I'd take care of her if I were you."

Buried owls, bad medicine men and witches, and threats to her and her loved ones? A chill rips through Maggie. Somehow the thought of Louise with special powers to protect her is meager comfort.

She says, "How about we go ahead and move the owl now?"

THIRTY-TWO

GOD SPARE ME THE MAN-COLD. Maggie is in Hank's passenger seat, and he's behind the wheel outside Walgreens, downing cold medicine. They'd driven to town separately, her with Andy, him alone. She left Bess in the Home Depot parking lot, where Hank will drop her when they're done with his doctor. Andy has a ranch shopping list for Home Depot and will wait for her there.

Maggie's still feeling a little anxious after what Michael said about the owl, but at least they'd moved it, so she won't worry about Hank's illness being her fault. Now she just has to worry about every other threat in the world to everyone she cares about.

She hands Hank lozenges and tissues. "Are we good?"

He moans. "Is it feed a fever, starve a cold? I'm really hungry."

"It's feed a *cold*, starve a fever. Lucky for you, we don't have time to stop for food."

"So I have a fever?"

She stares at him.

"Feel my forehead."

She obliges. He's cool and normal. "Nope."

"Are you sure?"

"Hank, I have bad news for you."

"What's that?" He reverses the truck.

"You're going to live."

"Maybe not."

"And I have a question for you."

"I might be too weak to answer."

She rolls her eyes. "Why haven't you guys brought in any female hands at Double S?"

"Well, we have you."

"I'm a volunteer. And this is my first day."

"Seriously, no women have ever applied for the job."

"Why?"

"Would you want to work in thirty-below weather if you had other options?"

"Good point. Now, where's your doctor's office?"

"New York."

Her head whips around to him. "Come again?"

"I Skype with him."

"So what are we doing in Sheridan?"

"Using the free Wi-Fi outside the library."

"We had Wi-Fi back at the ranch."

"Yeah, but you have to be back from Walmart in time for Trudy to cook dinner, and you wouldn't have made it if you'd waited to leave until after my call with Dr. Clark."

His logic is convoluted, but it works. "All right, then. I haven't been to the library."

After they park, he leads her to a wooden bench outside a picture window. "We'll get good signal here."

He unpacks his laptop and boots up. Maggie looks around outside while she waits. The library is a dark fortress of a brick building, but the grounds are spacious and well kept. Right across the street is a park with a sign that reads WHITNEY COMMONS, so the library green space—or tan space, this time of year—seems immense.

Hank says, "I'm making the connection, if you want to come sit with me."

Maggie scooches onto the bench beside him. "I don't plan on saying anything."

"You can if you want to."

"I just want to know what's going on. As long as you're completely open with him, you won't hear a peep from me."

He side-eyes her. "Right."

A surfer-dude-looking man in a white doctor's coat answers. "Dr. Clark."

Dr. Clark's voice is clipped and Bostonian, about as unlike a surfer dude as Maggie can imagine.

"Hi, Dr. Clark. Hank Sibley here for my checkup."

Dr. Clark doesn't waste a second on idle chitchat, but launches into a detailed quiz into Hank's condition and symptoms since they'd last talked. Maggie only has to jab Hank once when he squirms out of full disclosure about the problems with his headaches, mood, and mental functioning. He clears his throat and supplements his answer, then looks to her for validation. She smiles and bumps his knee with hers.

"Is there someone there with you?" Dr. Clark asks.

"My girlfriend, Maggie. She's been, um, concerned. She's here to keep me honest."

"Good. Maggie, did he leave anything out?"

Hank shifts the laptop so the camera lens picks her up.

"Hello, Dr. Clark. I think he downplayed everything a bit, but essentially that's it. And you're the brain doctor only, right? Not someone to talk to about an injury to his, um, man parts?"

"Man parts? You mean penis or testicles?"

Hank groans. "Maggie . . ."

"Penis. From sex. It's crooked."

"Any pain, Hank?"

Hank partially covers his face with his hand. "Right after it happened, but it's better now."

"Go see a urologist if it doesn't straighten out completely. They can fix it, usually. Better than I can fix your head."

Hank whispers to Maggie, "I'm going to kill you."

She gives him a smile worthy of a halo.

Dr. Clark shifts into a review of Hank's most recent lab work. When he's done, he doesn't take a breath before moving into regime changes for Hank. "You're not responding to the pills anymore. We need a better method of delivery. You're going to have to learn to give yourself shots a few times a week. If you don't see significant improvement within three weeks of starting that, set up another appointment."

"Got it."

"Stick with the rest of your regimen—food, sleep, exercise, low stress, and your other supplements and meds. It won't be overnight, but you're going to feel better, Hank."

Hank and the doctor discuss the details of the injections. Practice, timing, procedure. Maggie takes notes. They hang up.

"Well?" Hank says.

"He seems good. And he took your issues seriously and made changes."

"Yes. I like him. He costs me an arm and a leg, but he saved me, back when conventional medicine failed."

She's encouraged, but Dr. Clark's last words linger. "It won't be overnight." A lot can happen in a few weeks. A lot has happened. And there's a lot that might have happened that she prays didn't. *Thanks, Deputy Travis, for putting that in my head, however unlikely it is.* Hank's no killer, at least not when he's himself. But when he's not himself, how can she really know for sure?

THIRTY-THREE

"I'll meet you back at the truck, all right?" Maggie lifts the last bag into her cart from the checkout carousel. After Hank dropped her at Home Depot, she and Andy headed to Walmart.

Andy puts new work boots and several pairs of socks on the belt. "All righty."

Maggie's cart is full to the brim. She's shopping for the ranch table, mostly, and for herself and Hank, a little. She pushes the cart out to the parking lot and alongside Bess. As she hefts a fifty-pound bag of dog food into the bed, Andy appears with a bag on one arm.

"I could have helped you."

"It's a beautiful day, and I need the exercise."

And it is beautiful. The sky is a summery blue with only a few wispy clouds floating by. It's in the high fifties, and Maggie's in a short-sleeved T-shirt, jeans, boots, and the Frontier Days belt buckle. She's even wearing her long, white-streaked black hair down, since there's no wind to tease it into a fright wig.

She's getting out her keys to open Bess's old-school locks when she becomes aware of a big white pickup pulling into the empty space beside Andy. A bulky figure appears beside him.

"Ms. Killian." Travis tips a ball cap.

"Deputy Travis."

"I was on my way out to Piney Bottoms when I saw your truck."

"Well, she's hard to miss."

"True. I think this will save me a trip." He puts a hand on Andy's shoulder. "Andrew Yoder, you're under arrest for the murder of Paco Lopez." He holds up a pair of handcuffs. "Do I need to use these here? I can wait to put them on in the truck if you'll come peaceably."

Maggie runs around the truck. God forgive her, but her first reaction is gratitude that it isn't Hank. Her next is to wonder what the hell they have on Andy that Travis has arrested him. The boy's no murderer. It's crazy. And why is Travis doing this in a public parking lot? She wants to take him down with a knee to the balls, but she doesn't want to get arrested.

"What the hell?" Her voice is shrill.

Travis raises a hand to stop her. "No closer, Ms. Killian."

Andy stares at the deputy without a word, but Travis seems content to let him remain uncuffed for the moment.

"Mr. Yoder, you have the right to remain silent. You have the right to refuse to answer questions. Anything you say can and will be used against you in a court of law." Travis recites the rest of the Miranda warning to Andy. "Do you understand these rights as I've explained them to you?"

Andy's eyes are round and pale as a blue moon. Unlike most of his generation, he didn't grow up hearing the Miranda warning umpteen times a week on TV cop shows. The unfamiliar words must be confusing and intimidating. Despite the lack of cuffs, people are stopping to stare, too, adding further pressure to the situation. A young mother in yoga pants gapes, while her toddler son darts between parked cars. A woman closer to middle age, based on her less taut skin and muscles, grabs hold of him and puts her body between Andy and the child. Three teenage boys in high-tops, shorts, and tanks stop to watch, jostling and pushing each other.

"That'll be you, man," one says.

Another says, "Nah, cuz I ain't got no religion."

The third cackles appreciatively at their wit.

Travis ignores them all and says to Andy, "You'll need to answer verbally, son. Yes, you understand you have these rights, or no, you don't."

"I don't know, sir. I guess I do all right."

"Is that a yes or a no?"

"Yes. I understand."

"Good. Let's get you loaded up, then, and I'll take you in."

Maggie can't stand it any longer. "You're making a mistake."

Travis huffs at her. He opens the back door of his truck, then puts a hand on Andy's head to protect it as the young man climbs into the seat. "Why? You think I should arrest Hank with him?"

"Of course not. But there are other suspects. What about Mary's husband?"

"Who?"

"Mary. Paco's girlfriend."

"You're grasping at straws."

Maggie remembers what Andy had told her the day before, that he didn't have an alibi for the nights after Paco was last seen. "But you can't take Andy in just because he sleeps alone in a bunkhouse and can't prove where he was. It doesn't mean he killed Paco."

"No. But his fingerprints on the knife handle are pretty solid evidence. His knife." Travis gets in the driver's seat and shoots her one last look before shutting the door.

She knocks on the window.

Travis glares at her, but he lowers it. "What?"

"Can I come with him?"

"It won't do any good."

"What can I do, then?"

"He'll meet with a public defender later today, unless he gets his own lawyer. And I imagine he'll have a bond hearing tomorrow. You can help with those. That's all you can do." He raises the window and backs out of his space.

With Travis and Andy gone, the crowd loses interest and disperses quickly, but Maggie gazes after the truck as it leaves, feeling like she's failed Andy in some fundamental way. After a few moments, she gets her wits together enough to text Gene and Hank. *Andy arrested for Paco's death. In jail. Bond hearing tomorrow.*

Gene: *Shit. I hate that I'm not there.*

Hank: *Calling an attorney for him now.*

Maggie slumps into Bess and rests her head against the seat back. Then she bolts upright. Travis is wrong. The attorney, the bond hearing? That's not all she can do. If the sheriff's department won't look for the real killer, she can do it for them. For Andy.

THIRTY-FOUR

THE NEXT MORNING, Hank, Maggie, and Gene are at the county building for Andy's bond hearing. From its architecture, it's hard to tell if the courthouse wants to be a pagoda or the Wyoming homage to Frank Lloyd Wright. It doesn't put a best foot forward. The public entrance is almost like a loading dock. Half the walkway is cordoned with safety tape, cones, and warning signs so that visitors aren't killed by ice avalanches from the roof.

Outside the third-floor courtroom is a sign for the Fourth Judicial District Court of Wyoming and the Honorable Judge John P. Johnson. The inside has an Old West feel with vertical dark wood paneling and a beamed ceiling, green patterned carpeting and upholstery, and even a brass and velvet rope to mark reserved rows in the gallery. Because it's the new West, there are laptop-friendly counsel tables and a projector and big screen.

Andy is there, wearing his normal work clothes, dirty and wrinkled. At least he didn't have to wear prison garb. The attorneys, the judge, the bailiff, and the court reporter are all present, too. Paco's death isn't big news in the community. It's a murder, of course. That got people's attention. But Paco was a Mexican ranch hand from Texas, not someone from a local family, and that makes a big difference. There are a few people in the gallery, though. Reggie, glowering. Trudy, which warms Maggie's heart. And—surprise—Penny, which confuses her. She'd told her about the hearing in a text canceling the music lesson the day before, but she didn't think the girl was that into Andy. She doesn't get a chance to talk to her before the bailiff calls court to order, though.

The attorneys make their appearances, but the proceeding is anticlimactic. John Fortney does a good enough job for Andy, but he doesn't have a challenge. Hank and Gene have already pledged adequate bond, with the bondsman present to hand over the check to the court. One hundred fifty thousand is steep to them—they'll never see fifteen thousand of it again, the fee to the bondsman—and low to the county for murder, at least according to the heated objections of the county attorney. The judge seems to buy Fortney's argument that a twenty-year-old Amish man who doesn't drive, fly, ride trains or boats, or own a passport is not much of a flight risk.

Andy spares a brief smile for his supporters as he turns to walk up the aisle without cuffs, although he's rubbing his wrists like he still feels them there. He sees Penny, and his face lights up like the girl is the present he never dreamed Santa would leave under the Christmas tree.

Reggie steps in front of Andy, blocking his view of Penny. His face is cold, his tone harsh. "Come with me."

Andy ducks around him to keep Penny in his sight.

"Did you hear me, Andrew?"

Andy returns his gaze to his father. His jaw flexes as his head inclines. Maggie is sure he's about to say "Yes, sir" when Penny steps up beside Reggie.

"I'm happy they released you, Andy."

Andy's suddenly two inches taller, his shoulders rising up and back. That brief smile returns, directed straight at the brunette. "Thank you."

"I mean, I'm sad Paco died. But I'm sure you didn't do it and they'll find who did."

Maggie is torn between agreeing with Penny and the fear that the someone they'll find will be Hank. But she won't let that happen. He's standing ramrod straight beside her, no dimples, no smile, but his eyes are kind.

"Andrew, now," Reggie says, in a deep hiss.

Andy shakes his head. "No." He clears his throat. "No, sir." He turns and extends his hand to Hank. Then to Gene. "Thank you both. More than I can say."

Both of his bosses shake his hand.

"I'll pay you back."

Gene crosses his arms. "You're a good man, Andy. And we know you're a good investment."

Penny steps closer. "Could you use a coffee, Andy?"

Andy laughs, starting to seem more his age. "Yes, I believe I could."

Hank and Maggie share a look. *Maybe Penny has gotten over her religious objections*, Maggie thinks.

Hank says, "If you don't mind, we have some errands to run. But we could pick you up and give you a ride back to the ranch from there."

"Oh, and before I forget, let's reschedule that music lesson for the two of you. How about tonight?" Maggie asks.

"That will work for me," Andy says.

Penny nods. "And Java Moon is just down the street. The weather is so pretty. Would you like to walk, Andy?"

"Enough of this. You're defying the faith before my eyes." Reggie's face is so red it's almost purple.

Andy speaks softly, but firmly. "No, I'm not. Goodbye, Father."

Reggie storms out of the courtroom, looking like the poster child for a movie on Old Testament vengeance.

Gene whistles. "That's not a happy man."

"You staying in town?" Hank asks.

"Nah, I'll get on back to the ranch. See you there."

Fortney joins them as Gene departs. The attorney talks about Andy's next steps in the criminal justice system and promises to call the ranch to set up an appointment for trial prep. After the attorney takes his leave, Andy walks out with Penny.

Hank offers his arm to Maggie. "I thought we'd walk to the compounding pharmacy to pick up my prescription."

"That's sexy talk, cowboy. I'm so excited for you to start the new treatment."

They walk along busy Coffeen Avenue chatting and holding hands.

Maggie says, "I was thinking about Andy's defense."

"Fortney will do a good job."

"I know. But there's no substitute for someone who really cares about and knows Andy. Should we hire a private investigator?"

"Maybe. The state still has to prove he did it, though, and I don't see how they can."

"It would help if we could show them who did."

"But we don't know who did."

"I'd like to try to figure it out."

"So hire the private investigator."

"Okay. I'll just do a little digging first, so I can start a PI in the right direction."

"That sounds like a good way to get yourself killed."

They enter the pharmacy. Hank's prescription is ready. While he pays, Maggie Googles for private investigators in the area. She doesn't come up with anyone promising. Plus, she starts wondering about the impartiality of a small-town investigator when all the suspects are likely to be local, too. Everybody knows everybody here.

Hank shakes a white paper bag at her. "Got it."

"I'm proud of you."

On the way back to downtown, they talk about Hank's injection schedule.

"Are you scared to give yourself a shot?"

"I'm not looking forward to it, but I've given injections to animals nearly all my life. I'll be fine."

"Don't you get the vet to do the injections?"

"You wouldn't ask that if you knew what Doc Billy charges. We take very good care of our livestock. They're our income. But what we can do ourselves, we do."

"What about labor and delivery?"

"Now you're thinking about Lily?"

"Yes."

"She's done it by herself several times now. We'll be there to help her if she needs it. But unless there's a problem, we won't call Doc Billy."

Halfway down Main toward Java Moon, Maggie stops and stares into a window. "I love their displays."

"Twisted Hearts. Girly stuff."

"And what's wrong with that?"

"You might not have noticed, but I don't wear many dresses."

"On account of your bowlegs?"

"Very funny."

The door to the shop opens. Three women emerge with navy paper shopping bags.

Maggie groans. "Don't look now, but it's the Witches of Eastwick."

Hank says, "Shit. Well, Mary's nice, but June and Sheila aren't my biggest fans right now."

"Or mine."

Turn the other way, turn the other way, Maggie wills them. "Let's go." Maggie takes Hank's elbow and pulls.

But it's too late. "Hank Sibley, are you going to pretend you don't even see your ex-fiancée?" June asks.

The three women are upon them in an instant.

Sheila pulls a pair of pants from her bag. She drapes them across her. "I hope when I'm nearly forty I can still fit in these."

Maggie pulls her embroidered top up with her free hand, looking down at her tight tank. "I'm sure glad I don't have to stuff socks in my bra to look like a grown woman."

Hank clamps his hand over Maggie's on his elbow and propels her forward with two big steps. "Come on, before Penny and Andy run off and elope."

A mewling sound whips Maggie's head around. It's coming from Mary.

"Penny? I don't think so." She looks close to tears.

Maggie's strange feeling from earlier returns. What is it about Penny? She stops, which wrenches her hand out from under Hank's. "Why?"

"Don't listen to her," June says. "She's crazy when it comes to all things Paco Lopez."

"I am not. And Penny is the one obsessed with him. Paco'd been trying to foist her on Andy for weeks."

Sheila reloads her merchandise bag and leans to whisper in Mary's ear, but just loud enough that Maggie overhears it. "Mary, honey, why do you think he was using that religious freak as a beard? Because he could make it look like something it wasn't. Andy was a safe place to park his other woman. So quit lying to yourself. Up until the day he died, Paco was still giving it to Penny every bit as often as he was giving it to you."

THIRTY-FIVE

ON THE DRIVE back to the ranch, Andy is more like a lovesick puppy than a man charged with murder.

Maggie's still reeling from her interaction with the three witches. What's Penny's angle? Is she using Andy for something? Lying to the police and everyone else about her relationship with Paco? "You seem upbeat."

"It will all work out. I didn't do this. The lawyer feels I won't be convicted."

Hank turns right on Main, taking the back way out of Sheridan to US Highway 87 and on through Story. "But I don't think that's the reason you look so happy. I think it's the girl."

"A Cheyenne girl at that. I thought you didn't like Indians?" Maggie says.

"Depends on the Indian."

"Are you allowed to date non-Amish?" Maggie can still picture the glowering face of Reggie when Andy agreed to coffee with Penny. Maybe religion will save Andy from Penny. If he needs saving.

"During Rumspringa, yes. But outside marriages are against Ordnung— community rules. So if I go back and get baptized, I have to marry Amish."

The religion and the community fascinate Maggie. From growing up Wendish, she can relate to the isolation and the extreme views. "Can people convert to Amish?"

"It's very difficult. Rare."

"But not impossible."

He smiles. "No, not impossible."

The news isn't as good as she'd hoped.

THIRTY-SIX

THAT EVENING, Hank and Maggie exit the dining room with Andy, Michael, and Gene, to find Penny in the great room waiting for the music lesson.

"Hello, Penny." Hank kisses Maggie's cheek. "I'm going to take a shower."

"See you in a few." To Penny she says, "You ready?"

Andy's face turns the color of a beet. "Penny."

"Hi, Andy."

Michael's eyes narrow, and he looks confused. "What are you doing here? You could have called me if you needed something."

She hugs her purse to her side. "Sorry. I'm not here to see you."

Maggie's hackles rise. How widespread are Penny's affections?

"Oh?" Michael says. "Who are you here to see?"

"I'm taking a music lesson from Ms. Killian."

"Like Andy." His brows draw together.

"Yes."

"Is this lesson with him, too?"

"Yes."

Michael studies her face, then Andy's. The air is thick with something that Maggie wants away from.

She points at the stairs. "Let's go make some beautiful music together." She immediately regrets her word choice.

Michael stares after them as they go.

THIRTY-SEVEN

HALF AN HOUR after the music lesson ends, Maggie and Hank lay intertwined.

Maggie is limp and sweaty. "The bed didn't crash. That's good."

"I Maggie-proofed it."

Maggie laughs. In the background, Alison Krauss is crooning "Stay." "Definitely the afterglow. My favorite part, I mean."

Hank kisses her clavicle. "You think? I'm all about the pursuit."

"So if I'd stayed with you in Wyoming originally, we would have been over before we began? Because to you it's all about the pursuit?"

He runs his finger down the centerline of her body, from the hollow of her throat to just below her belly button. "In case you haven't noticed, you require a lot of pursuing."

"Don't try to talk your way out of this, cowboy."

He chuckles, and she touches the indentations in his cheek. "I believe I just pursued you to Texas. And up the stairs. And around the bedroom."

Maggie is mollified. She worries about leaving him to go back to Texas, if she can't get him to come with her. It's not that she'd require chasing, but she would want him to come after her. The thought of being apart makes her jangly and anxious. That reminds her she has two estimates sitting in her email inbox, a result of having no time to call the contractors back the day before. She hasn't even opened the emails.

"Hey, where'd you go?" he jostles her toes with his.

"Sorry. Thinking about Andy." She crosses her eyes instead of her fingers as she tells the white lie. "He and Penny were all googly-eyed on the porch after the music lesson. He's moony over her."

"You don't sound like you approve."

"I don't *dis*approve, but something isn't right with that girl."

"She seems nice enough."

"Harrumph."

He laughs. "You sound like Andy's mom."

Not what she wants to sound like when she's naked in bed with Hank. "Enough of that. Did you do your shot?"

"I did."

"Good."

Louise scratches at the door.

Hank growls. "Damn dog."

"She keeps getting shut out whenever we . . . you know."

"I don't need her watching my performance."

"You think she's going to critique you. Like, 'Hey, Mister, aren't those things usually straight?'"

"Too soon."

Maggie laughs. "About Louise. I have a confession on her behalf."

In the hall, the dog sighs and lies down on the floor with a loud, dejected thump.

"Uh-oh. As long as this isn't a story about Louise and one of your previous boyfriends, I'll be good."

"I got Louise here. In September. How fast do you think I work?"

"We were apart for a few weeks."

She nips at his nipple, eliciting a groan. "Louise has been keeping the ranch safe from small creatures. Rodents. Rabbits. Porcupines. Even an owl. I told Michael about it, and he thinks the owl was a witch, and that Louise saved me. That Louise is my protector."

"That's one bloodthirsty animal."

"Were you even listening to the punch line?"

He rolls her onto him and tips up her chin. In the moonlight, his face is shadowed, but his breath is warm and sweet on her lips.

"If Louise is protecting you, she's my favorite animal in the world."

Maggie nestles her face in the center of his chest. Hank holds her tight against him. Soon, his breathing is rhythmic and snuffly. Louise snores from the hall. Maggie is drifting off herself when she hears a screech and sees a shadow against the window. *Is it another owl?* But sleep pulls her under before she can decide.

Sometime later, Maggie wakes with a start. She's on her back, arms flung out.

"Waddafock," Hank mutters.

Her heart is kicking like the hooves of Lily's foal against the inside of her chest. She puts her hand on her throat. It's slick with sweat. There's an odor in the room. She sniffs. Something rank. Rotten. Dead?

Louise scratches on the door and whines. She sounds like she's digging for moles in the hall.

Maggie pushes herself to a seated position against the headboard. An image is fading from her memory. A dream? It's Paco's face, Paco's red boots running from the dead pile. He's pointing at something, or someone behind her. Hank is there. Gene. Michael. Andy. Penny. Her. She runs, gasps. Paco's image fades. What was he pointing at? Was he trying to show her something? His killer? She clutches at the covers pooled in her lap. Her hand closes over something warm, soft yet hard, and wet. She screams and rockets out from under it, landing on the floor with a thud on her side.

Hank is on his feet, fists swinging. "What? What? What?"

Maggie's voice is strangled. "Something was in my lap. I don't know what it is."

Louise scratches more frantically. Maggie doesn't tell her to stop, even though she'll have a sanding and staining job to repair the damage later. Hank switches on the bedside light. He hurries to her, leaning over to get a closer look.

"I'm fine. It's up there. On the bed."

He stands and searches the covers. She knows the second he finds it—whatever it is—because his expression of revulsion is unmistakable.

He crouches beside her, puts the back of his palm against her forehead. "Are you sick?"

"What? No. I was having a . . . a . . . nightmare, and I woke up."

"It's vomit."

She feels her chin, her neck, her chest, her mouth. "It's not from me."

"Or me. And Louise is in the hall."

The dog redoubles her efforts at the sound of her name.

"Having a cow."

Hank uses his alpha voice. "Louise, stop it."

Silence in the hall.

Maggie holds up her hands. "It's on me."

Hank grabs her wrists and gives them a gentle shake. "Go wash up. I'll try to figure out what's going on."

She nods and accepts his help standing up. Together they stare at the drippy bundle stuck to the covers.

"Are those *bones*?" she asks.

"Yes."

"And fur?"

"Yes."

"It's like something from a voodoo curse, or a witch doctor."

"Funny you say that."

"Why?"

"Last night you told me Michael thinks you had a visit from a witch."

"So?"

"This is from an owl."

"Owl vomit?"

"Yes."

"An owl couldn't get in our room."

Maggie runs to the door and lets her frantic dog in. Louise scrambles around the room, hackles up, growling. Hank and Maggie stare at each other.

"Hank, what the hell is going on?"

THIRTY-EIGHT

AFTER THE DISCOVERY of owl vomit on her in bed, Maggie and Hank can't get back to sleep. They decide to get a jumpstart on the morning chores and do the feedings together early.

After breakfast, Hank stops to hug her at the front door. He and Gene are on their way to meet Paco's family in Sheridan. "Don't let the dog out of your sight."

"I won't." She Eskimo-kisses him. "I hate that I'm not going with you."

"I'll be fine. Besides, I appreciate your help here."

"But the morgue."

"Not the first time I've been to one. Seriously, I'm good."

Gene walks up behind them. "You coming, Sibley?"

Hank picks up a travel mug of coffee he'd set on the sofa table on the way through the great room. The two men leave. Hank turns back for a moment, flashing her some dimples, and she waves to him from the open front door. Louise gives herself a side rub up against her leg. As the men back out and drive away, Maggie is alone, except for the dog. Her unease amps up.

Footsteps from the other direction draw her attention away from the ranch exit. She sees Andy walking up to the main house from the bunkhouse, his head down. His presence is comforting.

"You missed breakfast," she calls.

"Morning chores ran long." He doesn't look up.

As he skirts her to enter the door, she sees something dark around his eye. Purplish green, dark blue, and red. Like a blackened eye.

"Andy, wait."

He stops, not facing her.

"What's wrong with your face?"

"Nothing."

"Let me see."

He starts to walk away, but then he turns to her, revealing the mother of all shiners.

"Did you get kicked?"

He sighs, shaking his head. "Michael found out I like Penny."

"He punched you? But aren't you his boss?"

"Yeah." He clomps toward the kitchen. Then he turns back. "But I'm still going to marry her."

"What?"

"I asked her to marry me. She said yes."

"Whoa, what?" This doesn't feel like good news for Andy. "That was fast."

He trudges away.

"Wait," she calls after him. *And what the heck is Penny to Michael,* she wonders, but Andy doesn't hang around for her to ask more questions. She starts to chase after him, but decides she needs more information first. If she disapproves of their engagement, she'll drive Andy away. But if she figures out for herself who Penny is and what she's up to, well, then she'll have a better idea of what to do.

Maggie heads to the bedroom. Remembering her missed calls and emails, she quickly reviews the building estimate emails that came in two days before. The numbers are a little higher than she'd hoped, but one of them is close to workable. She sends a reply to that contractor, letting him know he's in the ballpark but needs to come down further.

She yawns. A quick makeup nap is in order after the rough night. There will be plenty of time after it to tackle the rest of her chores and her list of follow-ups, both in relation to Texas and to keeping Andy out of a bad marriage and prison. She's asleep almost before her head hits the pillow.

Loud knocking at the front door wakes her. No one answers the door, and the knocking just keeps going and going. She hears barking, growling, then yelling. *Shit.* Louise is outside. So much for Hank's request that she not let the dog out of her sight.

Maggie scrambles out of bed and downstairs, pushing wild hair out of her eyes and checking her breath on the run. She throws the door open. "Where's the fire?"

A puffy man dressed all in black is pinned on top of a Prius. Louise is lunging and snapping the air around it. She shoots Maggie a look as if asking what took her so long, then runs to her master and dances around her, tail wagging.

Maggie isn't about to scold the dog for protecting her. No one local drives one of these tin-can cars. It's a recipe for getting stuck on the side of the road in a pothole or snowdrift, or being killed when hitting one of the many deer who insist on suicide by vehicle. "Who's your friend, girl?"

Louise runs back to the muddy little car and resumes haranguing the visitor.

"Call off your beast, dammit." The man is holding his nose, giving his voice a nasally quality. Still, it sounds familiar.

Maggie crosses her arms. "Not a good idea to show up unannounced around here, mister. Who the hell are you, anyway?"

"Amos. We talked on the phone."

"Sic 'em, Louise."

His scream is high-pitched like a teenage girl. His arms flail the air, and he releases his nose, ducking his head and face. "No, no, no."

Louise doesn't know any commands. Even "come" and "sit" are still beyond her, no matter how many treats Maggie has offered her to learn them. But Amos doesn't need to know that.

"I told you not to come." Maggie's nose wrinkles up. "God, what's that horrible smell?" She's been so focused on the unwanted visitor, she just now realizes she's standing beside something dead and seriously rank. Not rank like owl vomit. Rank like . . . she searches the ground around her. Yep. Rank like a baby skunk. "Louise, bad girl."

"She smells like a skunk."

"You think?"

"It's making me nauseous."

The dog slinks to her, but she looks proud, not chastened. Her tail wags harder and harder. She smells as bad as the dead animal. Maggie is about to banish her to the barn until she can bathe her, but decides against it. She can take it, and it appears the sensitive flower from Colorado can't.

"If you don't like it, the interstate runs north and south, just a few miles that way." Maggie points.

His voice is icy. "Are you always this nice to people who drive hundreds of miles to see you?"

"No. Sometimes I call the cops." She opens the door to the house and starts to go back in. "Stay out here, Louise," she tells the eager dog.

"Wait! We got off on the wrong foot. Talk to me. Please."

She shuts the door. From the sound of the dog's growl, Maggie can tell she's rushing the Prius again. Amos screams. Maggie smiles and sits on the couch to check her phone.

Andy runs up, hollering at Louise. *Dammit.* After a short conversation, Andy pokes his head in the door. "Maggie?" he hollers.

"Right here."

"Oh. Sorry. There's a reporter here to talk to you."

"I know."

"What should I tell him?"

"That I'm not available. But I already did."

"Louise is terrorizing him. And she got a skunk. But I'll bet you already knew that, too."

"Sure did."

"I'm going to take her out to the barn and put her in one of the stalls."

"A shame. She was being such a helpful girl."

"Maggie."

She grins. "I'm kidding."

"He, um, he asked if he could interview me, since I know you."

"Suit yourself."

"You don't mind?"

"I don't recommend it. Reporters are vultures."

"I've never been interviewed for a magazine."

"E-zine. Blog. Or worse."

"What?"

"Do it, then. It's fine. Get it out of your system. Have fun."

"Can I bring him in here?"

Maggie nods. "I'll take care of Louise. I have work to do outside anyway."

Andy's eyes light up. "Thank you."

"I wouldn't thank me." Maggie follows Andy out, stepping over the skunk, and grabs Louise.

"You've decided to talk to me?" Amos asks from his dented rooftop.

He's finally looking at her without his hand clamped over his nose, and a bad feeling starts in her stomach, like the kind she gets from too much sugar. She knows this person. His salt-and-pepper hair is longer than she remembers it. He's wearing a beard on his formerly clean-shaven face. But she'll never forget the face of the man who used to be one of the top disc jockeys on the radio, until he harassed Maggie in an interview. Aaron cum Amos's fascination with her and his smears thinly veiled as news make sense now. He's got a hard-on for revenge.

"Not a chance. Especially not now that I see who you really are, Aaron Cryor."

"I don't use that name anymore."

"Freelancer now. My how the mighty have fallen."

"If that isn't the pot calling the kettle black, I don't know what is."

"No argument here. Come on, Louise."

Louise lifts a leg on the Prius like a boy, then follows Maggie to the barn. Maggie doesn't look back at the former shock jock. At the barn, she gives Louise a hose bath with skunk shampoo she finds with the dog supplies in the feed room. After Maggie rinses her, Louise shakes immediately, dousing Maggie.

"Stop." But Maggie laughs. She's going to smell like a skunk, too, but the temperature is a gorgeous fifty-five outside, and a little stinky water won't kill her. She goes for buckets and fills one with all-stock feed for the goats and another with sweet feed for Lily. They've already been fed, but she feels like spoiling them. She goes to the goats first. They're tethered behind the guest cabin she'd stayed at in August, before she and Hank were back together.

"I need to make you guys a pen before Mrs. Sibley has you butchered."

They don't seem overly concerned. She lets them loose. They follow her—and the feed buckets—to Lily's paddock.

"You're looking like an elephant today, my pretty one," she says to the horse.

Eyes on the feed, Lily jukes and jives as light-footed as if she weighed three hundred pounds less. She starts her funny *buh-buh-buh*, like a motor having trouble starting on a cold day. Maggie sets the goat bucket outside Lily's gate, then pours the horse's feed into her trough. The goats and horse eat quickly. When they're all done, she pushes the goats in with Lily. Louise squeezes in after them. The creepiness of last night and irritant of Amos's visit slip away in the presence of her favorite animals, just as she'd hoped they would.

She tips her head back, eyes closed, and soaks in the Indian summer sun. A flapping noise makes her open her eyes. A flock of Canada geese wing in front of blue sky and fluffy white clouds, then turn. She rotates with them and admires their silhouettes in front of the yellow orb of sun, like they're fleeing from a world on fire.

A blue-roan in the next paddock turns sleepy eyes on Maggie. The docile animal looks familiar.

With a start she realizes it's Crazy Woman. "Hey, superstar." She walks to her pen and holds out a hand. The horse rubs her nose on her foreleg, then goes back to dozing. "No love for your fans, huh?"

She's going to miss this in Texas.

Her phone rings in her pocket. Franklin. Finally they're going to connect. "This is Maggie. Give me some good news, Franklin."

"Oh, um, hi. I expected to get voicemail again."

"You need to learn what to do with it."

"What do you mean?"

"I've been waiting on this claim information, and you're holding it captive."

He clears his throat. "It's our policy not to leave it in a message."

"Then spit it out already."

The line goes dead.

She stares at the phone. "Dammit, T-Mobile. Dammit, Wyoming."

It rings again.

"Yes?"

"I lost you."

"Talk fast."

He gives her a number for reimbursement on rebuilding. It's less than half the amount of the lower of the two estimates she'd read earlier. And those were already for no-frills buildouts. Not nearly as nice as the originals.

"Come again?"

He repeats it.

Maggie is silent. She walks into the pen with Lily, the goats, and Louise. Omaha and Nebraska bleat at her and butt her legs. She reaches down and trades off between them, scratching behind their horns.

"Are you there?"

"I'm here. This is me being speechless."

"Are you okay?"

"How could I be okay? That amount won't pay for me to rebuild a shed, much less a house, a shop, and a barn."

Franklin hems and haws. Maggie doesn't listen.

"So what do I get if I don't rebuild?" she asks.

He names a far lower number. That, plus selling the land at the price the realtor suggested a few days before wouldn't give her enough money to buy a new place. She can't rebuild, and she can't afford to replace what she had. Not to mention she can't afford to give up the rental income on

Gidget's place, and she sure can't afford to lease Lumpy's place, nor can she qualify for a loan to buy ranchland for Double S. She'd been living in a dream world.

"What the hell was I paying for with my premiums all these years? You guys are screwing me."

"This isn't personal."

"Getting screwed is always personal. Expect a call from my attorney next."

He tries again to explain, but she ends the call in the middle of his sentence. Lily stares at her and swishes her tail.

Maggie kicks the gate. It hurts. "Son of a bitch."

THIRTY-NINE

AFTER FINISHING the rest of her ranch chores in a blue funk, Maggie takes her laptop into Hank's sitting room and plops onto the brown leather couch. It's worn but still feels plush under her. She puts her feet on the coffee table. Typing ninety-to-nothing on her phone, she shoots off an email to Michele about the insurance payout. Then she texts her: *SOS. Sent you an email. Getting effed over on insurance.*

As always with Michele, the reply comes fast: *See know more. Dammit. Trying out voice recognition. Quitting voice recognition. Seriously, I'm on it. Don't worry another minute.*

Maggie smiles for the first time since she talked to Franklin. *Thanks.*

"Maggie, is that you?" It's Trudy's voice from downstairs.

"Hi, Trudy. Yep, it's me."

"I have a surprise for you. Can I come up?"

"Of course." Maggie boots up her laptop while Trudy climbs the stairs.

The woman appears bearing a small plate in one hand and a steaming tin mug in the other. Maggie smells coffee.

"You seem to be sick of apples."

"I, um . . ."

Trudy sets the mug down by Maggie's feet, then hands the plate to her. On it is a sugar-sprinkled scone with some kind of reddish berries. "It's cranberry."

"I freakin' love cranberry scones."

"Good." Trudy brushes her hands on her jeans. "It's my own recipe."

Maggie bites into it. She moans. "It's still warm."

Trudy smiles. "Do you have a sec?"

Maggie pats the couch and takes another bite.

"Did Andy tell you he's engaged?"

Maggie nods and rolls her eyes, still chewing.

"Yeah. Me, too. Do you know anything about her?"

Maggie sets the scone on the plate and the plate on the coffee table. "She's a wonderful banjo player. She used to date Paco. Michael beat Andy up over her. And two days ago she thought Andy was too religious for her. That's all I've got."

"That's more than I had. What's her name?"

"Penny."

"Penny what?"

Maggie stares back at Trudy. "You know, I don't have a clue. I told myself I was going to do some hunting around for information on her this afternoon, but I'm not going to get very far without a name."

"She's Crow?"

"Well, Native American at least."

"No, I remember. Cheyenne. Andy told me."

That thickened the plot with Michael, for sure, since he was from the Cheyenne reservation. "Should narrow it down some."

"I have to admit I'm surprised. Andy hates Cheyenne."

"There's that."

"I'm worried this is just some kind of rebellion he'll regret."

"He's smitten with her, but I agree. Even if it's true love on his part, this relationship has regret written all over it."

"If you find anything out, let me know, okay? I can't stand the thought of him getting hurt."

"I will. You, too."

Trudy's face is pensive as she walks away.

Maggie's laptop is booted up. She eats the last bite of scone and sips her coffee. Time to do some good for Andy. She decides to research Mary, since she has a last name to go on. Martin. She types *Mary Martin, Sheridan, Wyoming* into Google. The search engine asks her if she meant Mary *Marton* Sheridan, Wyoming. She thinks about it, replays the sound of Hank introducing the woman to her in her memory. Mar-TAHN. Yes. *Marton.* She clicks to accept the change, and more search results appear on the screen.

Mary Sanders Marton. The Facebook profile picture is definitely the curvy brunette. Born in Sheridan, Wyoming. Graduated Sheridan High

School. Married to William Marton. His name is not highlighted, so it doesn't appear he's on Facebook. Mary graduated from Eastern Wyoming College. Works at Sheridan Vet Clinic. Occupation: Vet Tech.

Maggie scrolls down Mary's timeline. She finds pictures of her with June. With Sheila. With Sheila and June. One is at the Ox. She pulls it up and enlarges it to see the other people in the background of the shot. There's a flash of red on the feet of a cowboy sitting with his back to the camera. He has his arm around a woman in profile. A woman with a sheet of long black hair. Penny. The photo is creepy, since it brings life to a dead man, but it doesn't tell her anything new. She keeps scrolling. Mary likes to post selfies with her four-legged patients, as well as rescue animals from the local shelter. Maggie sees pictures of Mary on horseback at brandings, in the mountains on a four-wheeler, and fly-fishing in waders. What she doesn't see is any pictures of Mary with a man—Paco or her husband, or even friends or family.

She Googles Sheridan Vet Clinic. The website is factual and functional, with no pictures of the staff. Maggie reruns her search on Mary and sifts through the results. Mary has volunteered with rescue events, and she's competed in some 5K runs.

The sound of the front door opening and closing tears her attention away from Mary. Heavy boots clomp through the great room.

"Who's there?" she says, loud enough to be heard downstairs, but not shouting.

"Michael."

She pushes the laptop onto the couch and jumps to her feet. "Wait up." She runs down the stairs in her stocking feet.

He's waiting, and looking puzzled. "What's up?"

"Are you getting coffee?"

"Yep."

"I thought I'd join you."

"Free country, except on the res." There's an edge to his voice, and he doesn't meet her gaze.

She follows him into the dining room. It's empty and so is the kitchen. Michael grabs a mug from the stack by the percolator and pours coffee into one. He sets it aside and pours another, nodding at the first one. She doesn't need more coffee, but it seems like the right thing to do.

"Thanks." Maggie gets pumpkin spice creamer from the refrigerator. "I saw Andy earlier. He looks like shit." Michael had filled the mug nearly to the rim, so she's not able to get in as much as she likes.

"Yeah? Well, he had it coming." Michael walks to the door.

She stirs in her creamer. "It's a good way to get fired, and to hear you tell it, you really need the money."

He stops at the door. "Some things are more important than money or jobs."

She wishes she knew whether Gene or Hank talked to Michael about his time in prison. Bringing it up first herself wouldn't be right. "Like punching your boss?"

"Like Penny." He spits out the words like pellets from a gun, then turns on his heel to go.

"But why?"

He disappears without answering her.

FORTY

MAGGIE TAKES a late-afternoon shower to wash the day and dust off before dinner. When she gets out, she dries off, then uses the towel to turban her hair. She pads dripping into the bedroom. Hank is on the bed with his hat over his face. She removes the hat and kisses his cheek.

He opens his eyes, and his dimples are like the Grand Canyon. "Hello, beautiful." He reaches for her.

She wags a finger at him. "Time for me to dress for dinner. How was Paco's family?"

He sits, his long legs swinging over the side of the bed and his boots hitting the floor. "Sad. Nice. We took them to eat. Then they got on the road."

"Such a sad journey for them." Her dream image flashes back through her mind. She hopes his spirit went with them, if that's what it was.

"You sure you're in a hurry?"

She shimmies into panties. "I'm sure. I skipped lunch. But I'll take a rain check tonight." She doesn't tell him that she's still too depressed about the contractor estimates and insurance claim news to get her sexy on now. Somehow she doesn't think her bad news will be as bad to him as it is to her.

"Probably for the best. My head is killing me. I'm going to take some stuff."

"Did you do your shot?"

He mouths a pill in the doorway, talking around it, glass in hand. "Yeth-terday." He swallows the pill. "Don't be pushy, woman." But he smiles.

Her phone rings.

He swallows his gulp of water. "Aren't you going to get it?"

She picks up her phone and groans. "It's Amos, that reporter from Denver. He showed up here today uninvited. But get this: Amos is a pseudonym. It's *Aaron Cryor*."

"That asshole DJ you got fired?"

"None other."

"Give me that." He takes the phone from her and answers. "This is Hank Sibley. Listen, asswipe, leave my girl alone."

"That won't make it better." Maggie holds her hand out for her phone.

"And don't come on my property again without an invitation. That's a shooting offense up here."

"Give me the phone, Hank."

He slaps it into her palm. "I feel better."

She shoots him a look. "Aaron, don't bother me anymore."

"Amos. I texted you the link to today's article."

"Super." He must have written it in real time as he did the interview.

"Take a look. I'll hold."

"That's okay."

"Please. Your hand said he doesn't have technology. He wants you to show it to him."

"Fine." She puts him on speaker and switches to her texts, where she clicks the link he sent.

The first thing she notices—"Black Widow Steals Other Woman's Fiancé"—is a box quote from Sheila. *Maggie stole Hank from me. We were engaged to be married.* And then a picture of Maggie with Lily, Louise, and the goats, captioned *Country star to country girl.* Sneaky bastard taking pictures like some paparazzo with a telephoto lens.

Hank reads over her shoulder, squeezes her, and kisses her neck. "Want me to talk to him again?"

"I hear you, you Neanderthal," Amos says.

From downstairs, a woman's scream rings out.

Hank says, "Shit, that's Mom. You okay?"

Maggie points at the door. "I'm fine. Go."

Hank runs out.

"Maggie?"

"You're a jackal."

"The interest in you is huge after these murders you were involved in."

"I wasn't *involved* in any murders. Murderers were involved."

"Add all the rest to it, and you're great reading. You're dating a real cowboy, your superstar ex died, your old bandmate burned down your house, your father's running for president, and your new bestie is Ava Butler."

President? Oh, Boyd. That won't keep the scavenging press away. "I wouldn't call us besties."

"What would you call it?"

"We're . . . friends of friends."

"Well, people are interested. You can let me write about you, or someone else will."

"You have a grudge against me. No thanks."

"My articles are creating renewed interest in your music."

"Good—the record label that owns my tracks thanks you for helping line their pockets."

"Seriously, you should do something with it."

She doesn't tell him that Goliad Records had the same idea. "I don't want to do anything with it. I just want to be left alone."

"I'll be here a few more days if you change your mind."

"Digging up more dirt like you did with Sheila?"

"Satisfying public interest."

"That you create. Potato, potahto, shock jock."

"Have it your way."

After the call, she finishes dressing. While she's blow-drying her hair, another call comes in. It's not totally unexpected. Michele had warned her. Aaron had too, in his own way.

Maggie turns off the blow-dryer. "Hello, Ava."

Ava's island patois lilts over the line. "Maggie, you still up there freezing your backside off in Wyoming?"

"It's lovely here. And, yes, I'm in Wyoming."

"Girl, you need to do something with your music."

"It's not mine anymore."

Ava drops her accent. "I saw a video clip of you playing with some rednecks. You still got it—comes through even on a shitty cellphone video."

"Great."

"And that article. Some reporter asshole sent it to me. Amos. He said you referred him to me."

"I most certainly did not."

"He had my personal number."

"Not from me, he didn't. Please don't speak to him."

"I didn't. But listen, you're too talented and hot right now to let this go. And I have an idea."

"Why do I think I'm going to hate this?"

The accent returns. "Because you always been a sourpuss."

"Just tell me what it is."

A baby cries in the background. "I gotta make this quick. Collin is hungry. Collin Junior, that is. Well, probably his dad, too, but not that kind of hungry."

"Spare me."

"Let's do a mash-up."

"What?"

"Let me remix one of your old songs."

"I don't own the recordings anymore."

"But you own the songs. Like if someone records them, you get paid, right?"

"No. But I have lifetime rights to re-record them myself without paying royalties."

"That will work."

"Work for what?"

"We're going to record together. My producer is a genius. You'll make a mint, and I'll get tons of crossover fans from whatever it is you call what you do."

"I do antiques."

"Musically. Western shit."

"Texana. Or alt-country. Americana. Folk. Alt-rock. Any of those. But not Western."

"Yeah, well, that's what I want us to do together. Your shtick and mine. Your songs."

Ava is running her own show. Maggie wonders how much different her dead musical career would have been without an agent or manager calling all the shots and a label making demands. She has new respect for Ava. Not enough to cave, though. "Sounds fun. No."

"What do I have to do to get a yes?" She names a number. It's higher—three times higher—than the insurance payout. "Plus ongoing royalties, of course."

Maggie's breath hitches. It's more tempting than she'll admit. "Ava, I'm not part of that world anymore. I'm in Wyoming. Hell, you don't even like me."

"You've grown on me. But sleep with my man, and I'll cut you."

Maggie can't help it. She laughs. "Back at ya, sister."

The baby's cries escalate to earsplitting screeches. "Think on it. I'll be in touch again soon."

The call ends, and Maggie stares out the window, calculating whether Ava's offer would be enough to cover the delta between the chickenshit insurance payout and the cost of her Texas rebuild.

FORTY-ONE

MAGGIE SIPS A CUP of light and sweet coffee on the back porch after morning feeding and breakfast. She's in a red long-john top with her boots, jeans, and Hank's Frontier Days belt buckle. The clouds tumble like petals from a dandelion in the sky, and the breeze in her hair is mild and pleasant. On the mountain, the old summer cabin looks mysterious but inviting and close enough to touch. Louise is rolling in the grass—in something dead, from the smell of it—but even that can't spoil the glory of a perfect day. Last night she'd told Hank about Andy, Penny, and Michael and updated him on the status of her nightmare in Texas. It had felt good to share the burden, and Hank had been steady and helpful.

Things may not be perfect, but they're damn good.

The wooden floor creaks under Hank's boot treads. "What are you doing out here?"

"Admiring the view."

"Are those elk coming down the mountain?"

"What?" She squints. "Maybe. But I was admiring the summer cabin."

He drops a kiss on her neck. "I need to run up there to check on the old girl. Want a tour?"

Maggie adores old things, and she's dying to see the cabin. "I'd love it!"

"Grab a jacket. It's windier up there."

Half an hour later, the two are driving up a narrow, single-lane road in Hank's truck with Louise in the back seat. Maggie grips the armrest. It's one dead-man's curve after another, and she's on the uphill side, so all she sees is blue sky on the driver's side. The big cabin looms over them, straight up the road.

"It's crazy steep." She looks up at the cabin to take her mind away from the drop-off.

Hank grins at her. "It is. It took Dad and Grandpa two years to build this place. And half of that time was spent just hauling materials up this road."

"Does anyone come up here in the winter?" This road would be a ski jump with ice and snow.

"Sure. We used to a lot, but mostly on snowmobiles. There's a snow-plow in the barn, and an old Snow Cat." Hank spins the truck around a nearly one-hundred-eighty-degree switchback for the final approach to the house.

"Wow." Maggie can't find any other words that won't get stuck in her throat.

Somehow, the cabin site is just flat enough to accommodate a small parking area and the footprint of the cabin. It's as tall as it looks from down below, too—four stories built into the face of the mountain. The walls are hand-hewn logs encircled by a deck balancing over the drop-off below it. The green metal roof blends into the tops of towering ponderosa pines.

"Pretty cool, huh?"

"Amazing." Maggie jumps out and slams her door, then lets Louise out. The dog sniffs the ground like it's crack for an addict. After huffing for a few seconds, she takes off after a chipmunk that disappears into a woodpile. The air is thinner, crisper than at the ranch. "This is what Pine-Sol wishes it smelled like."

Hank laughs.

"And the view. Oh my God. This view." She points toward a ridge that juts eastward from the mountain range.

"It's special. Usually in this part of the state you're either looking at the mountains or you're in the mountains and see nothing but trees and rocks. Here you get both because of that ridge, plus the view of the buttes to the east, the foothills below, and the valley along Piney and Little Piney creeks."

"I didn't even know that gulch was there." She points at a fold lined with gray-and-red rock cliffs. "It looks like heaven for mountain lions."

"Oh, it is." Hank walks back and forth, staring at the dirt driveway, his lips pursed.

"What is it?"

"Someone's been up here."

"Is that bad?"

"Well, usually I'm the only one who comes all the way up to the cabin, at least unsupervised. I come up every week or two for maintenance. It's totally off the grid, so I make sure everything is working, keep the rodent population down, and arrange workers and deliveries." He points at several big propane tanks.

"Even in the winter?"

"Even more so in the winter. Can't afford to let it freeze or the pipes will burst."

"I didn't know you were up here so much."

"I have a strong sentimental attachment. And she requires a lot of care." He pats the edge of a log. "Come on in. I'll show you around."

They enter into a cozy kitchen with an old-fashioned wood-burning stove. The interior walls are simply the other side of the external logs. The effect is rustic and everything a mountain cabin should be.

"It's beautiful. Perfect."

Hank steps into a three-story great room with a black iron stove and tall chimney. "You should see it lit up with a giant Christmas tree and fires in all the stoves."

Maggie peers upward. The top floors overlook the lower ones with log railings instead of interior walls. She has a flash of inspiration. The Wyoming pieces she bought last summer, the ones that survived the fire, anyway, would look wonderful here. Music plays in her head, music she can picture making in this space. "The acoustics must be amazing. Why don't you live here? This place is magical."

"It's too big for a bachelor pad. And not convenient with Mom's condition. All these stairs and levels. Plus at the ranch house we're half an hour closer to help and have onsite cooking to share with the hands." He squats and examines the carpet.

"It's huge. How many bedrooms?"

"Six."

She's getting tingly, and she's not sure why. "And bathrooms?"

"Um, six and a half."

"It's big enough to be a bed-and-breakfast. A lodge. A guest ranch."

Hank frowns at the floor. "This boot print wasn't here last time I was."

"Maybe Laura came up?"

He traces the print with his finger. "Too big. And these are work boots, not cowboy boots like we wear around the ranch." He stands. "Damn, I wish I'd put up a game camera."

"Or you could use some of those Wi-Fi cameras you can check on the internet."

He nods slowly. "Maybe so." His phone rings.

"You have cell service up here?"

"Line-of-sight internet and 4G signal. It's better than down at the ranch." He looks at the screen. "I'd better take it. Laura and Mom were headed into town."

Maggie wanders off to explore on her own. She'll come up here and install the cameras herself, she decides. She is a ranch hand, after all, and it would give her another excuse to visit. In the dining room, wooden-framed windows show off the view. Deer wander down the slope, grazing. A mature buck, two does, a yearling spike, and some summer fawns that have lost their spots. Tears prick the corners of her eyes. How can physical beauty have this emotional impact on her? It's like this is the place she's been waiting to find her whole life.

Hank's voice booms with authority in the other room. "I'm leaving now. Hang on."

Maggie hurries back to the mezzanine and stands beside an old piano. "What is it?"

Hank's face is pale. "They're at the hospital. Mom collapsed. Laura thinks she's had a stroke."

FORTY-TWO

Louise hunkers down outside the cabin and refuses to load in the truck. The dog's no fool. She's found heaven.

"We don't have time for this." Hank revs the engine.

Maggie grabs Louise around her torso. "She's heavier than she looks." She hefts the dog into the back seat. Once in her own seat, she buckles up. "Ready."

The trip down the mountain is far faster than the one up, and Maggie presses her feet into the floorboard like it will help with the brakes. She closes her eyes on the scariest parts. Once they reach the relatively flatter road back to the ranch proper, Hank speeds up. The truck goes airborne between potholes. He stops so hard at the main house that Maggie's seat belt arrests her.

He puts it in park and turns to her. "I'm in a hurry."

"Then go."

"Aren't you getting out?"

"Not unless you want me to."

He throws it back in gear. "Thank you." His words are clipped, his face is stony, his eyes dark and sunken.

She reaches across the seat and touches his knee. "Of course."

He drives left-handed and holds her hand in a crushing grip the entire drive to Sheridan. Maggie texts Laura for him when they're five minutes out. When they park, Louise whines. Maggie had forgotten she was there. Hank doesn't seem to notice, so Maggie cracks her window.

"I'll come check on you in a little while with some water."

Louise wags her tail. Life is always an adventure to her.

Inside the hospital, Laura meets Maggie and Hank in the front lobby.

"No one is telling me anything." Laura collapses into Hank.

He bends down, and her head slides up to his shoulder. Maggie feels out of place. Until she acquired her two stepsiblings, she'd never had a brother or sister. She can't relate to Hank and Laura's reliance on each other. But she does understand they love each other, and that they love their mother. That they share the pain of the loss far too young of a father they adored. That once upon a time, their grouchy, confused, wheelchair-bound mother was a vital, loving spouse and parent.

Like her own father had been. A sob burbles up in Maggie's throat. She chokes it back. She rarely thinks about him. Feels sad about him even less often. But being here, remembering the change in her father and his death, knowing he had Alzheimer's like Mrs. Sibley, it all crashes down on her.

Hank hears her. His eyes find hers over Laura's head. His face is slick with tears, his eyes red-rimmed, and his lips tight and trembling. If Laura didn't have her arms around him, Maggie would scoop him up. His pain is her pain, and she aches to touch him. He reaches out to her, but they're interrupted.

"Are you the family of Evangeline Sibley?" A woman with white pin curls and a smock over her gabardine pants and polka-dotted blouse walks up on squeaky shoes.

Laura releases Hank and mops her face with her hands. "We are."

"The doctor would like to speak to you."

Maggie moves beside Hank. She slips her hand into his.

Laura holds up her hand. "Family."

Hank's face darkens.

"Please, Hank."

Maggie puts a hand on his elbow. "I'll be waiting for you here in the lobby."

His tight lips open, but Maggie interrupts before he says anything that makes the moment even harder.

"I'm good, Hank. I promise."

"Are you coming, Hank?" Laura says, avoiding Maggie's eyes.

Hank moves toward Laura, leaving a gap between him and Maggie. Every step he takes widens it. It's painful and surprising. Maggie wants to run after him. Instead, she settles into an uncomfortable seat in the lobby.

After a few minutes, Maggie's thoughts wander to her financial predicament. She doesn't have the money to rebuild her shop and her house. It's one or the other, unless she liquidates her inheritance: the Andy Warhol and the Jaguar have immediate value. She can put Gidget's little ranch on the market, but who knows how long it would take for it to sell? Or, she could take either Goliad Records or Ava up on their offers. Capitalize on her current resurgence of fame. In other words, sell out. She hates the idea of Goliad, but Ava . . . well, she's not completely opposed.

It might be fun.

But she hates Ava.

Or maybe she doesn't.

She's no closer to a decision when Hank pulls her to her feet.

Maggie moves to him, keeping their conversation private from Laura and her censure. "How is she?"

Hank looks like he's losing weight before her eyes, drawing in, winnowing out. "It's a massive stroke. They don't think she'll recover, even if she lives."

"I'm so sorry." She throws herself into his arms and squeezes him tight.

His lips move in her hair and his words are muffled. "Thank you."

"What can I do?"

"Love me forever."

She digs her fingers into his back. She already does. A flash in her mind foretells her future. Alone, in a hospital waiting room, losing Hank. A cry of pain escapes her lips.

"What is it?" Hank holds her away from him.

Everyone dies. One of them—her or Hank—will go first. Suddenly she hopes it's him. She doesn't want him to endure the pain she just felt at the thought of living without him. She doesn't admit to her terrors. "I hate this for you."

"Me, too." He draws in a long, deep breath. When he speaks, he turns to include Laura. "Let's go get some food, ladies. We have a lot to talk about."

Laura grimaces. "*We* have a lot to talk about, but not all of us. Did you bring your own car, Maggie?"

Hank wheels on her. "I'm sick of your shit, Laura. No more of it. Maggie is with me. If you don't like it, go eat by yourself."

"I know you're with her, and that's fine, but we need to discuss important *family business*, Hank."

"And we will. With or without you."

He propels Maggie with his body, arm around her shoulder. "Do you mind the cafeteria? I want to stay close in case they have news about Mom."

"Of course." As nasty as Laura has been, she feels sorry for her, but she doesn't know what to do about it. The younger woman's pain is palpable. It has been for the last week. Before this incident with Mrs. Sibley, and above and beyond any ill will she feels toward Maggie. Call it women's intuition or whatever. She may not have known her as long as Hank has, but she senses there is something else wrong.

Hank releases her at the cafeteria line. They fill their trays in silence. When they reach checkout, Maggie sees Laura in line behind them.

"I've got theirs," Laura calls out to the cashier, waving at the two trays in front of the register.

Maggie bites her lip.

Hank's voice is casual. "Thanks. I'll get us a table."

At a round table big enough for six, they huddle on one side. Hank pats Maggie's knee, and they eat in silence for several minutes.

Laura stares at a gravy lake in her mashed potatoes. "We've waited too long to talk about dividing property. Even if Mom lives, we have to figure this out."

"Say what's on your mind, sis." Hank takes a bite of meat loaf.

Maggie got it, too. It's a little dry, but surprisingly good.

Laura puts a thimbleful of potato on her fork. "I don't want the land."

"Land is all they have."

"Land can be sold."

Maggie holds her breath. Laura wants Hank to sell the ranch where he runs the Double S?

Hank pushes his plate back. "The value of the place is far greater than the price it would bring. To me."

"I understand that. But I need money. Mickey and I need money. Very badly."

"What are you saying?"

"I need us to put it on the market."

"You understand my entire livelihood is built around that property? Couldn't I just buy you out of your half of it?"

"How would you propose to do that?"

"In monthly installments."

She shakes her head and pushes back her tray. "I need the cash now. Could you get a mortgage?"

"Maybe. But I don't have W-2 type income. Banks don't like to lend money to guys like me. I don't own anything to put up as collateral."

"I'm sorry for your situation. But when it sells, you can use the money to get another place."

The sound Hank makes can't be described with mere words. The closest Maggie can come is a strangled cat in a dryer. "Did you have a time frame in mind?"

"As soon as humanly possible."

"Gosh, then, sis. You'd better hope Mom doesn't make it." He's on his feet like a jack-in-the-box. His hip jars the table and knocks over condiments and drinks. Ice and tea race across the table toward Laura.

Laura grabs napkins and sops liquids off her lap and legs. "Aren't you going to help me clean up your mess?"

"Not feeling helpful," Hank says from his clamped jaw. "And thanks for humiliating me and showing your true colors in front of Maggie."

Laura's voice escalates. "I warned you this was a family discussion."

Hank pushes down on his hat like he's walking into a stiff wind. "If only that felt like family." To Maggie he says, "Let's get out of here."

"I'll meet you up front."

He nods and strides off.

Maggie turns to Laura. "What's the matter?"

Laura finishes wiping down the table. "Other than my brother is a selfish asshole?"

"Why do you need the money?"

"That's none of your business." Laura lifts her tray with a jerk.

"Laura, I know you don't believe it yet, but I'm not the enemy. If there's something I can do to help, I want to."

"How can you help?"

Maggie follows Laura to a conveyor belt, carrying her own tray and Hank's. "I don't know. Talk to Hank, at least."

"I can talk to my brother myself, thank you very much." She slams her tray down on the belt.

"If you change your mind . . ."

"I know you'll be lurking around."

Maggie bites back what she wants to say, but she thinks it. *You don't have to be such a bitch about it.*

FORTY-THREE

GENE JOINS HANK and Maggie at the Mint Bar after Maggie sends him a distress signal text. Hank's been drinking for an hour. Maggie's taken Louise for a constitutional and drink of water. She's catalogued every animal head trophy and photo in the place. An email came in from the contractor in Texas, offering to work with her on a design that meets her budget. She made an appointment with him for the end of the next week. Now she's just trying to keep Hank upright.

Maggie side-talks at Gene. "I'm so glad you're here."

Gene holds up three fingers in a question to her. She holds up five. His eyes widen.

He nudges Hank with his shoulder. "Buddy, I'm so sorry about your mom."

"I lost all the rest of my fam'ly today."

"No, buddy, your Mom's still with us. And you've got me. Maggie. And Laura."

"Not Laura. Fam'ly doesn't try to sell your life out from under ya."

Gene looks to Maggie for interpretation.

"Laura wants the ranch to go on the market, ASAP." She takes a sip of her Koltiska original, straight.

Gene's eyes fly open like someone has cattle prodded him. "Put it on the market?"

"She's dead to me." Hank downs the whiskey in front of him. He holds up a finger.

Maggie curls it down. "You're getting too far ahead of me, cowboy." Like four ahead, but she doesn't tell him that.

He slant-eyes her. "You don't drink as much as you used to."

She realizes he's right. Not that she doesn't drink, but that she was drinking way too much for a while. She smiles. "You're the only drug I need. How about you?"

Hank locks eyes with her and shakes his head back and forth. "Doesn't appear so."

Ouch. She hopes he took his shot, because he needs all the help he can get. Grief and anger are doing a number on him. She rolls her eyes at Gene.

He's chewing his bottom lip. "We can make Laura an offer."

"We don't have the money to buy her out."

"Maybe she'll take a promissory note."

"She wants cashhhhh." Hank throws a twenty on the bar.

Maggie adds another.

"We gotta get back to the hoshpital."

"I'll drive." Maggie snatches the keys from his hand.

Gene says, "I'll be there in an hour. You got him until then?"

"Yep. He's safe with me."

A few minutes after Gene leaves, Maggie props Hank on her shoulder. "Time to go."

"Do you need a hand?" It's Penny's voice at her elbow.

"Hi, Penny." Maggie almost says no, then changes her mind. This is a good chance to talk to the girl. At least find out her last name. "Sure."

"I need to go to the bat'room," Hank announces. "Bleed the lizard. Drain the main vein."

"We can get you there, but after that you're on your own," Maggie tells him.

One on each side, she and Penny support Hank as he stumbles to the men's room.

"You gonna be okay?" Maggie asks him.

He salutes her as he falls through the door.

"Not good." Maggie leans against the pool table. She likes the small room in the back of the bar with historic ranch brands burned into the paneling, hand-carved wooden booths thick with varnish, and her favorite photographs in the place, all black-and-whites. A plane dating to the early days of flight with the mountains in the background. Snow-covered cattle and cowboys. Sheep at a mountain lake.

Penny nods. She gazes into the jukebox. "He's pretty hammered. His mom had a stroke, right?"

"Yes."

"Michael told me."

That's one of the subjects Maggie wanted to talk to her about. "Michael."

"Yes."

"You talk a lot?"

"Kind of. Not as much as we used to."

"You were close?" Maggie walks over to the jukebox, too.

"We still are. But we used to have an apartment in Sheridan."

"You lived together."

"Yeah." Penny dips her head. Her hair falls forward.

Maggie can only see part of the girl's profile. "Before you dated Paco?"

"Yeah."

"I heard you were still close with Paco when he died."

Penny closes her eyes. "We broke up."

"But you were still close?"

"Yeah."

Maggie breaks a long silence. "And now you and Andy are engaged. Congratulations."

She shakes her head. "I broke it off with him. It's probably for the best. But I thought he would be a good dad."

"Why did you do that?"

"Michael. But I didn't tell Andy that. I don't want to cause trouble between them."

"You mean trouble like Michael blackens Andy's other eye?"

"That was from Michael?"

"You didn't know?"

"No." Her hand covers her mouth, and she backs up to the jukebox.

"How did Andy take the breakup?"

She shakes her head. "He's okay, I think. I just told him. I guess this means I won't be coming to music lessons with him anymore."

Maggie is more confused than ever, but at least Andy is free from Penny. She thinks that's probably a very good thing. "I guess not."

Hank staggers out from the bathroom.

"I've got it from here," Maggie tells Penny.

The Cheyenne woman stares at her with inscrutable eyes. "Whatever you say."

How can she know less about this woman every time their paths cross? Penny walks away, and belatedly Maggie wonders what Penny was doing at the Mint.

"Give me your arm, cowboy." Hank throws it over her shoulders.

Maggie and Hank make their way to the door like the last-place team in a three-legged race. Once they're outside, Maggie turns right down the alley. They're parked in back. Not ten feet down it, they meet a man coming the other direction. A man dressed in the Amish style.

He looks up. The angry face is familiar. Reggie Yoder.

When Maggie is three feet from him, she gets a blast of the medicinal odor from his breath. If she didn't know he was Amish, she'd think it was moonshine. "Good day, Mr. Yoder."

"It ain't looking like a good one for my son's employer. What kind of man is drunk in public? Midday, no less."

Hank looks up, bleary-eyed. "I hear congraduelashions are in order, Reggie."

Maggie can't help but raise an eyebrow at his slurred pronunciation.

"What do you mean? My son is charged with murder and subject to any number of bad influences working for you."

Maggie tries to interrupt. "Hank, no—"

Hank bumbles on, pointing in the air. "Your son Andy is engaged."

Reggie hesitates for only a moment, then sprays spittle. "That's impossible. I would know."

Maggie tries again. "Hank—"

"You would know if she wash Amish, and if you wern an asshole."

"What do you mean?"

"Surely thish isn't the first time someone has told you you're a jerk?"

"Not that."

"Penny. You met her in court. Pretty Indian girl. Cheyenne, right, Maggie?"

"I think so. But—"

Reggie's face turns crimson and he punches the air. "This will not stand."

Hank grins drunkenly. "You jus keep thinking that. Have a good day, Yoder."

Maggie considers correcting the situation, but Reggie Yoder is so completely unlikeable, she decides he deserves to stew in it. Andy can set him straight later.

FORTY-FOUR

AFTER A QUICK STOP AT WALMART, Maggie and Hank return to the hospital. Something long-legged, blonde, and smelling like strawberry Lip Smacker rushes Hank at the door.

"Oh, Hank. You poor thing. Your mom. I'm so sorry." Sheila attaches herself to Hank like a baby koala to its mother, only a little less platonic.

Hank staggers back a step, but Sheila doesn't let go. Only the fact that Maggie is behind him saves them from toppling out the door and back onto the sidewalk.

"Uh, thanks." Hank pats his former almost-fiancée.

Maggie peels one of Sheila's arms off Hank and slings it back at her. Sheila glares from behind Hank's midsection. Maggie doesn't give a shit, so she slings off the other. Then she comes around Hank and gives Sheila a little push in the small of her back, to get her moving in the right direction. She nearly jams a finger on something hard. *Sheila's concealed gun, holstered high and tight.*

"Hello, Sheila." Maggie slides her arm through Hank's. "So nice of you to come."

"Well, when I heard, I just rushed right over. I've been comforting your sister, Hank."

Hank grumbles, "She's no sister to me."

Sheila looks confused.

Maggie mimes walking with her fingers.

"Where is she?" Hank's voice nears bellow level. "Laura?"

Sheila's voice catches. "She's up with your mother."

Maggie whispers, "It's about to get ugly."

Sheila's eyes flit to Maggie, to Hank, then back. She says, "I'll be praying for you, Hank," and leaves.

Suddenly, there's a loud, feminine wail from the far side of the lobby. "Hank."

Hank bows up, ready for battle, but when his tiny sister comes toward him, she's racked with sobs and walking with one hand on a couch back for support.

He runs to her. "What is it, sis?"

"Mom. Gone. Dead. Oh God, Hank. We've lost them both."

They fall into each other, their cries primal. When they release each other, Hank staggers to sit on the couch. He sinks down, his hat in one hand, his head in the other. Maggie sits beside him and slides herself under one of his shoulders. She wraps him in her arms and rocks him.

Long moments pass, and she becomes aware that Laura is sitting on the other side of Hank. Maggie looks across Hank's chest. The tips of Laura's hair are plastered against wet cheeks. Her face and neck are splotchy. She encircles her brother with her arms and grabs Maggie's elbow. The skin on Laura's hand is calloused and a little sandpapery, the palm small, and the fingers like the talons on a raptor. Her eyes meet Maggie's. She's given Maggie plenty of reason to hate her. But Laura is Hank's baby sister, and their mother and father are dead. Maggie puts her hand on Laura's elbow, so they're locked forearm to forearm.

"I'm sorry. I'm so sorry." Maggie gives the words a lullaby quality, repeating them over and over until both Sibleys start to breathe normally. "I'm so, so sorry."

"I know it's for the best." Laura's fingers dig even harder into Maggie's elbow. "She wouldn't have wanted what was coming for her. With the Alzheimer's."

Maggie feels a kinship with Laura in that moment. "My father had Alzheimer's. It was horrible. So bad that he killed himself."

Laura sits upright, her jaw slack and eyes round. "I didn't know. I'm sorry."

Face against Hank's chest, Maggie nods.

Laura stares out the window into the parking lot traffic. "Mickey's dad has cancer. And no insurance. That's why we need the money. For his treatment."

Hank lifts his ravaged face. "God, sis, why dincha just tell me?"

"He's embarrassed to be a hardship to his family. And Mickey feels like a failure because we don't have the money to help him."

"Thank you for telling us," Maggie says.

Laura gets to her feet, scrubbing at her eyes with her fist. "I told the nurse I'd be right back. There's paperwork."

"I'll come, too." Hank doesn't move.

"No. It's fine. I'll be back as fast as I can."

"I wanna say goodbye."

"They promised they'd let us know when it's time for that."

Hank nods. She leaves, looking back once at Maggie on her way out. Maggie wipes tears from Hank's face.

He focuses on her eyes. His words come out in a low croak. "Don't let me end up like my mom."

She grabs his face with both hands. "Oh, Hank. We all go somehow. Sometime."

"Promise me."

Maggie can't do that. "It will be okay, Hank. It won't be like this."

"I never gave her a gran'child."

"She had Farrah."

Hank shakes his head. "Who'm I kidding? I'll never have a child."

Maggie feels like a cold wind is blowing through her. They haven't talked about kids together. She hadn't thought about it much, but she realizes she assumed that they would have them, some way, somehow. "Why is that?"

"Because you're going back to Texas. Arnchoo?"

"I don't want to be anywhere without you," she says carefully, and reaches for his face again. Of course she has to go back and salvage her professional and financial situation. Is now really the time to discuss the complexity of her options, though?

He shucks her off, and stomps away unsteadily. Each step feels like it's landing in the middle of Maggie's chest.

FORTY-FIVE

A man's voice breaks through her consciousness. "Maggie. Wake up, Maggie."

Her eyes fly open in the dark. She throws an arm out, feeling for Hank. His side of the bed is cold and empty.

"Come to the window, Maggie."

"Hank?" She tries to crawl out from under the covers, but she's stuck, her pj's like Velcro against the flannel sheets. "Dammit." She kicks and makes it worse.

"Hurry, Maggie."

She stops, clutching the sheet. *It's not Hank's voice.* Her eyes drill into the dark, searching for movement or a shape, but she sees nothing. "Who's there?"

Downstairs, she hears a cracking sound. Her eyes jerk from the window to the door. She holds her breath. Two long, high-pitched scrapes. Then a thud.

Louise, she thinks. She calls for the dog. "Are you in here, girl?" There's no response. *Yes, it must have been the dog.*

The voice is a hiss now. "You've got to hurry."

Something about it is familiar. Compulsion overcomes fear and she finally wrestles out of the bedsheets and runs to the window. No one is there. She's hearing things. She presses fingertips to glass and gets her face as close to it as she can without fogging it over. The glass is cold.

"What is it?" she asks, then she snorts. Like she expects an answer from someone who isn't even here.

"Too slow, Maggie."

She gasps. Someone *is* in the room. But where? She scans the nooks and crannies, but movement snaps her attention outside. There's a shadowy figure moving along the road, toward the barn. Her eyes lose it in the dark. It must be Hank, which would account for his absence from bed. Or Gene. Or one of the hands. People move around the ranch at all hours, depending on weather or the needs of the animals.

An image mirrors in the window glass, a man behind her. Compact. Muscular. Dark. Handsome. Mustached. Paco?

She wheels. "Paco!"

But there's no one there.

A coldness seeps down Maggie's face that isn't from the window glass or the fall chill. What had Michael told her about knowing when she sees the spirits of dead people?

She knows.

She hugs herself. *There's nothing to be scared of, Maggie. Paco won't hurt you. If it's even him.*

But where is Hank?

She burrows back under the covers, knees to her chest, shoulders against the headboard, eyes popped wide and brain spinning over all she saw and heard, until the sun finally makes its dramatic morning appearance across the eastern sky.

Finally, she sleeps.

FORTY-SIX

MICHAEL ATTACHES a wireless camera to a mount on a tree facing the front door of the summer cabin. Maggie is logged into the cabin's password-less Wi-Fi, setting up the system through her laptop. The cameras' base station she put in a cabinet by the front door. Maggie bought a two-camera package at Walmart the day before, when she was taking a drunk Hank back to the hospital. Hank. The Hank she hasn't seen since dinner at the ranch the night before. At breakfast, Gene told her not to worry, but it's hard.

She examines the feed on her laptop. "Looks good. Now let's sync the other camera and mount it facing the back door."

They quickly sync it and install it. Michael says as little as possible during the whole process. He seems to be waiting for the boom. For her questions about Penny and Andy. But she's too exhausted to quiz him.

It's more than that, though. After the weird events in the middle of the night, she's unsettled. In the barn at the feeding earlier, she kept looking over her shoulder. Here, now, she has a strange sensation that someone is watching her. She doesn't know if she's looking for the mysterious shadowy figure or Paco, but she knows her sonar is pinging like mad.

Maggie closes her laptop. "I think we can take off now. Thank you." She heads for Bess.

Michael follows her. It's his first time at the cabin, and while he has played it cool, she's seen his big, amazed eyes. She knows just how he feels. It's an impressive place.

He stops, head cocked. "Is someone living here?"

"Why do you ask?"

"The tire tracks on the road when we were driving up. And I thought I saw someone in the window upstairs just now."

Shadows and light, she thinks. *Don't let this rattle you, too.* But Hank had said the same thing the day before. "Hank and I were up here yesterday. But I don't see a vehicle. How could someone be up here without one?"

Michael shrugs. "They could park in the barn."

Her eyes cut to it then back to the cabin. He's right. It could be an unwelcome visitor. Or maybe this is where Hank hides out when he's not fit for human companionship. Could he have stayed here last night? For a second, she considers knocking on the door, but then gets in the truck instead. If Hank's in there, she doesn't want to talk to him in front of Michael. She can come back later, if Hank doesn't show up by lunch. *Or not,* she thinks, remembering the footprint Hank saw yesterday.

An hour later Maggie and Michael are back at the ranch building a goat pen. Michael warms slowly as it becomes clear that Maggie won't be badgering him. She clamps a goat panel to a green metal post. Michael drives in another post with the T-post driver. She hears a grinding sound she can't identify and looks around for the source. Nothing seems to match it.

Michael's voice ends her search. "Last one." He wipes sweat from his brow with the inside of his shirt neck.

He's driven four more posts while she's been standing there in a daze. She's a mess. Maybe he won't notice.

"Thanks." She puts another clamp in place and grips it with pliers. Her hands shake.

"You okay?"

She twists the thick metal ends of the clamp. "I'm just thinking about Mrs. Sibley. I wish I'd built this pen for the goats before she died. They drove her crazy."

"I don't think the pen would have helped with that."

She half smiles. "You're probably right. I just feel guilty."

A shadow falls across the panel she's working on. "I've got it from here, Michael."

Michael snaps to attention. "Yes, sir, Mr. Sibley." He disappears with the driver and an extra post before Maggie can disentangle herself from the panel.

"I saw you coming back to the ranch in the truck with him."

But from where, Hank? She holds in the game of twenty questions she wants to throw him into, right before she whups his ass. It will go better if she lets him tell her of his own volition. "So?"

"He's a felon, Maggie. Trouble. You need to stay away from him."

"He *works* for you, Hank."

"For now."

His eyes are black and hollow. Maggie knows what that means. It steals her breath away. "Gotcha."

She brushes dirt from the seat of her pants. Hank takes the pliers from her and leans over at the waist to get a clamp, then kicks a leg out for balance. With his tool and clamp, he squats and fastens the panels to the posts far faster than Maggie. He works without speaking. When the last panel is secured, he leaves one side loose as a temporary gate. Maggie hands him a chain latch. He loops it through and clips it back on itself, testing it.

"You can keep Louise in here, too."

"Why? Is she causing problems?"

"She left a dead squirrel on the porch this morning."

"That. Okay."

The awkwardness between them gets worse as they walk to fetch the animals. She halters the goats. Hank takes Omaha, and she leads Nebraska. She whistles for Louise. The goats bleat and fight the leads the whole walk over. Louise meets them at the pen. Maggie closes the gate when all three are inside.

"Crap. I forgot to put their food and water in."

Hank walks to the barn without further comment.

Maggie stands at the pen, fuming. So he's done and just walks away, without even explaining where he was last night? Why can't he just tell her he runs to the summer cabin? Give her that little bit of comfort? Anger propels her forward. She marches into the barn with a head of steam. A farrier's truck is pulling away when she gets there. Grinding. Horseshoes, she realizes.

"Where the hell were—?" She runs into Hank, and a full bucket of water sloshes on her.

Hank lifts the bucket shoulder high. "Watch out."

Maggie slings water off her arms and brushes it from the front of her jacket and her jeans. Her indignation fades. "Thanks. I'll get their feed."

She catches up with Hank at the pen. Louise is sitting in front of the gate, sweeping dirt with her tail and looking hopefully into Hank's eyes.

"I think you're all set." His face is inscrutable. He turns to go.

"Wait."

He stops and faces her.

"Thank you."

"Of course." He takes a step back, pivots, and starts striding toward the barn again.

She raises her voice. "I was up last night. You were gone."

He freezes but doesn't turn back.

"I was worried. Where were you?"

"Couldn't sleep."

"Like I asked. Where were you?"

The pause is heavy.

"I needed to be alone."

His boots start crunching again, but she doesn't watch him go. She's too busy staring at the dirt. The old Maggie would tell him she didn't deserve his bullshit. But his mother just died. His brain injury is an issue. So the Maggie who's trying to make the relationship work won't rip him a new one yet. But she's not sure how much longer she can hold out.

FORTY-SEVEN

Laura and Hank leave for the funeral home before lunch. Maggie only knows this because she runs into them on their way out when she's coming to the house to wash up. Laura nods at her in a more friendly way than she has in the past. Hank isn't unfriendly. He just isn't anything, other than factual.

Maggie walks them to Hank's truck.

"Back before dinner," he says, and gets in the driver's seat.

She watches them drive away. They turn north at the ranch gate toward skies dark gray with the promise of a storm. Well, she's not just going to sit around here and mope all day. Andy is still facing trial for murder, and she needs to figure out whether Mary or her husband are viable suspects. And she has an idea about how to finagle a conversation with Mary.

Louise. The dog needs vaccinations, heartworm medicine, and an exam. She can't get signal, so she returns to the house and makes a call to the clinic.

"Sheridan Vet." The voice is raspy and bleak.

"Is Mary Marton working today?" Maggie asks.

"You a friend of hers?"

"Uh, yes, sort of."

"Yeah, she's here."

"I've taken in a stray. This will be her initial visit. Do you have any time to see her today?"

"Doc's going into surgery at one. How fast can you get here?"

"Forty-five minutes."

"Yeah, we can squeeze you in."

Maggie makes it to the clinic on the southeast side of Sheridan in forty-six minutes from the time she ended the call. Louise strains against the leash on the sidewalk, pulling Maggie along for frantic examinations of garden gnomes, dog statuary, and a sign that says DOG RELIEF AREA. Once inside the tiny lobby, Louise goes bananas. The bags of dog treats. The Chihuahua in her owner's lap. The cat carrier, filled with a hissing cat, sitting on a chair. Maggie hauls her to the front desk, away from the cowering Chihuahua owner with the judgmental eyes.

The woman behind the desk looks like she's wintered outside for forty years, with wind-tanned skin, furrows instead of wrinkles, and hair like a Brillo pad.

Maggie says to her, "I called about bringing in my new stray."

The woman nods. "Can you control it?"

"The dog?"

The woman looks down her nose at Maggie. "I'm not talking about your bladder, lady."

Maggie senses a soul sister. "Not so much."

"I'll put you in an exam room to wait, then."

"Thanks."

"Yes, thanks," the Chihuahua owner says, her voice snotty.

Maggie considers letting Louise go and imagines the satisfying havoc. But instead she and Louise walk behind the receptionist to a boxy room with a stainless steel examination table and a bench on one wall.

"Mary will be along shortly. Doc, too."

"Sounds good."

Not a minute later, the staff door opens. Mary's curves are mostly covered by blue scrubs.

Her face is puzzled. "Have we met before?"

Maggie sticks out her hand. Mary takes it and shakes before Maggie answers.

"Yes. I'm Maggie. Hank Sibley's girlfriend. We met at the Ox last week. And a few other times."

Mary's eyes widen. "Oh. Yes." She smiles. "Sorry about Sheila. She's not taking the breakup well."

Maggie doesn't want to talk about Sheila. "This is Louise. She's a stray from Piney Bottoms ranch. I'm pretty sure she's never had vet care before."

"They do their own preventative care out there."

"She's my personal pet."

"Gotcha." Mary runs through a list of questions about Louise, most of which Maggie can't answer. "We need to test her for heartworm before we can put her on a preventative. But I'll go get the rest of the vaccinations ready." She rattles off their names. "Do you want all of them?"

"Yes."

"Doc will be in to examine her in a minute."

Before she can leave, Maggie says, "So you dated Paco."

Mary's face blanches. "Can you keep it down?"

"Sorry." Maggie lowers her voice to a conspiratorial tone. "Penny said Paco told her your husband wasn't very happy about it."

"We're trying to make things work." Mary puts her hands on her hips. "Paco had a big mouth. Penny still does."

The staff door opens again. Doc Billy enters.

Maggie says, "Hello, Doc Billy. We've met, out at Piney Bottoms. I'm the one who rides Lily."

He nods distractedly. "I remember. Sorry to be in a rush. We've got a dog about to go under sedation." He starts examining Louise, poking and prodding her, and says over his shoulder, "Honey, tell me about the dog."

Mary shoots a look at Maggie. "Sure, Billy." She repeats what she knows about Louise to him.

Maggie stares between the two of them. She remembers Mary's Facebook page. Husband: William Marton. William. *Billy*. Doc Billy. Of course. Gears start to mesh in her mind. How nice that with Paco dead the two of them can try again. Then Maggie flinches like she's been poked with a cattle prod. Whoever killed Paco had to have access to the ranch. Doc Marton is out at the ranch a lot. Sure, so are a lot of people. Even the farrier today. But Doc Billy had motive. And he knows about the dead pile.

"Maggie, are you okay?" Mary says.

"Fine. Yes. You were saying?"

"I asked you whether or not you'd like Louise on a flea, tick, and tapeworm preventative?"

"Um, sure."

"She looks healthy as a horse," Doc Billy says. He takes off his exam gloves. "Nice to see you again, Maggie."

He puts his hand on Mary's shoulder, and they walk out together.

"Holy shit," Maggie says to Louise. "Holy frickin' shit."

On her phone, she looks up the website of John Fortney's law firm for his contact information. Email, that's what she wants. She writes one to the attorney as fast as she can thumb-type and hits SEND. Her next call is to Travis. She leaves him a message about what she's learned. She hasn't completely lost faith in Sheridan County yet.

FORTY-EIGHT

Back at the ranch, Maggie is still riding high from her discovery at the clinic. She puts Louise back in with the goats. The weather is continuing to worsen, and it looks like the rest of the day will be best spent inside. She goes in and washes her hair. While she's drying it she checks her phone. She has an email from Fortney.

"The other-guy-did-it defense. Works for me. Thanks!"

She feels a sense of progress. When her hair is dry, she decides to bring Louise up to the house. She puts on a sweatshirt and a fleece jacket. As she's walking out to the pen, she hears a commotion at the barn over the sound of the wind.

Andy's voice. He's yelling. "Get back in there. No. All of you. No. Bad dog."

A barreling gust of wind hits. The temperature feels like it's dropping a degree a second. She zips her jacket collar to her chin. A fully enclosed Ranger approaches her. Andy and Michael are in it, dressed for a norther. She hustles to meet them. At least Andy doesn't know Michael is the reason Penny broke off their very short-lived engagement. Still, they both look tense.

On the passenger side, Andy cracks his door open.

"Louise let the goats out." Andy points in the distance. "And Lily."

"How'd she do that?" Maggie shouts to be heard over the idling engine.

"No idea."

"I'm sorry."

"No, I am. There's a storm coming, and we've got to tend to the rest of the livestock. That dog is trouble, but she's crazy smart. They'll probably come in them own selves. But if they don't, best you wait for Hank, okay?"

She looks north. The dark gray sky feels like it's closing in on them. Already her fleece jacket isn't enough to ward off the cold. "Do you need my help out there?"

"No, but thanks. It's a two-man job."

"Be careful."

Andy salutes and Michael accelerates toward the ominous wall of clouds. The wind rumbles like a runaway freight train. Dirt swirls in the driveway. Even the eaves whistle. She scans the pastureland and ridgelines within sight. No big black mare. No little red goats. No fast, low-slung dog with flapping ears. Andy told her to stay put, but she can't do nothing. She'll just look around the central ranch grounds, stay close to the compound. But first she needs better clothes for the conditions.

While she's upstairs changing, she hears the front door slam against the wall.

"Hello?"

No one answers her. The sound of the wind increases, and it beats the door rhythmically against the wall downstairs. Whap. Whap. Whap. She hears scratching and bumping on the stairs, then a knock against her door.

Her heart does a flip-flop. "Who's there?"

The familiar sound of Louise trying to dig her way through the door breaks her tension. She opens the door, and fifty pounds of cold fur barrels into her legs.

"You're a bad girl." Maggie rubs the dog's ears to warm them.

Louise flops on the floor and wriggles. Maggie goes to the window to look for the other animals. Icy snowflakes pelt the glass, but she can still see down to the barnyard. Omaha and Nebraska are standing in the entrance to the barn, no fools they. But Lily is nowhere to be seen. Not at the barn, the paddocks, not grazing in the yard to the house. Somehow the thought of her with two noisy goats and a superhero dog wasn't as terrifying as the thought of her alone. Big and quiet, with a horse's predilection for injury, and a baby on board—Maggie doesn't like it.

Maggie runs down and shuts the front door, then finishes gearing up. She grabs her knife and scabbard along with the ATV driving goggles she uses against dust and sun. They should help with the blowing snow.

She opens the door, letting the storm in the great room with a whoosh of wind. "Come on, Louise."

The dog cowers behind the couch.

"Oh no. This is your fault. I need your help."

Reluctantly, the dog comes after her, hunkering low and moving fast. At the barn, Maggie puts the goats up in a stall. She grabs the keys to an extra Ranger and fires it up. Louise jumps into the seat beside her. Maggie drives out of the barn. Even with the plexiglass windshield and plastic doors, the wind comes right through. Louise hops down onto the floorboard, where she's more protected.

For fifteen minutes, Maggie drives in circles around the house. She grows more confident about driving and more concerned about Lily as time passes. By now, Maggie is wise to Lily's favorite flight paths. She's exhausted all her close-in spots. Maggie will have to go farther out.

For a moment, she second-guesses herself. Lily is a big, strong animal, and she's smart. But she's alone. And if anything happens to her, especially after fucking Louise let her out, Maggie will never forgive herself. If only she'd kept Louise inside. It's her fault.

Despair wells up in her. She's failing at this ranch-hand thing. Failing like she fails at everything. Faking it like she's faking everything these days. Faking at being a Crow. At being a Wyomingite. At being a girlfriend. Things are so much easier for her in Texas. She knows how to be a junker, a washed-up singer, and a free-and-easy single woman. Suddenly, it's hard to breathe. All her life she's been the risk-taker, ready to jump. Running off to Nashville at seventeen. Touring the country playing for tips at eighteen. Even trading the rights to her recordings for her shop and house in Giddings in her early twenties had been a huge risk.

But those risks had been about her music and her livelihood. Now that it's her heart at stake, it's not nearly so easy to be brave and real. To tell Hank she loves him. To commit to a future with him. To confront him about not shutting her out.

Going after Lily isn't nearly as hard as those things. She points the Ranger into the wind and guns the engine. Whether Maggie is faking it or not, Lily is out there, and Maggie's the only one who can help her.

FORTY-NINE

AN HOUR HAS PASSED, and there's been no sign of Lily. The snow is falling horizontally, and it's almost a whiteout. Maggie follows fence lines to keep herself from getting lost. Twice she's come upon hulking black objects, but both times she finds cows huddled in small groups. Sweat drips down her face. How can she be so cold and so hot at the same time? She wiggles her fingers. There's barely any feeling in them or her toes. She's not sure how much longer she can stay out here. The gas gauge on the Ranger doesn't work, and running out of gas in this storm would be bad news for a flat-lander like her.

It's time to head back in. She hates it, but she knows it is.

She decides to make a circuit of the fence in one last pasture, even though it's not one of Lily's haunts. The land out here is wild, she knows, prone to unseen gulches, rock formations, steep hills, mini-cliffs, and irrigation ditches. There's no two-track inside this fence as there has been in the others. The Ranger putts along slow and steady, up, down, and over terrain and obstacles unfamiliar to her.

Suddenly the steering wheel is wrenched from her hands, and the whole unit tips. With no seatbelt to hold her in place, Maggie braces herself against the steering wheel and floorboard. The Ranger lands on its side, ripping its door apart. Louise falls on top of Maggie's side, but Maggie manages to hold them both suspended over the snowy, rocky ground. The roof is on the downhill side, and the ATV begins to slide. Snow and mud cover Maggie head to toe in seconds. There's a painful scraping sound and the Ranger comes to a jarring stop.

"Oomph." Maggie shakes her arms and legs and rotates her neck. She's all right.

But the Ranger isn't. She opens the other door. Dog and woman crawl out. Maggie takes a few steps around the Ranger to inspect it. There's no way she can right the thing. She feels as much as hears a crunch and finds her driving goggles under her boot.

"Come on, Louise." Maggie scrambles on her hands and knees to the top of the ravine. She holds her hands out and walks slowly until she finds the fence, which just skirts the top of it, leaving no room for an ATV to pass, which would explain why she ended up at the bottom of the little gulch.

Just as she's about to retrace their path and start the long, cold walk home, she hears a whinny.

"Lily!"

A horse whinnies again. In the wind and weather, Maggie can't get a fix on the direction the sound is coming from. She doesn't even know for sure if it is Lily. But she can't go back in without checking, when the horse is so close.

She follows the fence out in the direction they'd been headed, calling every few seconds. Without the goggles, Maggie is nearly blind, even with her scarf wrapped around her forehead as a shield. She and Louise trudge on.

Then Louise barks once, a shrill yip. Maggie takes another step, then another, calling for Lily, and runs into something large and unyielding.

FIFTY

MAGGIE SCREAMS AND JUMPS BACK, but not before she realizes the something is also warm, and it snorts. She moves back to it and brushes snow from a big animal's back and uncovers black fur. She works her way to the head and gets a big puff of Lily's breath in her face.

She smashes her face into Lily's long, hard one, holding the horse's head with both hands. "You big, dumb horse. What are you doing out here? Why do you always have to be so damn independent? Look what it gets you. In trouble. Alone." She lifts her head, kisses Lily's velvety muzzle. "Let's go home."

Maggie is wearing a halter and lead over her torso, bandolier style. Lily submits easily to them. But when Maggie gives the lead a tug, the horse doesn't move an inch. Steadily increasing pressure does nothing either. Lily huffs.

"What's the matter, girl?" Maggie strokes her nose. She gets out her phone and uses the flashlight to inspect the animal.

Barbed wire is wrapped around three of Lily's legs. Panic rises like a tsunami in Maggie's chest. "Oh no, Lily. Don't move."

She pulls her knife from the scabbard. But Lily isn't in rope and bramble like last time she'd rescued her. This is wire. And what good is a knife against wire?

Think, Maggie, think. She's going to have to unwind the wire to get Lily free. Thank God the horse is standing still instead of giving in to the instinct to fight against pressure. Squatting, Maggie searches hand over hand for an end to the wire. She can't unwrap Lily only to send her into more. She traces the piece to a post, where she finds four individual strands attached, all of which lead back to Lily. A whole fence's worth.

There are no ends. The fence is down. Lily walked into it.

Okay. That's all right. You can do this. One strand at a time.

She crouches by the least tangled strand. Louise presses against her, and Maggie appreciates the dog's warmth and loyalty. "It's okay, Lily. Good girl." She takes a deep breath and starts pulling the wires apart, inch by inch. Her gloves are shredded in seconds. She takes them off and works bare-handed. Now the wire nips at her skin. Blood drips into the snow, and she's not sure if it is coming from her or the horse. The cold makes her fingers stiff. She can barely feel the wires. Lily snorts and shifts her weight, but she doesn't move her feet, even when Maggie removes barbs embedded in her hide.

"Such a good girl, Lily." She strokes the horse's belly, then gets back to work.

It takes about ten minutes for Maggie to liberate the first strand. She moves it as far as she can out of the way, then repeats the process with the other three pieces. It's hard to stick with it. Her feet feel like pincushions from the cold. The wind is burning her face and making her eyes water so badly that she can barely see what she's doing. But she can't give up, and she's desperately glad she came. Lily was—is—in trouble and needs her.

When she finally has all the barbed wire far to one side of the mare, she runs her numb hands up and down Lily's legs. Her fingers come away bloody. She sweeps her forearms under Lily's enormous belly. The foal kicks out. Her arms come away bloody.

Maggie tries not to panic. It's a long way back to the ranch house, and Lily is injured. It's too dark to see how badly. She can only assume it's better to walk her in than to leave her out here, but what does she know? Moving her could make it worse. There's no one here to make the decision for her, though. She puts her tattered gloves back on and makes the call—they're going home.

"Come on, big girl."

This time, Lily offers no resistance to being led. They walk the fence in the blowing snow, the only sounds their breathing and the wind. Occasionally, Maggie has to high-step through drifts above her knees. Louise lunges and leaps to get through them and disappears under snow with each landing. The exercise keeps Maggie's core warm, although now she's sweating so hard her clothes are wet from the inside out. The only thing really cold anymore is her face, feet, and hands, and the ripped gloves aren't helping matters much. At times she can't feel the rope in her hands. Or, when she does, the line is so slack she doesn't think Lily is back there. But she is. The horse knows where they are going, and she's on board.

Time slows to a crawl. Maggie isn't sure how long it takes them to reach the two-track at the corner of the pasture. It could have been fifteen minutes or it could have been an hour. She's tired. Very tired. And sleepy. In her flashes of alertness, she has a new worry. What if she passes out?

In the distance, she sees lights blinking. At first, she's worried she's taken a wrong turn. Those can't be the ranch lights. But then she sees them moving. It's some kind of vehicle. But who, and how far away?

"Hey!" she yells. "Over here." *Idiot. They can't hear you. They can't even see you.*

She urges the horse and dog faster, worried about Lily hurting herself worse, but even more worried they'll freeze to death in their own dead pile. The snow is packed somewhat from her Ranger tracks, so the going is easier. Trotting, they make the next fence line, intersecting the path of the approaching lights. Maggie waves frantically, which makes Lily back a step. Maggie loses her balance and falls after the horse onto her butt. She hears the puny honk of an ATV, and Maggie waves from the ground in relief.

FIFTY-ONE

MICHAEL DOCTORS Lily as the storm rages against the barn walls.

"Is she going to be okay?" Maggie asks.

"Yeah." He pats the mare's haunch. "Horses heal fast. Faster than people. You'll hurt worse than she does."

Maggie's hands had looked like bloody pincushions, purple and swollen from cold, but they're washed, dabbed with ointment, and wrapped now. "Do we need to call in the vet?" Doc Billy isn't someone she trusts or wants to see. But she'll suck it up, if Lily needs him.

"Nah. She's good. Can I walk you back to the house? We'll be fired if we lose you twice in one day."

Andy walks into the barn, dusting snow off his jacket. He doesn't look at Michael, and Maggie feels the ongoing tension between them.

"How'd you know I was gone the first time?"

Andy answers. "I was closing up the barn, and the Ranger was missing. Didn't take much to figure after that, since you and that mutt were gone, too. You didn't even take one of the walkie-talkies." He puts one back on the charging station. "So I took one and waited here, and Michael went with the other in the ATV."

"I'm so sorry. I feel like an idiot. I'll take the offer of the escort, Michael, but let me feed Lily first."

Maggie mixes an ounce of Mare Magic in sweet feed. She hopes it's helping strengthen Lily's uterus, because it hasn't stopped her running off.

Maggie opens a stall door and pours feed into a trough. Then she leads the horse in.

"What will I do about you when I'm back in Texas?" Lily doesn't appear to listen, all her attention on the oats, corn, and molasses. "I sure can't go until after your foal comes." She thinks about the appointment she made to meet with the contractor. Maybe she can push it back some.

"What happened here?" Hank is standing in the doorway to the barn.

Andy has disappeared. Michael is cleaning up veterinary supplies. His hands and clothes are stained with blood.

Michael looks nervous. "Lily got out, then caught herself in some barbed wire."

Hank's eyes lift. He looks in Lily's stall and sees Maggie, with her two bandaged hands. "Maggie." He hurries to her and grabs her by the wrists, holding her hands in the air. "What happened to you?"

"Lily's barbed wire."

"You went out with them to get her?"

"Not really."

Hank frowns. "What does that mean?" Then he turns to Michael. "Give us the barn, please."

Michael doesn't need to be asked twice. "I have to meet someone in town anyway. Chores are all done. Good night."

"Good night, Michael." Maggie lifts her chin at Hank. "I went alone."

"How?"

"A Ranger. And I remembered to take this." She holds up her knife in its scabbard, hoping to lighten the mood.

He glowers, his eyes taking inventory around the barn. Maggie sees the second he starts counting machinery and comes up short.

"Where's the Ranger?" he demands.

"About that. I'll pay for the damage."

"You wrecked it?"

"I'm really sorry."

"You could have gotten yourself killed out there."

"But I didn't. And Louise and Lily are fine, too."

"You're too damned independent for your own good. But I guess that shouldn't surprise me. You've been running off since the day I met you."

"I didn't run off. I went to find Lily. That fucker Louise had let her out. Michael and Andy told me not to go, but I wasn't going to be able to live with myself if she got hurt or died."

"Great. You could have gotten the hands killed, too."

"But I didn't."

"And every time I turn around, you're holed up with Michael."

"That's ridiculous."

"Maggie, I'm having a rough week, in case you haven't noticed. I need something I can count on. You're not it."

Her first thought is that his brain injury is making him irrational. "Bullshit. You can count on me and you know it."

"Really?" He points at her. "I read your phone last night."

"You what?"

"You have meetings set up with contractors in Texas. Next week."

A meeting. Singular. Her second thought was that the pot was sure the hell calling the damn kettle black, but she's too busy defending herself to point it out. "I was going to tell you. There hasn't been a chance."

"But you didn't." Hank stomps out of the barn.

"I was going to reschedule," she calls after him. Then, softer, "I'm sorry."

He disappears into the snow. Then she realizes what she should have said instead, those words she can't get out. That she loves him. Because she does. She's in love with Hank, and she wants to help him through his injury and the loss of his mother. She's in love, and it feels fucking . . . terrifying. Can she do this love thing? Because right now it feels like she's messing it up big-time.

Maggie shuts Lily in her stall, then walks alone through the storm back to the house. She enters, then sinks back against the door and sits on her heels with her head in her hands.

FIFTY-TWO

Maggie wakes to the sound of loud snoring. She smiles. Hank. She rolls over, and Louise licks her face.

"Not you, Fucker."

Thump-thump-thump goes a tail.

Hank had been here when she fell asleep—sullen, uncommunicative—but he's clearly not here now. She wishes she'd found the courage to tell him how she feels. She kept waiting last night, waiting for a perfect time that didn't come. But in the light of day, she knows the perfect time is a fallacy. *Now* is the perfect time, and *now* passes by all too quickly. Case in point, Mrs. Sibley's funeral is set for Tuesday. Time marches on. People lose each other. She needs to make the most of every moment with Hank.

"Hank?" she calls.

No answer from the bathroom or hallway. He's probably already out working, because of the storm. Animal welfare comes first. Maggie's nose is cold and her breath makes an icy cloud in front of her face. Sunlight is streaming through the window. Her phone sounds a notification from the bedside table. She picks it up. It's a motion alarm from the cameras at the summer cabin. In the small picture on her phone and with her bleary eyes, she sees the figure of a man, thick like he's bundled against the weather. Then her phone rings. *Hank.* She can't read the caller ID. She picks up anyway.

"Hello?"

"Hello, honey. It's Mom."

"Mom. Good morning. What time is it?"

"Seven thirty."

"Which makes it six thirty here."

"Oh no, did I wake you?"

Ya think? "It's fine. What's up?"

"I led women's Bible study at my house last night, and I just wanted you to know that it came over my heart that we should pray for you. We set up a prayer chain, and I've been calling the entire congregation this morning."

"Why? What did I do this time?" She checks the irritation in her voice. She shouldn't complain. She can use all the help she can get. "Never mind. I know why."

"Is it so bad to want you where you belong?"

"And where is that?"

"Back here, happily married, within your own faith?"

"Mom, I think we've been doubling back on this tired old gene pool long enough. Besides, don't you think that's ironic coming from a woman who just married outside the faith?"

"He's a Christian."

Maggie thinks of the Amish Christians, the Wendish Christians, Edward's Catholic faith, and Hank's cowboy Christian. There's Christian, and then there's Christian. "So is Hank."

"Everyone needs their own people, Maggie."

"I've got what I need."

"Do you? You're just like your mother."

"You're my mother."

"No, your birth mother. Running off from everyone and everything good in her life."

"Who says I'm running?" Her mother's words ring in her ears, an echo of Hank's. "Mom, this conversation is going nowhere. Thank you for praying for me. I love you. Now, I have to go. It's time for breakfast here. I'll talk to you soon."

"Maggie—"

Maggie ends the call and presses her fist to her mouth. Her mother thinks she's running from Texas. Hank's accusing her of running from Wyoming, and him. They can't both be right. But they could both be wrong. She's not running. She isn't.

And she's nothing like her birth mother.

The phone rings again. Sighing, she answers. She shouldn't have hung up on her mom.

"I'm sorry."

"Good, so meet me for breakfast at the Busy Bee." Not her mother.

"Who is this?"

"Amos. Is your caller ID not working?"

"I'm hanging up now."

"No. Not until I tell you I'm sorry."

"This I have to hear. Sorry for what?"

"For before. When you were on my radio show. I was a different person back then. I was angry at you for a long time. I blamed you that I was fired after that. But I don't anymore. I caused my own problems. And if I hurt you, I'm sorry."

"That's a lot of sorry to absorb."

"I think that's why I started writing about you. I've been following you a long time. For no good reason. I don't want revenge. I just needed to say that."

"What if I don't forgive you?"

"That's okay. And I still want to finish my story on you. Can you meet me?"

Louise noses her hand—sore, but unbandaged—and Maggie massages the dog's floppy ears. She wriggles until her upper body is splayed over Maggie's. Maggie chews her lip. She hasn't made up her mind about recording with Ava, but if she does, publicity sells records. The redemption of Aaron Cryor and Maggie Killian, two for the price of one. And isn't it far better if it's on her own terms? He's going to write about her anyway. This could be a trial balloon. If it were to go well, maybe she'd give Amos an interview with her and Boyd.

"Fine."

"One of these days, you're going to—Wait. Did you say 'fine'?"

"Yes."

"You won't regret it. What time?"

"How are the roads?"

"Bad, I think. But this is Wyoming. The plows have probably been out all night."

"Give me an hour. If I'm not there, order me scrambled eggs, hash browns, and bacon. And coffee. A lot of coffee."

FIFTY-THREE

Trudy is changing channels on the big-screen TV in the community room when Maggie gallops down the stairs in heavy winter boots. She fastens her scabbard to the belt loop of her jeans, then pulls her long, loose sweater over it. She straightens the Frontier Days belt that makes the sweater like a tunic. Today she's not driving off anything less than fully prepared for whatever Wyoming has to dish out.

"Wait. You missed breakfast. Let me bring you a biscuit and some coffee."

"I'm having breakfast in town. But thanks. Hey, have you seen Hank?"

Trudy returns her attention to the TV. "He took off after breakfast in the truck."

So he was at the ranch for breakfast. Maggie doesn't like that he didn't say good morning or goodbye. In fact, she's pissed about it. He could have texted. Left a note. Called. She's sick of him acting like the world is ending and she's not his partner. His mother died. It's very, very sad. But not her fault.

Maggie's voice is bright as she adds a scarf, wool cap, and mittens to her gear. "Okay, thanks. If you see him, tell him I'm in Buffalo."

"Will do. Be careful. The roads are bad."

Fingers flying, Maggie texts Hank. *WTF, cowboy? Maybe I should start taking off without telling you, too?* Her thumb hovers. She can tell him herself that she's going to Buffalo in this text. Or not. She hits SEND.

Maggie waves goodbye to Trudy, who heads back into the kitchen.

Maggie opens the door. A frigid wind knocks her back. She tucks the scarf into the neck of her puffy jacket and wraps the end over her face. Louise bounds out, dipping her nose in the snow and tossing some in the air with her mouth. Maggie stomps to her truck. It isn't deep—maybe three or four inches—and it's powdery soft. She turns on her truck to let it heat up while she gets after her windshields with an ice scraper. This isn't going to be a warm or fun ride to town. A quick double check confirms she has a shovel, towrope, and chains in the bed and a blanket, bag of kitty litter, waters, flares, a first aid kit, and food bars of some sort under the front seat. Absent a satellite phone, she's remote-Wyoming-ready.

Forty-five slow and careful minutes later, she pulls into Buffalo. Amos was right. The plows were out, and the interstate is snow- and ice-free. But when she nears the Busy Bee, she discovers a police blockade in front of the courthouse.

She rolls to a stop and an officer comes to her window. It's Detective Lacey, a cop she became much too familiar with back in August when he zeroed in on Maggie as a murder suspect. His white-blond hair almost blends with the snow. His light blue eyes crinkle at the corners when he recognizes her. She'd pretty much solved his case for him, and she's not sure how he feels about that. Spoiler alert: the murderer wasn't her.

"Ms. Killian. Good to see you back. We've got a detour. If you can just turn right here, and skirt the downtown area, please."

"What happened?"

He checks the road behind her. It's clear of approaching vehicles. "Don't quote me on this, but there was a double murder back there." He points at the parking lot behind the courthouse.

Maggie's familiar with it. She'd parked there just last week when she and Andy went to the Thursday Night Jam at the Ox. "Oh my God. Who was it?"

"I don't know anything other than they're early twenties, an Indian girl and boy. And if I did know, I couldn't tell you until we notify next of kin. But keep it to yourself, okay?" He motions her on as another car pulls up behind her.

Maggie coasts along, thinking about the boy and girl found dead. Her stomach clenches. It's not like there aren't lots of Native Americans in the area, plenty of them in their early twenties, but the fact that she knows two has her heart in a vice grip. She cuts her wheels hard to the left, sliding across two lanes of oncoming traffic. Her tires lose traction and she slams into the curb hard enough that a newer truck would have deployed airbags. Her forehead bangs against steering wheel.

"Shit."

She takes a moment to straighten the truck, then pushes in the clutch, shifts into park, and turns off the ignition. She run-skates as fast as she can across the lawn of the Sheridan College annex, to the courthouse parking. When she's almost there, she slips on an icy patch and goes down hard on her tush.

"Son of a bitch."

She stares at the sky, her neck jarred and her butt smarting, a painful reminder of being thrown by Lily. When she's back on her feet, she moves more slowly, all the way to the police tape. An ambulance is parked fifteen feet away. She sees booted feet, pointed toes-up. Another set with the toes of the boots splayed. Nothing definitive for identification, until her eyes fall on the beat-up banjo case covered in bumper stickers. Even from where she's standing, she can see her own signature scrawled on it.

Penny.

With all the death in her life in the last few months, Maggie should be used to the blow to her solar plexus. But she's not. She clutches her midsection. Penny was an enigma. Maggie hadn't been in favor of Andy marrying her. But she was a living, breathing person, a beautiful girl, and a talented musician. She didn't deserve to be killed. Few people do.

One of the crime scene techs stands up, holding something in her gloved hand. Her movement leaves a sightline to the two people on the ground. The boy has a strong, recognizable profile.

It's Michael, Maggie is sure of it. She stifles a cry with her mittened fist. She can't tear her eyes away. She'd grown to care about him. Talks to Eagles had been kind to her. He'd be telling her right now that his spirit is heading skyward for another conversation with his friend.

The crime scene tech turns. A black object in her hand catches Maggie's attention. It looks like a knife. Maggie leans as far as she can across the barrier, then nearly collapses when she gets a crystal-clear view of a Double S logo. Hank's knife.

FIFTY-FOUR

MAGGIE CAN'T GET BACK on the road to the Double S fast enough. She drives without conscious thought, the miles flying by without her worrying anymore about the conditions. Just as she's slowing to take the exit from the interstate, an owl flies in front of the truck. A witch, Michael would have said. *And Louise not here to protect me.*

Maggie jerks her foot off the gas and fights the urge to swerve, but her automatic reaction is faster. The truck rumbles off the highway. If she over-corrects now, she'll flip back onto the blacktop. If she doesn't correct, she'll go over the embankment and down a good thirty feet before she hits the bottom. Holding her breath, she steers gently back toward the off-ramp and braces her leg under the steering wheel. The wheels grab pavement, and she navigates into the lane. The exit is steep and curved, so she isn't able to stop until she's made it safely through her turn and is on flatter road.

She pulls over, panting.

Her life is so out of control. She could have died back there. She could have died yesterday in the ravine under a Ranger. Or frozen to death on top of the ridge tangled in barbed wire and stomped by a giant, pregnant horse. And all the deaths around her. She's never been around so much death as these last three months. Just within the last week, Paco was murdered, Mrs. Sibley has died, and now Penny and Michael are gone, too—Hank's knife beside their bodies.

She shudders. Hank's knife may have killed them. A knife that anyone who enters the ranch house could have taken, but that was in Hank's bedroom. Hank, who had disappeared in the night. Who's volatile and physical, and under emotional and physical pressure right now. Who's protective of her when it comes to Michael.

No. Other people have stronger motives. Mary was jealous of Penny. Andy had reason to hate Michael, and to resent Penny for breaking their engagement. It can't be Hank.

She realizes she's clutching the steering wheel with both hands, and that her arms and shoulders are rigid. She lets go, flexes her fingers. Her breathing slows down. Her heart eases in her chest, although it feels like it's left her bruised from its wild pounding. She picks up her phone, not to call anyone, but because it makes her feel connected to the rest of the world. Convinces her she's not dead in a snowdrift on the side of the interstate.

But of course she sees messages.

Amos: *Are you coming?*

Hank: *Where are you?*

Charlotte: *Why did you hang up on me?*

She gets a strong image of Lily in the barbed wire, except in her mind she's the one trapped.

To Amos: *Almost home. Must reschedule. Sorry.*

To Hank she thinks about telling him about the murders over text, but decides against it: *On my way back from Buffalo. I have to talk to you. Are you at the ranch?*

Her mother she skips. She'll deal with her later. Right now, she has to get back to the ranch and break the news to Andy before he hears Penny is dead from someone else.

Maggie runs into the house. Hank's truck isn't out front, but she calls for him. "Hank?"

Trudy appears, wiping her hands on a flour-dusted apron. "He's not back."

Maggie is out of breath. "Andy?"

"Nope. What's wrong?"

Maggie sprints to the barn without answering Trudy. "Andy, are you in here?" She hears a vehicle engine outside, then it shuts off. Footsteps, soft thuds in the snow, approach.

Andy appears from the hayloft. "Yes?" His head cocks, his eyes study her. "What's wrong?"

Maggie doesn't have time to explain before a Buffalo police officer walks in. Lacey.

"Ms. Killian."

"You're off traffic duty."

He nods and looks up at Andy. "Andrew Yoder?"

"Yes."

"I'm Detective Lacey, Buffalo Police Department. I'd like to ask you to come with me."

"Is he under arrest?" Maggie steps between the detective and Andy. Her need to protect him is strong, even as a horrible place inside her tells her that if they focus on Andy, they won't suspect Hank.

"No, just some questions for him."

"About what? What's going on?" Andy's confusion is giving way to panic, and his voice rises in pitch.

"Do you know a Penny Short and a Michael Short?"

Short. Both were named Short. Maggie doesn't understand. Were they *married*? Separated? Divorcing? That might explain Michael's reaction to Andy.

"Yes. Why?" Then he groans. "Oh God, no. Please, God, no. Don't let something have happened to Penny." Andy lurches and falls a few steps into the wall, where he holds himself up.

"Where were you last night, sir?" the officer asks.

"I, um, here?"

"Do you have any witnesses to corroborate your whereabouts between ten p.m. and four a.m.?"

Andy's eyes are wide and wild. "N-n-no, sir."

"They were murdered. We'd like to talk to you about it."

Andy nods. Tears gather in his eyes.

"Can't you talk to him here?" she says.

"We'd prefer not to."

She knows what Andy will say before he says it.

"It's fine."

Maggie takes his arm. "You know the drill, Andy. You're riding with me." She'll just have to tell Hank and Gene later. Andy is the first priority now.

FIFTY-FIVE

IN THE POLICE department reception area, Maggie waits for Andy. She kills time rearranging her schedule for the next week and soul-searching her options in Texas—Hank's absence makes it impossible to reach a decision. She'd thought Hank would respond after she group-texted him and Gene about Michael and Penny. Gene had. He was upset and also understandably worried about the ranch and finding a replacement for Michael, even more so after she told him the police had Andy in for questioning. She hadn't heard back from Hank.

"Ms. Killian?" the receptionist says.

Maggie gets up and walks over to her. "Yes?"

"Detective Lacey asked me to tell you he expects a long interview. Would you like me to text you when they're done?"

"Yes. Thank you." She recites her phone number.

Freed, Maggie walks down Main Street, with no enthusiasm for the cute stores. Luckily, she runs into Amos. She lets him interview her over a cup of coffee at the Busy Bee. It goes well enough. He'd heard about the murders and their link to Double S, but he doesn't spin it as related to her. At least not to her face. When they're done, she gets up to go.

"I really am sorry about before," he says.

"Thank you."

"I'll send you a link when I post an article."

"I hope I didn't make a mistake talking to you."

"You didn't. And text me if you have any news. Please."

"I'm not newsworthy."

"Let me be the judge of that."

Back outside, she stands at the railing of the bridge over Clear Creek and calls Travis, even though he'd never called back after her message about Mary and Doc Billy.

He picks up. "Ms. Killian."

"Deputy. Thanks for taking my call."

"I got a call from Lacey in Buffalo."

"So you already know about the deaths there."

"Long since."

She takes a quarter from her pocket and feeds it into a machine that dispenses fish food. Doling the pellets out one by one, she watches the trout dart from the shadows for the treats. "You're the one that pointed them toward Andy, aren't you?"

"I mentioned his name."

She throws another pellet. "I'm in Buffalo now, waiting on the police here to be done with him."

"And you're calling me why?"

"Andy and Penny were engaged." *With an emphasis on were,* she thinks, but doesn't elaborate. With Michael and Penny dead, who will there be to contradict the old information?

"So?"

"He adored her. He wouldn't hurt a hair on her head." A fish jumps out of the water to beat a competitor to a pellet.

"The greater the love, the greater the crazy. That's what we've been discussing with respect to your relationship."

She tosses the rest of the food, creating a frenzy in the water below. The fish thrash, their bodies like writhing serpents. Then the food is gone, and the turmoil ends. "I've never discussed my relationship with you."

"Fine. We've talked about Hank, then."

This is a subject she wants to avoid at all costs. "Did you follow up on the information I gave you about Mary Marton and Doc Billy yet? There's got to be something there. Mary was very jealous of Penny."

"Maggie, you're like a horse with blinders on. I'm doing my job. Now, if there's nothing else?"

Horse with blinders? Takes one to know one. "No. Nothing. You have a nice day, Detective."

She hangs up, fuming, and checks her texts. *Travis is so . . . so . . . so . . . smug. And close-minded.* Nothing from the police department receptionist. The gurgle of the creek is less now that the water level is fall-low, but it's still soothing. Taking deep breaths, she lets it do its magic on her until she's breathing calmly and freely again. She can only think of one more way to pass time, so she takes Bess to the gas station, parks at a pump, and starts filling her up.

"Maggie." A female voice makes her name a statement instead of a question or greeting.

Sheila. *What the hell is she doing in Buffalo?* Maggie looks at the display on the pump. She has a long way to go before the tank is full. "Sheila. You get around."

"I'm interviewing for an assistant principal's job here, not that it's any of your business."

Young, pretty, and ambitious. God, how Maggie hates this woman. "Do they need a character reference? I'd be happy to talk to them."

Sheila flips her hair, with her middle finger raised. "Where's Hank?"

Maggie gives her a dirty look.

"You don't know where he is, do you?" Sheila's smile is wide.

Maggie doesn't answer.

"I'll bet you were wondering if he was with me."

"As a matter of fact, no."

"Go ahead, ask me."

"Eff off, Sheila."

Sheila's boot heels grind salt as she walks into the c-store. Maggie swears she can hear her laughing. The nozzle clicks off. She returns it to the gas pump and puts the cap back on the tank, seething at Hank for going AWOL, at Sheila for general bitchiness, and at herself for letting Sheila manipulate her. Suddenly Maggie remembers that when Hank was sort of engaged to Sheila, he'd disappeared and ended up tied up in Maggie's bed. Never mind that Maggie wasn't the one who tied him up and that he nearly died, the fact remained that Hank had gotten cold feet and come after an ex.

No. That was different. He hasn't been with Sheila. Maggie and Hank are meant to be together. They both know it. It's why she's in Wyoming and sticking by a man with traumatic brain injury and unexplainable behavior. *Shit.* It doesn't sound good when she thinks about it that way. Is she being a fool? Even if Hank hasn't done anything worse than act erratically, is she crazy to hitch her wagon to him? She doesn't have to sign on for a life of helping him through the ups and downs from his old injury.

Does she?

A text notification comes in from the receptionist at the police station.

Andy is ready for her. She pushes her worries about Hank to the back of her mind for now.

Less than five minutes later, Andy is in the truck, wringing his hands. "Thank you. For everything."

"Of course. I'm so sorry about Penny. And Michael, although I know the two of you didn't get along that well."

His eyes are vacant. "She was in a family way."

Maggie doesn't understand. "What?"

"Penny. She was going to have a baby."

"Oh my God." Whose baby? She can't ask Andy.

"She was going to let me be the father, too. Until Michael messed it up."

Panic laps at Maggie. Did Andy kill Penny and Michael? "What are you saying?"

"I have to go home."

Even if he killed them, he's not a danger to her. This is Andy, after all. What was done in the heat of passion is not the core of who he is. "I'll get you back to Piney Bottoms as fast as I can."

"No, I mean I need to go to *my* home. In Montana."

She knows he's devastated. He's also even more exhausted than she is. But she doesn't get it. If anything, the Andy she knows would feel an even greater sense of responsibility to the ranch with Michael gone. "What's going on, Andy? Why home now?"

He wipes tears from his eyes, a furtive gesture. "I have to talk to my mother. I've brought shame on my family. She has to know from me I ain't done this, before she hears it from anyone else. I should have done it before, after Paco died, but it didn't seem real. Now it does. And I have to get to her."

Maybe he didn't kill anyone. God, she hopes not. "Okay. Do you want me to make a call for you to find a ride?"

He stares at his hands. "Could you maybe take me?"

"Um, no problem." She gets her phone out. "I need a minute, then we can be on our way."

His voice is strangled. "Thank you."

She texts Hank. *WHERE ARE YOU? I'm taking Andy home to Montana. I need your help.* She stares at the phone. *I need YOU.* She sends it, willing Hank's text bubble to appear. Willing a response to come in from him.

She gets nothing.

She gallops her fingernails on the steering wheel. Who is she kidding? Trusting Hank was a huge mistake. She needs to kick the rest of her life into gear. What was the name of that real estate agent who offered to list her place? She scans through her emails until she finds what she's looking for: an email from Trish Jasper. The woman's number is in it. Her finger hovers over it. She has to move forward. She can't stand still. She pushes it.

"This is Trish Jasper. May I help you find your dream home today?"

"Maybe. This is Maggie Killian."

"Maggie! Are you calling to list your property? That ranch you had your eye on is still for sale, too."

"I want to list my place. Ten acres and a damaged barn—the house and shop are a total loss and I'm bulldozing what's left of them. Then I need you to find me a new place, less land, with a house and barn already in place. Not the ranch. I'll be using the sale proceeds to pay for the new place, and not a cent more." She doesn't mention the insurance payout. She'll need that to finish out a new store and restock inventory.

"How exciting. Are we in agreement on a listing price for your place?" She names the number from their last conversation.

They're not, but what choice does she have? "That's fine."

"Great! I'll get the listing up within the hour and have someone out to take pictures later today. But honestly, I think one of my clients will have an offer in to you by tomorrow. And watch for an email from me tonight with some properties for you to preview."

The answer should make her feel good, but it does the opposite. "Thanks."

Maggie hangs up and puts the truck in gear. Her skin prickles with the sensation of Andy's eyes on her face. "What?"

"If I had someone who loved me I'd choose that over any place. Much less some new place that means nothing to you."

She thinks about Hank. How much does he really love her if he keeps hiding from her? *Not enough. Not nearly enough.* A sob threatens, but she swallows it down and presses Bess's accelerator.

FIFTY-SIX

A LITTLE MORE THAN two hours later as the sun is setting, Bess bounces onto the rutted road into the Amish community. It's surprising to Maggie. As hardworking and conscientious as Andy is, she'd expected it to be clean and orderly. Instead, it's broken-down farm implements, cobbled-together fencing, and a hodgepodge of buildings that don't look sturdy enough for Montana winters. The muddy snow doesn't improve the picture, even though the community is set before a beautiful mountain ridge overlooking the Tongue River.

There are horses everywhere, pulling carts, carrying kids of all ages, milling in corrals. She sees a few women, all in drab dresses down to their ankles and with white scarves on their heads. They're standing in front of houses with babies in their arms. Men converge on the houses, looking like they're coming home from work.

"That's my house." Andy has been perking up ever since they left the Cheyenne reservation fifteen minutes before. He points at a large, boxy structure that boasts a roof, covered windows, and a door, but doesn't have much else to recommend it as a place to live.

"We've made it."

He smiles, eyes soft, and waves at some children who are hanging off a wooden fence.

Maggie pulls to a stop in front of the Yoder home. "I'm glad you're going to get some time with your family. Will you need a ride back to Piney Bottoms?"

"I'll hitch with someone tomorrow afternoon."

Stern-faced Reggie approaches the vehicle.

Andy gets out to greet him, leaving the door open, so Maggie can hear their exchange. "Father."

"Why are you here?"

"A weekend visit. There was a tragedy today. My friend—" His voice breaks and he tries again. "Penny is dead. So is Michael. He worked with me."

Reggie grunts. "Well, there's plenty of work to go around," he says, as if he didn't hear the last of Andy's words.

"Yes, sir."

A short, round woman with friendly eyes joins Reggie. She whispers in Andy's ear. The two have a brief conversation.

He turns to Maggie. "Can you stay for dinner before you drive back?"

"I can't impose."

Again, the woman whispers.

"It's no imposition."

"Thank you, then. That's very kind." Maggie follows them into the house, conscious of curious eyes on her back.

The conditions of the house are worse inside than outside. The walls are partially Sheetrocked. The floor is bare plywood. Black tar paper is tacked up over the insides of the windows. There are children everywhere, but they grow silent when they see her. Gene had mentioned before that Andy has nine siblings. Ten kids. Two parents. Twelve people in this house, plus her makes thirteen. It hardly seems big or strong enough to contain them all.

A large table is already set, and a teenage girl ushers her to a seat. The trapped feeling from earlier returns, the one she had when she was driving home from Buffalo. It was a mistake to accept the dinner invitation. She feels suddenly desperate to get out of the house. To get out of the state of Montana, then Wyoming, and all the way back to the safety of Texas. But Maggie sits and steels herself with a deep breath. She doesn't have that choice right now.

After the rest of the family has filed in and sits down, Reggie begins the meal with a lengthy prayer. Maggie sneaks a glance around the dining and cooking area while he's still at it. She sees a mortar and pestle on the kitchen counter. At first, she thinks it looks a lot like Sibley's family heirloom. Then she grows suspicious. Is it the same one? Did Andy take it and give it to his family? She can't believe she's having doubts about him. His moral code doesn't allow for stealing, so it can't be the same one. Mortar and pestle sets can't be all that different anyway.

After grace, they eat quietly. The food is simple but good. She takes homemade bread and butter, then serves herself stew with carrots, potatoes, onions, and some kind of meat she can't identify. Andy's mother and oldest sisters clear the table when they finish and bring out dessert, a rhubarb crisp. Maggie takes a no-thank-you bite and starts the countdown until she can leave. She'll be out of here in ten minutes. Fifteen tops.

Andy unfolds some printed pages from his wallet. "I was in this article. It's about Ms. Killian. She's a music star."

His family passes it around, rubbing their hands over it and his picture in it.

When it reaches the head of the table, Reggie wads it up and throws it to the floor. "Pride, Andrew. You're indulging in pride. That's a sin. I hope now that the Indian whore is out of your life, you will sin no more."

Everyone looks down. Andrew's neck flushes. The silence is sharp as razors.

Maggie bites back a comment. This is not the environment for it. Instead, she puts down her spoon. "Thank you for the delicious dinner. I hate to be rude, but I have a long drive back on dark roads."

"And the snow." It's the first time Mrs. Yoder has spoken to her directly.

Maggie smiles at the woman. "Exactly. You have a lovely family. Andy, I'll see you later."

He stands, fists clenched. "She wasn't a whore, Father. And Michael may not have been a good brother to her, but he was a good person who tried to protect her. It's terrible that they died."

Brother. Michael was Penny's brother. Things begin to make more sense to Maggie. The baby had to have been Paco's.

Mrs. Yoder speaks with her eyes down, cutting off Maggie's line of thought. "Of course it is, son. Please sit back down."

He does. Maggie doesn't. She feels twenty-four eyes watching as she hurries out.

FIFTY-SEVEN

Maggie opens the door to her truck. This has been one of the weirdest days of her life. Time to get the hell out of here and back to the ranch.

She smells cheap booze, then a male voice close behind her says, "Drive me back to Sheridan with you."

She jumps, startled. In the dark, she can't make out a face, but she knows it's Reggie, and that he's a secret drinker. "Mr. Yoder?"

"I need to pick up Andy's things. He won't be coming back."

"I can't let you do that without hearing it from him."

"I am the head of this household, and my word is final."

"But you're not head of household at Piney Bottoms, Mr. Yoder."

"Fine. I have to work in Sheridan tomorrow. I can stay out at the ranch in his cabin."

Internally Maggie resists, but manners win out. "Not my call. You can certainly ask." She knows he's still going to try to take Andy's belongings, but Gene and Hank can deal with that when the time comes.

The two of them pile into her cold truck. She checks her phone. No signal, so of course no new messages, from Hank or anyone. Despite her earlier dip about him, he's the one she wants to talk to now. She types him a text. *Heading home from Montana with Reggie Yoder. He wants to stay in Andy's cabin. Yes or no? He's giving me the creeps. So much to tell you.* She'll send it when she's in range.

As she drives out of the gate, she says, "Thank you for dinner with your family, Mr. Yoder."

He doesn't respond.

Maggie fiddles with the heat, trying to get more of it flowing. "Do you have a ride into work tomorrow?"

He nods.

Her mind returns to the Yoder's home, her disquietude there. "The mortar and pestle in your kitchen. Where did you get them?"

"Them's women's things."

"So you don't know if they came from the Double S?"

He grunts noncommittally.

So this is how it's going to go, then. Maggie finds a staticky station on the radio and fills the silence with country music for the rest of the two-and-a-half-hour drive, with the occasional grumble about heathen music from Reggie. It's dark as pitch when they arrive at the ranch gate.

"You've been to Andy's cabin, before, right?" she asks. Her voice cracks from lack of recent use.

He nods.

Maggie realizes she forgot to call and ask permission for Reggie to stay, but she's too tired to take him back to Sheridan anyway. It will just have to be okay. In front of the bunkhouse, she takes her foot off the gas. Something hard jabs her in the side.

"Ouch." She turns toward the pain and Reggie.

"Keep driving."

"But we're here. What is that?"

"A gun. I don't prefer to use it."

"I—"

He pummels her with his words. "Drive. Now. Or I shoot."

Maggie's brain feels like it's stuck in quicksand. This doesn't make sense. Reggie is unstable. He's upset. He has a gun. She needs to do what he says and calm him down, even if she doesn't understand why yet. "Fine. Fine. Where am I going?"

"Where I say. Turn here. And throw your phone out the window."

She hesitates, hand on the window crank. They're heading into the south pastures. Her phone is the only way she can summon help, but she won't have signal much further anyway. She glances at the screen. Her message to Hank is still in a text box, unsent. She hits SEND.

His voice is edgy, cracking to let a higher pitch through. He jabs her again. "Do it now."

"Okay, okay." She opens the window and tosses it out. They reach the first gate and she stops. "Are you going to get the gates?"

"No. You are."

"I'm not strong enough for some of them."

"I suggest you will be."

"What's going on, Mr. Yoder?"

He doesn't answer.

"What do you want from me?"

He doesn't even look at her.

Maggie's adrenaline spikes, making her light-headed. She's still close enough to make a run for the house. She gets out of the truck. Instead of walking to the gate, she bends low and takes off at top speed, which isn't very fast over the rough, slippery ground, in cowboy boots. The ground wins. She goes down.

Reggie's door opens. "I'm a good shot. If you make me shoot you, I'll still have a mostly full magazine left. Who do you think I'll go for next? Your boyfriend? His partner? Your dog?"

The snow on her sore hands is wet and cold. She pushes to her feet. Now she's really scared, but she does her best not to show it. Without looking at Reggie, she goes to the gate and opens it, returns to the truck and pulls it through, then closes the gate and returns once more.

The road through the next pasture is rough. Maggie barely notices. All of her energy is going toward a plan to get away from Reggie. Her brain cycles through one useless idea after another. Jump on him and wrestle the gun away? Wreck the truck? But into what? And what would she do then, without wheels, alone with him and his gun?

She sees a horde of eyes shining in the headlights. Expensive, mean rodeo-bull eyes. She slows down.

"What are you doing?"

"Trying not to hit a bull."

"They will get out of your way. Keep driving."

"You'd think that." But she speeds up, and, luckily, the eyes in front of her shift to the side and soon are behind them. Her mind churns again, and she decides her only option is to figure out what's wrong with Reggie and try to talk sense into him. "I know you're upset. I'm sorry about everything that has happened. If you want to pick up Andy's things, I'd be happy to help you."

"Open the gate and turn."

It's too far back to the compound to make a run for it, plus he still has his gun, so Maggie does as he asks. As she struggles with the wire loop, she hears a bovine snort and a heavy hoof pawing the snow. "Whatever you're thinking, no. He's got a gun, you big dummy."

He doesn't back away. What if this is one of the star bulls? And he charges, and Reggie kills him?

She waves her arms in a crisscross over her head. "Shoo. Go away." She gets the gate open, then drives the truck through. The bull barrels through the gate and past them. *Great.* This one is going to have a sexcation with the cows, because that's what's in the pasture.

She shuts the gate. When she returns to Bess, Reggie is in the driver's seat. He points her to the passenger side. She gets in and Reggie drives on. As they cross the next pasture, Maggie's fear turns to terror. She sees the mound in the distance and knows exactly where Reggie is taking her.

FIFTY-EIGHT

IT ONLY TAKES five minutes to reach the dead pile, and they're the shortest minutes of Maggie's life. Reggie parks so close to the edge of the cliff—the old buffalo jump, where the dead pile gets pushed over with a tractor—that she's scared the ground will crumble and drop them the hundred feet to the rocks below. Her hands start shaking violently in her lap. She clutches them together.

"I'm putting the truck in neutral. We're going to get out. But don't try anything stupid. I have the gun pointed at you."

She exits the truck, looking for a place to run and hide. There's nothing. Nowhere and nothing.

Reggie is out and around the truck before she can come up with a plan. "Now you're going to push." He jams the gun between her shoulder blades, forcing her to the tailgate.

She stares at her truck and shakes her head.

He digs the barrel in harder. "Push."

A silent wail reverberates inside Maggie. She puts both hands on the truck she's loved since first sight. "Too heavy."

"Push!" Reggie shouts. "Now!"

She bends at the knees and waits and pushes. The truck doesn't budge. She crouches further and uses all her strength and weight. The truck starts to roll, and her feet slide out from under her. The truck stops. On the way down, her chin smashes into the trailer hitch. The pain is blinding.

"Ow." She cradles the gash with her palm. To buy herself time, she asks, "Why are you making me push my truck?"

"Everything about you is evil. I have to destroy it all."

"Bess hasn't done anything wrong. I haven't either."

"Get up. Be quiet."

"I—"

"Shut up or I shoot."

Maggie crawls to her knees, leaving a bloody handprint in the snow that she can just barely see in the dark. Her head spins as she stands.

"Push again."

"I've tried. I'm not strong enough."

"Like with the gates, tonight you will be."

Maggie swivels and digs her heel in the snow until she reaches the grass below, then does the same with her toe. She repeats the digging with her other foot. Once she has traction, she pushes again, every muscle in her body straining. Her chin pulses with pain. She cries out, and it turns into a long scream of effort, fear, and rage.

The truck moves forward again.

"Don't stop."

She takes a breath and lets out another scream. Bess rolls another few inches, gathering momentum on the slight decline. Bess. Her beloved truck. He is making her push a piece of herself over the cliff to its death. She can't. She just can't. Maggie hates this man. She desperately wants to turn the tables on him. But try as she might, she can't think of a way to do it. Best to play along a little while longer.

She empties her lungs on a final war whoop of a scream, and the truck topples over the edge. When she hears it hit something hard down below, Maggie crumples to the ground. "Bess."

"Walk."

She hesitates just too long, and he smashes her ribs with the gun.

Again, she cries out, but at the same time, she fights to get to her feet. "I'm g-g-g-g-oing, asshole."

He marches her to the dead pile. "I hereby judge you as the corruptor of my boy, forcing your immorality on him. Playing the guitar is nothing but prideful vanity. I won't let you continue to ruin him. Just like that Paco who took him to bars. And that whore who was tempting him with her loose ways."

His words are horrifying. This isn't a one-time break brought on by the stress of Andy being a suspect in the murders. This is madness. Reggie Yoder is a multiple murderer.

She has to keep him talking. "What about Michael?"

"The Indian boy?"

"Yes."

"May God forgive me for him. But he showed up as his sister's protector, and I had no choice. Just as I have no choice with you if I want to save my son."

"I haven't been corrupting him. I promise."

"Hush!" He holds up his gun and points it at her. "This time, no one will pin it on my Andrew."

She'll never be able to talk him out of this. Her mind whirls. She has to fight back, now. She searches around her for something to use as a weapon. Her size and strength are no match for his, much less for his gun. But in all the snow, she can't see anything heavy, even though she knows there are rocks and debris near the pile.

She makes one last try to keep him talking. "Doesn't the Bible tell us to let God judge?"

"You have no understanding of God's words or commandments."

"Help me understand. Please." Suddenly, she remembers the knife and scabbard concealed under her sweater. The one Hank made her promise to carry. The one Reggie will thrust in the back of her skull if he sees it before she can use it. How had she forgotten it? Her sweater is already partially hiked up over one hip. Slowly, she pushes the bottom edge up further until she can rest her hand on the hilt of her knife.

"Impossible." Reggie strikes her across the temple with his gun. "You'll never understand."

She falls toward the snow, time slowing, a metronome in her head counting out the ticks of seconds passing. Her face hits first. It's cold, cold, cold, especially in the cut on her chin. Thank God for the cold, because it keeps her awake. She closes her eyes and wraps her fingers tightly around the handle of her knife, using her thumb to open the snap on the strap that holds it in place.

Suddenly everything is clear to her. She wants nothing more in the world than to stay alive, here with Hank, on this ranch, in Wyoming. The emotion is so strong that it paralyzes her for a beat. Why has she been too proud to tell Hank she loves him? To fight for him and help him through his treatment change and the death of his mother? She's been distant. Short-changing him with her emotions. She wants to give him everything she has and is. She needs to tell him she loves him. And that's not all. She sees that Charlotte is right, but also that she's wrong. Maggie does need her people, but what her mother doesn't realize is that Maggie's people are *here*. Maybe she had to run to find them, to find Hank. Like Gidget did. And maybe being like her birth mother isn't the insult people have always intended it to be.

Reggie grunts. "I thought you'd have more fight in you."

He steps closer, snapping her out of her haze of thoughts. He pushes her with his foot, but she plays possum. After a few moments, he holsters his gun. She hears his breath as he leans over her. Through slitted eyes, she sees him reach for her wrist. His legs are by her torso. She rips the knife from the sheath and stabs backward into his calf.

His shriek is inhuman, the cry of a screech owl, and scarier than anything he has said to her all night. She pulls the knife out of his leg with a twist. She rolls away, pushing herself, and her knife jams in the ground and rips from her hand. Reggie leaps on top of her. He lands a punch on her cut chin. Stars flash in her vision. Then he's pressing down on her chest and something above her glints.

He has the knife, and he's a witch.

She braces for the blade, her eyes closed. Then she hears a noise like the rhythmic beating of a bass drum. Her eyes fly open. Reggie looks startled, and he hesitates. Seconds later, snow sprays in Maggie's face. Reggie grunts and falls to the side, all of his weight off of her except a leg. She crab-walks out from under him as fast as she can.

When she's free of him, she glances back. She barely processes what she's seeing. It's like a Tasmanian devil is attacking Reggie. Their bodies are writhing and turning, so intertwined it's as if they're one. Reggie is stabbing at the thing with his knife hand. The little devil is black. A bear? A wolf? No, it's too small. Wolverine? No, there are none in Wyoming. Tasmanian devils either, for that matter. The black fur is long, with white markings. Too big to be a skunk. The sound it's making is like a growl. Or a whine. Or a . . . bark.

"Louise!" she shouts. She has to help her dog before Reggie stabs her wonderful, loyal, hero of a dog to death.

But it's not just Louise. Lily is stomping, pacing, and pawing behind them. There's no time to wonder how they got there. As she scrambles to her feet, her hand touches something icy cold, smooth, and hard. Really hard.

Reggie's gun. It must have dislodged from his holster in the struggle with Louise.

She's no gun expert, but it's big and black and looks deadly. She fumbles with it. If there's a safety, she can't find it. She holds it up and aims it at man and dog. They're a churning mass, slamming over and over into a small tree. There's no way she can shoot Reggie without risking Louise. She gets as close to their fray as she can without being swept into it, then she smashes the gun down with all her strength. Louise yelps, but she doesn't loosen the jaws she has clamped over Reggie's arm.

"I'm sorry, Louise."

Without hesitation, she hammers the gun down again. She hears a sickening crack and Reggie cries out, then releases Louise. He rocks on the ground in the fetal position. Conscious? That's not good enough for Maggie. She has better aim now that he's not wrestling the dog. Grunting, she hits him again with the gun, harder, this time on the back of his head.

"Umph." Reggie's body goes limp and silent.

Louise barrels into Maggie, licking her and trying to push her away from their attacker at the same time.

Maggie hugs her tight. "You are such a good, good girl. Such a good girl." She looks up at Lily. "I rescue you, you rescue me. Good girl." She checks Louise for injuries. Sticky blood mats her fur, whether hers or Reggie's, Maggie doesn't know. But Louise doesn't seem to be in pain or distress.

Maggie paws through the snow around Reggie looking for her knife. She's not taking a chance he'll wake up and jump her with it. The blade finds her first, drawing blood. She sucks her hand, then jams the knife into its sheath. As she starts to snap it in place, she stops. Thinks. Decides. She drags Reggie to the tree and props him against the trunk. Then she pulls the pigging string out of the scabbard, pulls Reggie's wrists behind the tree, and wraps the pigging string over and over around them before tying it off. *This wasn't on the list of things Hank told me I could do with a knife and a string.*

When she's done, Maggie's hands are like ice. She walks over to Lily. "Help me out, girl?" She warms her hands between her body and the mare's belly. Lily turns her neck and puts her muzzle on Maggie's hair. Louise leans into her leg.

Maggie's adrenaline has worn off, and her energy is sapping out of her quickly. "Let's go home, guys."

Louise leads the way in the dark. After ten minutes of high-stepping through snow and going through one gate, Maggie begins to wonder if she'll make it back. Her clothing and boots aren't made for winter hiking. Wetness has crept into her boots, and her feet are now as cold as her hands. After another ten minutes, she's fairly sure she won't make it.

Louise seems to sense the quit in Maggie. She whines and bumps against her. Losing her footing, Maggie falls. She reaches up and her hand lands on the dog's collar.

Time stops. Her face hurts. She can't remember where she is. It's snowy and quiet, though. Louise barks and head-butts her.

"Stop it."

She's holding something. Louise's collar. The dog strains and Maggie allows herself to be pulled until she's standing up. With one step, though, she slips again and lurches forward, headfirst into something big, warm, and unyielding. She touches it with her hand. A horse. Lily. The mare bumps her muzzle into Maggie's face. Reaching up, up, up, Maggie clutches a handful of coarse mane and buries her face into warm fuzzy horse hair.

The warmth rejuvenates her, and her brain tries to make sense of everything again. She realizes she's in the ranch pasturage. Because? Reggie. She's out here because Reggie brought her. She groans. He made her push Bess off the buffalo jump. And he tried to kill her and put her on the dead pile. He's still out there. Tied up, but he could escape. She has to get home. Get help.

"You gonna help me, girls?"

With Louise pressing into her lower legs from one side and Lily's wide barrel against her head and shoulder from the other, Maggie keeps a tight grip on Lily's mane and stumbles along between them. Little, big, and bigger, abreast, they keep moving for what seems like forever. Maggie's feet, hands, and face are like ice, and she still slips, but Lily keeps her upright, and the warmth from the animals is a big improvement. They don't do much for her brain, though, and she has trouble keeping the story she's fought so hard to remember straight in her mind.

Headlights appear in the distance.

"Over here," she says, her voice barely above a whisper. She feels a strange sense of déjà vu. "Over here."

She's babbling incoherently when a truck pulls up beside her.

Hank jumps out. "Maggie, oh my God. We've got to get you warm." He lifts her in his arms.

"Lily and Louise saved me."

He pushes her into the truck and turns his heater on full blast. "Are you okay?"

Louise jumps into the front seat with Maggie. Hank ties Lily to a metal loop in the side of the truck bed, then he gets in and closes the door.

Maggie shivers. Her hands and feet feel like they're being stabbed with needles. Her face burns, except her chin, which throbs. "I tried to text you."

He starts rubbing her hands briskly between his. "I got your message about dropping Andy in Montana."

"Montana. Yes."

"I'm sorry, Maggie. I'm ashamed of how I've been treating you. I can't lose you. I had to get away where I could protect you from what I was becoming, until the treatment started to work. So I went to Denver to get something for you. While I was there, I started to feel better, more human again. I think it's working, the program and the shots."

Maggie groans. She's only partially processing his words, but the sound of his voice is soothing. The rubbing isn't.

"I came home as fast as I could. You should have been back already, but your truck wasn't there, and I couldn't find you. You weren't answering your phone. When I saw Louise and Lily were missing, too, and there were fresh tire tracks out toward the south pasturage—not ranch truck tracks, but skinny like the ones from your funky old truck—I was so scared."

"Bess," Maggie whispers.

"What?"

She shakes her head. He puts his warm face against hers.

It hurts so good. She sighs.

"Wait, where is your truck?" Then he holds up her arm. "Is this blood?"

Maggie smiles at him. It hurts her cheeks. "You didn't do it."

"What?"

"Neither did Andy."

"I'm not following you."

Maggie shakes her head. Her brain starts to come back to her. She points in the direction of the dead pile. "You'll understand when you see the surprise waiting for you and two counties worth of deputies at the dead pile."

FIFTY-NINE

An unfamiliar truck pulls up the lane toward the ranch house two mornings later—looking like it shares a birth decade with Bess, but hasn't aged as well—with Travis in his Sheridan County truck on its bumper. Maggie is walking back from the barn, where she's been feeding Louise and Lily a special thank-you breakfast. She would have done it the day before if she hadn't spent all of it either being questioned by doctors or law enforcement personnel. It's not only the animals that have had to wait. She and Hank have barely had a moment to themselves either.

A toothless man at the wheel of the ancient truck leans out the window and spits a stream of tobacco juice. Part of it splatters behind him on the rear door. He parks in front of the house. A light snow begins to fall as Andy gets out of the passenger side and walks toward the entrance. Travis pulls in beside him but leaves the motor running.

Hank meets Andy at the door, and Maggie begins to trot, her long hair falling from the stretchy headband she'd pushed it up and back in. The headband falls down to her neck like a scarf, sticking to her ChapStick for a second on the way. She catches Hank and Andy mid-conversation.

"You're welcome back here, any time." Hank has a hand clamped on Andy's shoulder.

"Thank you, sir. I know that. But I'll be staying in the community. My mother needs me now, to help with the family."

Maggie is only a little out of breath. "Is that what you want?" Returning to the community means baptism and is a point of almost no return.

"My father ain't my religion. I can keep the pieces separate. This is what is right."

The lump in Maggie's throat nearly chokes off her air. "You're a good person, Andy Yoder."

"So was my father. Before. I wish you could have known him then."

Hank holds his hand out to Maggie and she takes it, gripping it tight.

"Before what?" Hank says. "You've lost me, son."

"Before the rotgut ate his brain."

"Alcohol." Maggie isn't surprised. It confirms what she has smelled and suspected. And she knows substance abuse can destroy a human one brain cell at a time. She wonders if they'll find bottles up at the summer cabin—she'd reviewed the new security camera shots in the hospital the day before. The mysterious figure she'd seen in the alerts? Reggie Yoder. "You knew?"

"Others did. The truth is out now."

"Maybe he can get treatment in prison?"

"That ain't the Amish way. We don't always understand God's will, but I know my father never would have done those things before."

Maggie isn't sure how it could be God's will that Reggie kill off the people Andy cared about, but now is not the time to wrestle her theological demons. Whatever God's will, Reggie's quest is fulfilled: Andy is returning to the community. But if she remembers one thing from all her religious upbringing and education, it is not to confuse God's will with man's. Reggie made the choice to start drinking, not God, and that was the choice that led to all his other ones. Or that's the way she sees it as a two-time survivor of rehab, and success story of sorts, anyway. Her head hurts from even that little bit of religious contemplation, so she forces her attention back to the conversation.

Hank is saying, "If it's about money, Andy, we can help."

"That's a very kind offer. Especially after all my father did. I'll be sure my mother knows about your generous nature. Maybe someday she'll support me coming back."

"I'd like that." Hank pulls him into an embrace.

Maggie takes her turn hugging Andy. She expects him to hold back from her touch, but he surprises her with a warm bear hug. "We could continue your guitar lessons."

Hank shoots her an odd look.

"I'd like that. Well, I'll just pick up my things, then, and be off. I'm visiting my father and his court-appointed attorney before I go home."

They wish him good luck, and he returns to the passenger seat of the decrepit truck. It isn't even in gear before Travis gets out and walks over to Maggie and Hank.

He shakes hands with both of them. "If you're going to make a habit of solving our cases for us, we'll need to put you on the payroll, Ms. Killian."

"If nearly getting killed by the murderer is what you call solving a case, then I don't want the job."

"You knew who didn't do it, and you never quit trying to prove it."

Hank clasps her around the shoulders. "Don't let her good looks fool you. She's stubborn as hell. And no one gets to tell her the sky is blue. It's whatever color she damn well says it is."

"Well then, I guess you two are a good match."

Maggie watches the old pickup pull up to the bunkhouse then says, "I hope you're not here to tell us someone else is dead."

Travis smooths his shirt and adjusts his belt. "Nah. I just dropped by to tell you I'm sorry. It was nothing personal."

"You mean about Andy?" Hank says.

Something on the horizon becomes mighty interesting to Travis. Then he sighs. "Hank, you're one volatile and physical son of a bitch. I don't take that back. But I was wrong about Andy, and I was wrong to suspect you. Don't get me wrong. It's my job to question everything. I just want you to know that everyone out here at Piney Bottoms is A-OK, as far as I'm concerned."

Hank looks at Maggie. "You had my woman questioning me, too."

Maggie holds up her thumb and forefinger. "Only a little bit."

Hank makes a wider space between his hands. She shrugs. Travis chuckles.

"Looks like you've got her snowed again, then." Travis backs a few steps. "I've gotta hit the road. Stay out of trouble."

"No promises," Hank says.

Maggie waves.

As soon as Travis closes the door of his truck, Hank flips Maggie around so her shoulders rest against the front door of the house.

"What was that about? The thing you said to Andy."

"What?" She gives him an innocent smile.

"Teaching him guitar lessons if he ever comes back someday. I thought you were on your way back to Texas."

"Well, how can I be, with no truck?"

He grins at her. "About that."

"About Bess?"

"Yes. I took a look at her. She got lucky on her landing. I think we can fix her back up. It'll take a while, but if you're not going anywhere soon, maybe we'd have time."

Tears threaten the corners of Maggie's eyes.

From the barn, Gene's voice interrupts them, shouting. "If y'all hurry, you'll get here in time to see Lily's latest. She's about to drop it."

Gene and Hank have been working since four a.m. with the day hands and some neighbors who insist on pitching in until the Double S can find help, now that Paco, Michael, and Andy are gone. The two men have to be exhausted, but they don't show it.

Hank grins and takes Maggie's hand. A laugh escapes her throat as they trot to the barn. The snow falls faster—big, pretty flakes. When they reach the entrance, Maggie pulls him to a stop as she catches her breath and a whiff of sweet-smelling hay.

"I'll always be on my way somewhere, Hank. That's who I am. And it so happens I have things—people, too—in Texas. From time to time, I'll have to take care of them."

"What do you mean?"

"I'll leave sometimes. But I'll always come back where I belong."

Hank takes her other hand. "Jesus, Maggie. Are you leaving me or not?"

"Not. I'm staying. I've figured out how to support myself here." She lets go of one of his hands and holds up a finger. "I can teach music lessons." Then another. "I can be your first permanent, part-time female hand." She lifts a third. "I can sell my salvage pieces on consignment or at rodeos with you." When her pinky finger rises, so do the corners of her mouth. "And maybe I can use some of them to decorate the summer cabin."

He pulls her to him and kisses her long and hard. "That is the best thing I've ever heard. All of it." Then his face falls. "If we can keep the place, which Gene and I are going to try like hell to find a way to do."

"About that. I have an offer for you and Gene."

Gene appears. "Hank and *me?* I'm not into that kind of thing, thank you very much, Maggie May." Then he laughs. "You two look like snowmen. Come on."

He leads the way to the birthing stall. Maggie and Hank drop snow as they follow him.

Maggie turns to Hank in the corridor. "I have insurance money coming, and I'm going to sell my place." And according to an email from Michele, she should expect double the number the insurance company offered. "I was thinking you might let me buy in. Not in the Double S. But in the property. Piney Bottoms. I could run a music camp in the summer cabin a few times a year. And, um, Ava has offered me a deal to record together." Maggie had called Ava just that morning, and the two of them had reached a deal. If Ava keeps being so reasonable, Maggie is even going to have to admit she likes her. And after Maggie's meeting with Amos, he'd sent a link to a semi-positive piece on her, with a promise he'd be all over any collaboration with Ava. "She'll front us the rest of the money to buy Laura out, an advance on royalties. So that Laura and Mickey can cover the cost of Mickey's dad's treatment ASAP."

Hank's fingers grip her arms so tightly it hurts, but she's not about to ask him to let go. "Are you serious?"

"Holy shit," Gene says.

"It's taken me a while to work through the options, but I think this is the best one. So, yes, I'm serious. What do you think?"

Hank's eyes shine. "We can live there together. At the summer cabin. With lots of room for your friends and family to visit."

"No, thanks, I've got a place," Gene deadpans.

Maggie makes a raspberry at Gene and says to Hank, "Your friends and family, too. Except Laura, because she hates me."

"She doesn't hate you. She's had a tough time. But thanks to you and Ava, things will be much better for her soon." He kisses her forehead and lowers his voice so that only she can hear. "But what about my condition? My brain—that's forever."

She moves her mouth by his ear and speaks softly. "You said yourself the treatment is helping. And I've got a few issues myself. If you haven't figured them out already, I'll let them be a surprise."

He presses his forehead against hers. "Then you can't run off again when things get tough."

She leans back to give him the evil eye. "Look who's talking, Mr. Denver."

"Oh shit. I forgot. I have a present for you. The thing I went to Denver to pick up."

"It had better be damn good."

He grins. "Only if you like signed prints of *Front Porch Pickin'*, a Gidget Becker original. And a pair of snow boots, which I think I'm delivering a few days late."

"Oh my God, Hank. It's the best gift ever. Thank you. Thank you. Thank you." A signed print of the prized original she'd lost in the fire, plus boots? This man gets her. She locks her lips on his, crushing their faces together. Steam rises around their bodies as snow melts from the heat of their kiss.

When they come up for air, Hank says, "I'm serious. You'll crush me like a grape if you ever leave."

"I'm not just your lover, Hank. I'm your partner. We'll do the hard stuff together. Like your mother's funeral tomorrow. Like telling my mother I'm staying here."

"Yeah, you can do that last one by yourself if you want."

She socks him in the chest, and he catches her fist, laughing.

Gene's voice comes from inside the birthing stall. "If you lovebirds don't mind the interruption, Lily has something to show you."

Hank and Maggie tear their eyes from each other and lean over to look in the stall. Lily is licking a bundle of wet black fur that's mostly long legs that seem to stick out in every direction.

"Way to go, Mama. Is it a boy or a girl?" Hank says.

Gene approaches mother and baby. "Hey, girl. Let me take a look at what you got there."

Lily nudges at her foal, and not gently. It begins scrambling and rocking. She keeps pushing it insistently until it stands, only to wobble and tumble immediately. Maggie clutches her throat, but Gene and Hank laugh.

Gene says, "I got a glimpse down under. Looks like a girl to me."

Maggie claps. "Go, Lily. Bucking girl power."

Hank turns to Maggie. "Are you sure you're ready for that kind of partnership? The forever kind."

"I am."

"Promise on the life of that little one in there?"

"I promise on the life of the Black Widow."

"The Black Widow?"

"Those spidery legs. She needs a killer name for a killer bucking career, so she can follow in her sister Crazy Woman's footsteps." Maggie spits on her hand and sticks it out with a grin. "And oh, by the way, I love you."

Instead of shaking it, he pulls her into his arms, but not before she sees the dimples that curl her toes. "Now that didn't hurt so much to admit, did it, music girl?"

DO YOU LIKE FREE STUFF?

Do you like free stuff, exclusives, and finding out about new books before they hit the market?

Visit https://www.subscribepage.com/PFHSuperstars to become a PFH Superstar.

Plus, you'll get to know all of the kick-ass women sleuths from the entire *What Doesn't Kill You* romantic mystery series.

ACKNOWLEDGMENTS

The Maggie books are set one foot in Texas and the other in Wyoming, while Maggie's life is a little bit junker and a little bit rock and roll. My own love affair with Wyoming started at an early age when my family moved to Buffalo. Then my parents "ruined my life forever" by moving us back to Texas a few years later. I didn't return to Wyoming until 2014, and then only because I took Eric for his first visit in July, as opposed to January. My mama didn't raise no fool.

Two cabins later, my Virgin Islands–native husband drives a snowplow and owns more coats than his famous sandals. I wrote all the Maggie stories from our Snowheresville, Wyoming, in a big, beautiful, remote, off-the-grid, and, above all, *rustic* cabin on the eastern face of the Bighorn Mountains. It's not easy shuttling between two homes in Texas and one in Wyoming, but Eric does it with a smile on his face and adventure in his heart. I am beginning to think he loves me.

The animals in this book are based on Pippin, one of our granddogs, and Katniss, my Percheron cross mare. The truck, Bess, and store, Flown the Coop, are rooted in the lives of Tiffany and Jeff, who live near our Nowheresville, Texas. I am grateful to a colorful cast of Wyoming characters (Jeff, Christina, Brenton, Colter, Mandy, Travis, Ron, Eric, and many others) for endless anecdotes. Thanks for the inspiration, all of you!

Thanks to my husband, Eric, for brainstorming the *Maggie* stories with me despite his busy work, travel, and workout schedule. He puts up with me recycling bits and pieces of our lives in the stories as well. I'd say he does it without reservation, but that would be a lie. I guess that makes it even more remarkable that he smiles about it in the end.

Thanks to our five offspring. I love you guys more than anything, and each time I write a parent/child (birth, adopted, foster, or step), I channel you.

To each and every blessed reader, I appreciate you more than I can say. It is the readers who move mountains for me, and for other authors, and I humbly ask for the honor of your honest reviews and recommendations.

Thanks mucho to Bobbye and Rhonda for putting up with my eccentric and ever-changing needs.

Maggie editing credits go to Rhonda Erb and Whitney Cox. The beta and advance readers and critique partners who enthusiastically devote their time—gratis—to help us rid my books of flaws blow me away. Special love this time goes to Angie, Caren, Pat, Tara, Karen, Ken, Candi, Kelly, Vidya, Jim, Ginger, Mandy, Linda and Ridgely.

Thank you Alayah Frazier, for working with Bobbye to create amazing vector art for the covers as we took Maggie into (for *What Doesn't Kill You*) uncharted visual territory.

SkipJack Publishing now includes fantastic books by a cherry-picked bushel basket of mystery/thriller/suspense writers. If you write in this genre, visit http://SkipJackPublishing.com for submission guidelines. To check out our other authors and snag a bargain at the same time, download *Murder, They Wrote: Four SkipJack Mysteries*.

OTHER BOOKS BY THE AUTHOR

Fiction from SkipJack Publishing

The *What Doesn't Kill You* Romantic Mystery Series

Act One (Prequel, Ensemble Novella)

Saving Grace (Katie #1)

Leaving Annalise (Katie #2)

The Jumbie House:

(Katie Short Story/Expanded Excerpt from Leaving Annalise)

Finding Harmony (Katie #3)

Heaven to Betsy (Emily #1)

Earth to Emily (Emily #2)

Hell to Pay (Emily #3)

Bombshell (Ava #1)

Stunner (Ava #2)

Knockout (Ava #3)

Going for Kona (Michele #1)

Fighting for Anna (Michele #2)

Searching for Dime Box (Michele #3)

Buckle Bunny (Maggie Prequel Novella)

Shock Jock (Maggie Prequel Short Story)

Live Wire (Maggie #1)

Sick Puppy (Maggie #2)

Dead Pile (Maggie #3)

Box Sets

Murder, They Wrote: Four SkipJack Mysteries
by Pamela Fagan Hutchins,
Ken Oder, R.L. Nolen, and Marcy Mason

Nonfiction from SkipJack Publishing

The Clark Kent Chronicles
Hot Flashes and Half Ironmans
How to Screw Up Your Kids
How to Screw Up Your Marriage
Puppalicious and Beyond
What Kind of Loser Indie Publishes,
and How Can I Be One, Too?

**Audio, e-book, and paperback versions of most SkipJack titles
available.**

Books from Other Publishers

Eve's Requiem (anthology), Spider Road Press
OMG - That Woman! (anthology), Aakenbaaken & Kent
Ghosts (anthology), Aakenbaaken & Kent
Easy to Love, But Hard to Raise and
Easy to Love, But Hard to Teach (anthologies),
DRT Press, edited by Kay Marner & Adrienne Ehlert Bashista

OTHER BOOKS FROM
SKIPJACK PUBLISHING

Murder, They Wrote: Four SkipJack Mysteries,
by Pamela Fagan Hutchins,
Ken Oder, R.L. Nolen, and Marcy Mason

The Closing, by Ken Oder
Old Wounds to the Heart, by Ken Oder
The Judas Murders, by Ken Oder

Pennies from Burger Heaven, by Marcy McKay
Stars Among the Dead, by Marcy McKay
The Moon Rises at Dawn, by Marcy McKay

Deadly Thyme, by R. L. Nolen
The Dry, by Rebecca Nolen

Tides of Possibility, edited by K.J. Russell
Tides of Impossibility, edited by K.J. Russell and C. Stuart Hardwick

My Dream of Freedom: From Holocaust to My Beloved America,
by Helen Colin